AF663863

The Four Moons in the Human Body The Mysterious Tales of the Bauls of Bengal

(Introducing 'BaulOlogy')

Books Published by Allied Publishers for Dr. Siddhartha Ganguli

1. Live Happily, Work Happily - 2009
2. SUCCESS Can be Planned and Earned - 2010
3. Greying Gracefully: Planning for Retirement and Old Age Happiness - 2011
4. Conscious Management - 2011
5. The Making of a Winning Child - 2012
6. Smart Leading and Parenting of Teenage Kids in the Digital Era - 2021
7. Music is Magic Music is Medicine: Impact of Music on Body, Brain, Mind & Soul - 2023

The Four Moons in the Human Body The Mysterious Tales of the Bauls of Bengal

(Introducing 'BaulOlogy')

Dr. Siddhartha Ganguli, *Ph.D*

ALLIED PUBLISHERS PVT. LTD.

Noida • Mumbai • Kolkata • Chennai • Bangalore

ALLIED PUBLISHERS PRIVATE LIMITED

D-5, Sector-2, **Noida**–201 301
Ph. Nos.: 0120-4320295/2542557/4352866
E-mail: delhi.books@alliedpublishers.com

17 Chittaranjan Avenue, **Kolkata**–700072
Ph.: 033-22129618 • E-mail: cal.books@alliedpublishers.com

15 J.N. Heredia Marg, Ballard Estate, **Mumbai**–400001
Ph.: 022-42126969 • E-mail: mumbai.books@alliedpublishers.com

No. 25/10, Commander-in-Chief Road, Ethiraj Lane (Next to Post Office)
Egmore, **Chennai**–600008
Ph.: 044-28223938 • E-mail: chennai.books@alliedpublishers.com

P.B. No. 9932, No. 15, 3rd Floor (Next to Vijaya Bank), 5th Cross, Gandhinagar, Karnataka, **Bangalore**–560009. Ph.: 080-41530285 / 22386239
E-mail: bngl.journals@alliedpublishers.com / apsabng@airtelmail.in

Website: www.alliedpublishers.com

© 2023, Dr. Siddhartha Ganguli

ISBN: 978-93-90951-76-5

The thematic sketch for the front cover has been prepared by the author's friend Andy J. Peters of Manchester, U.K.

No part of the material protected by this copyright notice may be reproduced or utilized in any form or by any means, electronic or mechanical including photocopying, recording or by any information storage and retrieval system, without prior written permission from the author.

Published by Sunil Sachdev and printed by Ravi Sachdev
at Allied Publishers Pvt. Ltd., D-5, Sector-2, Noida–201 301

This book is

dedicated to

The Bauls & Fakirs of
West Bengal, India and Bangladesh

Appetizer

"The study of man is the study of man's religion."

—**Max Muller**
German Indologist & Philosopher

The Bauls of Bengal: Mystery Number One

From the compendium of the immortal songs of the King of the Fakirs and Bauls, Fakir Lalon Shah, let me share one 'moon-full' song:

"There are moons around the moon,
Tonight, how would you catch that star?

There are a million moons that make it a great spectacle.
In between those is the glow of the moon that is uncatchable.

Moving around the moon market,
The moving moon may affect you
So, watch out lest you lose your senses.

There are moon fruits hanging from the branches of moon trees,
Like lanterns—dazzling beauty!!

Look at those and your eyes will sore,
So amazing is the glare of the rays!!" (Reference 1)

Moons have been galore in the Baul path. There was a period in the 19th century when there were several groups where the members had chosen Baul singing as a hobby. Young persons from respectable families having a good voice used to sing dressed up in loose costumes and putting on wigs and false moustache and beard. They were named after moons ('chand' is the Bengali word for 'moon'): 'Fakir Chand', 'Rasik Chand', 'Ajab Chand' and the like. *(Reference 2)*

There is a fascination for 'moon' in the Baul path. Amazingly, the Baul path is not bound by any religion. It is a specific way of performing devotional rites which are quite different from any religious concept or philosophy. It is largely based on the doctrine of the body (they believe that the 'body' is the seat of God and, I suppose—although I'm not sure, that God exists in every living 'body') which makes it totally different from any mainstream religion like Hinduism, Islam, Christianity, Judaism, Buddhism, Jainism and Sikhism.

Why I find the Bauls of Bengal most mysterious? I'm sharing with you one of their most weird practices that make me regard them as so much shrouded in mystery.

While in school, my parents used to take me and my younger brother to different places within India during long vacations. Many a times, we would spend our holidays in Shantiniketan, where Rabindranath Tagore's Viswa Bharati University has its sprawling campus. And, I used to get fascinated by the colourful attire, the melodious songs, and the plucked sounds on the strings of the mono-stringed ektara of the Bauls, who would be wandering around the University campus as well as in the nearby open spaces surrounded by trees and beautiful bowers. We would meet them on the train also, while travelling in chair cars. Many of them would be out on their 'madhukaris'—that is, moving with their begging bowls seeking alms, like bees collect honey from flowers ('madhu' in Bengali is 'honey' and 'madhukar'—'bee').

At home, during the pre-television days, I used to listen to the Baul songs broadcast from the All India Radio-Calcutta with apt attention. So, while I would meet them in person and would be in close proximity, that would be a most exhilarating experience for me as I would follow their rhythms by tapping my feet. At times, I also dared to talk to some of them—the soft-looking ones and ask their names and home addresses.

During my college and university days, Purna Das Baul, Gostho Gopal Das, and Sanajit Mondal became my favourites and some of them would also come to perform on stage during our annual socials. During my second year of engineering at Jadavpur University, Kolkata, by strange coincidence, our University selected me to be a part of the musical choir for participation in the Inter-university Youth Festival at the Talkatora Gardens, New Delhi, and the song that we had to perform was a famous Bengali Baul song and our music coach was the legendary folk singer Late Nirmalendu Chowdhury—who was unparalleled in musicality and style. This was my first real exposure to the Baul music; and we not only earned great applause after our stage performance, but also bagged the 1st prize for group singing. Incidentally, another group from Calcutta—the Calcutta University drama group stood first in drama where Late legendary actor Soumitra Chatterjee, Dada Saheb Phalke awardee had acted in the hero's role. Those were the golden days!!

Thereafter, I'd lost touch with Baul music except for occasional exposure on the radio, television, or cassettes. In 2018-19 I took up the leadership in a self-sponsored research project on 'Bio-musicology & 3H Music' in collaboration with over 100 musicians from all over the world. 'Bio-musicology' is a term coined by me and it deals with the impact of music on body, brain, mind and soul. According to yogic, tantric & ayurvedic principles, 'Body' and 'Brain' represent the 'Gross Body' or 'Sthula Sarira' and 'Mind' and 'Soul' represent the 'Subtle Body' or 'Sukhsma Sarira'. '3H Music' stands for 'Music for Health, Happiness & Healing'. The massive first phase of my research is over and the findings have been combined and published as an epic volume under the title of 'Music is Magic/Music is Medicine' in June 2023.

During this exhaustive study, I bumped on to some of the Baul practices for the first time which really intrigued me, being a scholar studying the human body and the brain. One of them is known as the 'Chari Chandra Ved': 'Piercing of the Four Moons'. 'Four Moons' is a much-discussed topic in the Baulsphere and it denotes four products manufactured inside the body and ejected outside the body through bodily exit outlets. These are: the male semen containing the 'sperms' ejected by the penis; the female menstrual blood and vaginal discharge containing the ova, ejected by the vagina; urine ejected by the urinary organs; and, faeces, ejected by the rectum or anus.

The first one is the seed to be sown in the female vagina, which is comparable to the soil of the field where it eventually meets the anxiously waiting yet most choosy ovum—both uniting to form the zygote, turning into a foetus inside the female womb. Urine and faeces are both waste products of the body, but like a chemical plant waste, these can be consumed for recycling to get the reclaimed benefit of some minerals and salts which are beneficial for us but get inter-mingled with the body waste and get released. An integral part of the Baul sadhana is that the sadhak Baul has to consume these four excreta from the human body without feeling bad. This ritualised practice has been a characteristic feature of 'Baul Sadhana' as a part of Baul philosophy ever since it got a start hundreds of years ago. Modern biomedical sciences have now enough evidence to recommend the consumption of the male semen and the female menstrual blood as well as human urine and faeces for health reasons. Really amazing!!

To quote John Gegory Bourke, who had authored a well-researched classical treatise on the medicinal uses of human excreta: " ......religion and medicine, among primitive races, are almost always one and the same thing, or at least so closely intertwined, that it is a matter of difficulty to decide where one begins and where one ends." *(Reference 3)*

Just get the public idea about 'faeces' from the following quotation from Robert Keith Wallace and Samantha Wallace's book:

> *"The zinger in my last night's lecture was that one of the most powerful discoveries in gut research is the success of faecal transplant, a procedure in which a doctor inserts stool or 'poop' from a healthy donor into the lower gut of a sick person. Before I finished this sentence, I could see looks of 'disgust' and discomfort pass over the faces of my audience." (Reference 4)*

Let me get into the depth of the 'Chari Chandra Bhed' ('CCB') practice so common amongst Baul sadhaks. Prof. Shaktinath Jha, has mentioned that the 'Chari Chandra' signifies the 'Chandra' or the 'moons' that come out of our body. *(Reference 5)* I have no idea whose brainwave was this metaphor but I have a feeling that whoever had conceived it got the idea from the relationship between the Earth and the Moon. I appreciate his flight of imagination!!

The Earth formed over 4.6 billion years ago out of a mixture of dust and gas around the young Sun. It grew larger—thanks to countless collisions between dust particles, asteroids, and other growing planets, including one last giant impact that threw enough rock, gas, and dust into space to form the Moon. So, one can say that Moon was formed by the rejected debris from the Earth. *(References 6, 7 & 8)*

Or, did he get the 'moon' idea from the mystic poet and saint Kabir (1398-1518), whose poem I quote below:

> *"There's a Moon Inside My Body.*
>
> *The moon shines in my body, but my blind eyes cannot see it.*
>
> *The moon is within me, and so is the sun.*
>
> *The unstruck drum of Eternity is sounded within me,*
> *but my deaf ears cannot hear it.*
>
> *So long as man clamours for the 'I' and the 'Mine',*
> *his works are as naught:*
>
> *When all love of the 'I' and 'Mine' is dead,*
> *then the work of the Lord is done.*
>
> *For work has no other aim than the getting of knowledge:*
>
> *When that comes, then work is put away.*
>
> *The flower blooms for the fruit, when the fruit comes, the flower withers.*
>
> *The musk is in the deer, but it seeks it not within itself: it wanders in quest of grass." (Reference 9)*

Prof. Shaktinath Jha in his Bengali book "*Bastubadi Baul*" says: *(Reference 10)* "In the protection of the body, protection of the semen, protection of self by preventing diseases, the 'Char Chandra Sadhana' of the Baul culture is an unique effective practice." To follow the 'CCB' ritual in practice, the Sadhak Baul has to consume semen, urine and faeces of his own and the menstrual blood of his female companion regularly, without having the feeling of 'disgust'. And, I wouldn't be surprized if some of the very aged and experienced Sadhak Baul gurus had developed folk medicine techniques for assessing the quality of the four moons by looking at them physically without testing those in a pathological lab. In this context, let me mention that in western medicine, the Bristol stool chart, also known as the Meyers scale is a diagnostic tool designed to classify the form of the human faeces into seven categories *(Reference 11)* Interestingly, under normal gut conditions, the faeces that come out do resemble 'sausages' which are a processed meat delicacy.

Our brain has a very efficient 'Error Detection Circuit' ('EDC') which is designed to detect any stimulus or input into the system which is not good for us. Any such bad input of worst nature will be regarded as 'disgusting'. An overactive 'EDC' will lead to the psychological problem of 'Obsessive Complex Disorder' ('OCD'). An OCD patient will wash her hands again and again and would not allow anyone to enter her over-sanitised environment. Once I had a young male patient who had arrived at the appointed time but disappeared into the washroom and came out after a shower and said that as he was travelling by the metro, he was feeling that everyone was spitting over his body.

While an efficient EDC is a security guard for us, if it can be tamed to reduce the intensity of our feeling of disgust, our brain can reduce its demand for energy as it is an energy-costly equipment. If we can save the expensive neural energy and mobilise energy capital, it can be utilised for different positive purposes including for health management, disease prevention and living on very simple almost zero-protein diet.

Just read the verse of a smart Baul song written by the Bengali poet 'Din Sarat' (translated into English by me) which talks about the 'Four Moons': *(Reference 12)*

> *"My mind is keen to know about the doctrine of the body,*
>
> *Oh, my Guru! Please tell me about the doctrine of the moons*
> *which are twenty-four and a half in number!*

Oh, my Guru! Tell me where are the sun, and the moon—
where do they rise and they set,
Tell me about the full moon and the moonless nights,
and when does the moon get eaten up during lunar eclipse.

Please tell me which moon is located in which part of my body.
Which moon is located in the sky and which one is on this planet.

Oh, my Guru! Please talk to me about the ritual of the 'Four Moons'
I am keen to know which Moon serves us in
what ways and what do we gain
I am keen to know about the benefits that we derive from the
Four Moons!
Baul Din Sarat is keen to know: at the time of 'eclipse',
Which monster devours which of the Moons,
And consumption of which of the Moons
makes us free from the birth-death-rebirth cycle."

Din Sarat writes wonderfully in another song: (*Reference 13* – translation mine)

"If you want to know about the doctrine of the body,
first go and touch the Guru's feet,
And, if you follow the ritual of the 'Four Moons'
you will get an immortal body, conquering disease & death.
The doctrine is one of the twenty-four and half Moons.
You have a Moon in your lips and one more in your forehead.
And two half moons on top.
Get to know about the Four Moons now
One is poison, one is insane; another one is like a nine-year
old just-menstruated damsel and the fourth one is arrow-like.
Please note that what seems to be poisonous is sweet as nectar.
From the seed of the Moon nectar oozes which, when consumed,
man becomes immortal.

> *The poet Din Sarat says the planet 'Rahu' carries the death toll.*
>
> *The day when both the sun and the moon will get the eclipse together,*
>
> *On that very day, the twin eclipse will cast darkness on the house that the body represents."*

Having been able to crack the mystery of the 'Four Moons' ritual, I got tempted to go deeper into the lifestyle, culture and the philosophy of the Bauls of Bengal. Thus 'BaulOlogy' was born.

I will conclude by quoting from a very old book by the English anthropologist Edward Burnett Tylor (1832–1917):

> *"Few who will give their minds to master the general principles of savage religion will ever again think it ridiculous.... Far from its beliefs and practices being a rubbish heap of miscellaneous folly, they are consistent and logical in so high a degree as to begin, as soon as even roughly classified, to display the principles of their formation and development; and, these principles prove to be essentially rational, though working in a mental condition of intense and inveterate ignorance."*

– ***"Primitive Culture"***,
EB Tylor, London: John Murray,
Revised 3rd Edition, 1891, Vol. I, p. 21.

Baul *versus* Fakir: Role Minimalisation

"Nothing in a living organism is just one thing. Nature's economy lies above all in making maximum use of what is a process that we may call 'pleoaptation', the adaptation of an organ or system to multiple uses. The liver, for example, the largest gland in the body, performs more than five hundred tasks, including processing glucose, protein, fats, and other compounds the body needs, generating the haemoglobin that is the soul of a red blood cell, and detoxifying the poisons we consume when we drink wine or eat those fibrous packets of natural toxins called vegetables." *(Reference 14)*

I am a multi-cellular biological organism. Like one of my body parts, liver, in my own life, I also perform multiple tasks. I play different roles at different times, in different places, with different people, under different circumstances, which involve performance of multiple tasks of different kinds.

I used to be my parents' son, my brother's brother, my parents-in-law's son-in-law, my brother-in-laws' brother-in-law, my sister-in-law's brother-in-law, and my cousins' cousin.

My parents, my brother, my parents-in-law, my one-brother-in-law, most of my cousins—all have left this planet, so I don't have to play, any more, the roles that I used to play with them. With the brothers-in-law and the sisters-in-law who are still there, I don't remain in touch, so those roles are diffused. Amongst my cousins, I'm still in touch with only one on my mother's side because we share the same interests, so that role I'm still playing; with another living cousin, my role is totally diffused.

I am husband to my wife and father to my children and their spouses, and grandfather to my grandchildren, father to the boys whom I'd groomed up, teacher to my students, Dr Ganguli to my WhatsApp friends, but most of the roles are being played in a detached fashion except for the one with my wife and a handful few. That way, I'm saving a lot of my 'Emotional Energy' ('E-E'). With a very simple balanced diet and extra light exercise and physical output by way of household work, whatever energy I've is being utilised as 'Intellectual Energy' ('E-I') for intellectual work.

A Baul's or Fakir's aim is to minimise roles so that 'E-E' spent is very little. But, there is a difference between the Bauls and Fakirs in this respect. A Baul may get married, but they are against having children, so there is no 'Parent-to-Child' role to be played. Sadhak or Devotee Bauls may not get married, but they have 'Sadhan-sanginis'; so in that relationship, although there is high libido and desire to ejaculate, since semen release is controlled, 'Dietary Energy' ('E-D') is saved as semen is built on dietary inputs, but 'Breath Energy' ('E-B') is spent as control of ejaculation is achieved by performing special breathing feats, and 'Emotional Energy' ('E-E') is expended especially when the conjugation is 'Prem Rati' (union out of 'love' and not 'lust'). So 'Baul Sadhana' is energy-costly. Besides, for walking on the Baul path, having a 'Guru' is a must and with the 'Guru' the Baul devotee has to spend 'Spiritual Energy' ('E-S') which is related to the 'Anandamaya Kosha'. *(Reference 15)* So, the total energy available to a Devotee Baul gets divided as it has to be spent in different channels for playing different roles. And the more roles one plays, the more his Soul gets split into different pieces or segments. So, a Devotee Baul is a 'Split Soul' person (in Bengali: 'Khandita Satta' and not 'Akhanda Satta').

Let me tell you that there is a heaven-and-hell difference between following the Baul path and the Fakir path. A pure Fakir, or a devotee who is a 'Fakir' in the true sense (who roams and begs for his livelihood) is so much engrossed and meditative in his thoughts about his 'Guru' that to get attracted towards a female partner outside his own body is almost an impossible task. He is free from any attachment; his 'E-E' income as well as expenditure both are almost zero.

A 'Fakir' is free, independent, different from others, without any friends, totally attachment-free noble man. Fakir Lalon Shah's life is a glaring example. He had never accepted any wife or female partner, whereas in the Baul path, it is not possible to perform any devotional task without any female partner.

"Chari Chandra Bhed" for Fakirs is not the same as the Bauls observe by consuming four things released by the body. A Fakir's four moons are four progressive stages or phases of development, starting with the 'Sthul Desh' or the 'Gross Phase'. It is followed by the 'Prabarta Desh' (the 'Initiation Phase'. Thereafter, comes the 'Sadhak Desh' (the 'Devotee Phase'). And, finally, we have the 'Siddhi Desh' which is the 'Success Phase'.

The 'Sthul Desh' or 'Gross Phase': 'Gross Body' ('Sthula Sharira') means which is made up of bones, flesh, marrow, and blood. The body which grows from a 'zygote' after the fertilisation of the father's sperm with the mother's egg. The 'Gross Body' is dependent on the working tools ('karmendriyas') and knowledge tools ('jnanendriyas'). This makes us weak as we are entirely dependent and attached to these tools for our survival, replication and bonded human relationship-building.

'Gross Body' has two connotations. The first connotation is related to the feelings inside the mother's womb and the second one is related to how it feels like being in touch with the external world. The 'Gross Phase' is where there is birth and death—creation and destruction. The parents are the creators of the vessel for the 'Initiation Phase' (that is, 'Prabarta Desh').

The 'Gross Phase' is meant for having a family, and running a household; to be groomed with the help of love and affection of the parents, observing obedience to them so that the body and mind get consolidated leading to expansion.

There is a beautiful song by Fakir Lalon Shah (translation mine), representing the 'Gross Phase', that I would like to share with you here, with some minor relevant changes that I've made:

"You spent your time being driven by
what is natural for your age
(in the 'pre-human' existence that you're in)!!
Now, in your youth, you're being driven by lust,
You simply do not know how to get rid of this obsession & addiction.
You are deluded by the physical fun, frolic and pleasure.

Day after day, you lost your semen
(the wealth that you'd inherited from your father).
Your solar power has gone, your eyes have lost their capacity.
You never know when the end will come to take you away
(from this birth to be reborn).

Those with whom you spent your life,
Eventually, they will turn into your foes, displaying envy.
Oh, My Mind! You do not know what dirty games
those people want to play.
(This is the reality of 'human' existence.)

All the wealth of energy that you'd inherited got lost
dealing with your sensory organs which cost energy
in coping with the people who

All are big-mouthed, quarrelsome, dividers.
They cause hindrance to allow you to complete the
'Initiation', 'Devotee' & 'Success' phases of 'Sadhana'
(For you to transcend the 'human' and get into the 'post-human' consciousness)
A person who is supposed to be the principal actor in this transformation,
Lalon, you're caught up in greed & lowly lust!!"

During the 'Gross Phase', one follows the practice of an external religion, observing standard rituals and scriptural recommendations. Those who are lucky, they get a sudden trigger for preparation for the next phase to free himself from the fetters of the bondage of family and worldly life. The next phase is the 'Initiation Phase'.

The 'Prabarta Desh' or 'Initiation Phase': During the 'Initiation Phase', you've to follow a Guru's instructions meticulously. During this phase, you're going to shed off all attachments, liberate your mind totally and take shelter in the magnetic field of a 'True Mentor' (an 'Authentic Guru'). This is the phase to know yourself—who or what you really are, why are you here, and so on—questions that you'd never asked yourself when you were totally engrossed in the delusive 'Gross Phase'. In this phase, each devotee has a different lesson to learn, a different path to follow under the direction of the Guru. The Mentor decides his course of action for initiation according to the capabilities and limitations of the vessel or the receptacle that the devotee represents. The Guru becomes much closer to the devotee than his parents, brothers, sisters, and friends.

The body having twenty-four moons is known as the 'Subtle Body' ('Sukshma Sharira'). This subtle body contains the subtle energy fields which draw energy from the cosmos via the external environment. The devotee has to understand and appreciate this subtle phenomenon which is beyond normal perception. He will be endowed this realisation by his 'Guru' who would cite practical examples and share case studies. He will be taught the difference between 'temporal' existence and 'permanent' existence; the former following the birth-death-rebirth cycle, whereas the latter is 'eternal'—where there is no birth, no death, no rebirth.

The 'Sadhak Desh' or 'Devotee Phase': One 'key' purpose of this phase is to tame the body so that its energy cost or energy expenditure is reduced to the minimum. Purification of the body leads to the purification of the mind. Our body is nothing but a device which is the collection of many instruments and tools. Its overall and different functions are controlled by the mind. The body contains the brain, the brain contains the mind and the mind contains intelligence and imagination, which are mental powers. The mind also contains the 'Ego'—the 'I am' feeling.

Unless the body and the mind are absolutely free from any complexities as well as health problems, you cannot be devoted to anything. Pure mind is essential for realisation of the 'Self'. Effective breathing as well as certain other practices are essential requirements for the 'Devotee Phase'.

The 'Siddhi Desh' or the 'Success Phase': This phase is attained when the devotee is successful after being purified in body, brain, mind and soul, by the fire of the knowledge of a True Mentor or a 'Sadguru'. During this phase, the mind is tamed totally so that its energy loss is almost nil.

The receptacle of the 'Success Phase' is the main soul. It is groomed in such a way that it does not want to 'pro-create'—it only 'creates'. It has no attachment to anything. (Rebirth takes place because you're attached to your worldly desires; you want to fulfil them by being born again). In this phase, your entire consciousness is beyond all calculations of profit and loss, good and evil, blessing or curse, credit or discredit.

The whole exercise is aimed at evolving the consciousness from 'pre-human' to 'human', and from 'human' to 'post-human'. The supermen, who are 'post-human', highlight the truth to the general people of the world in their own way, in their own language, because they have realised it—the purpose of this life. They have realised the truth that everything is an illusion, that attachments are impermanent—they are not long-lasting.

Following the 'Chari Chandra' Fakir Sadhana, the devotee acquires the power to restrain his semen from getting out and thus prevents his downfall. He becomes stable. He acquires the rare power of self-control and self-restraint—thus conquering two enemies of the mind directly—'Kam' (or 'Lust') and 'Lobh' ('Greed' to enjoy the partner's body). Indirectly, the other enemies of the mind—'Krodh' ('Anger'), Mad ('Ego'), Moha ('Infatuation/Attachment') and 'Matsarya' ('Jealousy') are all tamed.

As long as he is not able to restrain the release of his semen, he is totally unstable, ungrounded. Unless you can preserve your semen, you cannot be a 'Fakir'. Those who do not have the procreative and ejaculative power under their own control, they have to suffer a lot throughout their lives. *(References 16 & 17)*

Fakir Lalon Shah expresses his thoughts about the life and style of a Fakir in one of his songs: *(Reference 18)*

"Oh, my friend!
Unless you get to know what is not known to you
How would you lead the life of a 'Fakir'?
How would you do 'Fakiri'?
The light that shines from the prophet, the God's messenger
I wish that it showers on me.
That flow of light...that glow of light is embracing all other lights.
But when you try to catch it...you try to touch it
It becomes dangerous lightning!!
The light that shines in the lowest of the 'chakras'—the 'Muladhar'
Without that light everything immerses into darkness

(Here, the poet is possibly referring to semen ('bastu' or 'pitridhan', which is potent with the power of 'creation' of life. If semen is ejaculated and not retained, then the light will be lost and everything will plunge into darkness)

He, in whose mind, the seed of pure love has been planted,
He only can see the shine and feel the power!!

Siraj Sai says, 'Lalon, get your body ready for the merger of lights
And witness that spectacular sight'!!

Backward Bauls, Yet most Advanced in Certain Respects

Only recently, the New England Journal of Medicine reported about the outstanding success of a faecal transplant (transplantation of the faeces of one person to another). The faecal transplant proved so much more effective and less expensive than a treatment using a strong antibiotic that the hospital deemed it unethical to continue giving the antibiotics to the patients and stopped the study.

There was another more revolutionary procedure in which researchers took faecal transplant to the next level, "Poop in a Pill". Children infected with *C. difficile* were given an oral faecal transplant with great success. *(Reference 19)*

This is an example of a research study of a most advanced level. Bauls and Fakirs have already been taking poop tablets (faeces mixed with soil and made into pills), in pockets though, for their health maintenance with good success. So, although this community is backward in many respects, they are advanced in certain other aspects. This practice is also reported in Traditional Chinese Medicine.

As a part of the 'Chari Chandra Bhed', by consuming the menstrual fluid, urine, and the stool of a female, the male—I presume, is acquiring some feminineness in him which makes him more understanding and care-giving than being all too individualistic.

What is 'BaulOlogy'

Why Bauls and Fakirs, the wandering minstrels of Bengal are different from the members of all other sects? They are not followers of any of the standard religions—Hinduism, Islam, Christianity, Judaism, Buddhism, Jainism, Sikhism, yet they have a distinct identity of their own. All these religions are scriptural and regimented—designed to transform 'Pre-human' consciousness to 'Human' and, in a few cases, to 'Post-human' consciousness. Bauls and Fakirs have the same aim, but they are less philosophical, less abstract, more physical, more practical. They are (Bauls especially) are relentlessly searching for the 'Man of the Heart' ('Moner Manush') not in any sacred text or religious ritual like offering any oblation or 'namaj', but in the field, amidst human crowds and congregations. Nevertheless, when he comes and when he disappears—nobody knows. Who is the Baul's 'Man of the Heart'? What are his special qualities that he will get a permanent place in your heart? Or, is he a heartful and soulful person who will win you over easily at the first encounter?

Some researchers are of the opinion that the Bauls and Fakirs have been influenced by the 'Sahajiya' concept. What is this 'Sahajiya' concept- I was curious to know. 'Sahajiya', I gathered, was a form of Hindu Tantric Vaishnavism (influenced by Bengali Buddhist tantric tradition known as 'Sahaja') focused on the romantic relationship between Radha & Krishna. The 'Sahajiyas' believe that such an innate desire exists in everyone and that is what is 'Sahaja' meaning 'simple', 'natural/innate' or 'spontaneous'. The 'Sahajiyas' seek to experience the union between two romantic lovers through its physical enactment in tantric ritual. Thus, they often made use of sexual intercourse in their 'sadhanas'. They understand 'Krishna' as being the inner cosmic form ('svarupa') of every man and likewise 'Radha' was seen as the inner form of every woman. However, was it easy to acquire such 'bhava' (feeling) and 'rasa' (emotional flavour) unless the male and female partners performing the 'sadhana' were very close and intimate with each other—was an enquiry that bothered me. Could it be effectively practised when the relationship was just mechanical? *(Reference 20)*

Such questions intrigued me to delve deep into their lifestyle, philosophy and practices—especially their songs and style of singing and dancing. The outcome is 'BaulOlogy'.

'BaulOlogy' is a term coined by me. Baul songs and dances feature most prominently amongst all types of folk art and culture of India. There are several articles, books, and scientific papers published by Indian, Bangladeshi and Western scholars on the Bauls and Fakirs of Bengal. These publications primarily deal with the historical, sociological, and philosophical facets of the culture, rituals and practices followed by them. Although superficially mentioned, nobody has attempted to delve a little deeply into the biological and psychological aspects that form the core of such practices. 'BaulOlogy' is an endeavour to try that out. Nevertheless, it is just not a treatise covering the 'Deha Tattva' (the 'Doctrine of the Body'), the 'Srishti Tattva' (the 'Doctrine of Creation') and the 'Atma Tattva' (the 'Doctrine of the Self') which play prominent roles in the Baul parlance, I've made an attempt to look at the Bauls and Fakirs holistically.

In this project, I have received help from several publications and people. The people have included practicing Bauls and Fakirs and others who have closely mixed and moved with them in their ashrams and akhras as well as different melas and folk musical gatherings in West Bengal, India and in Bangladesh.

References

[1] Shaktinath Jha, *Fakir Lalon Sai: Desh, Kal ebong Shilpa* (in Bengali), Kolkata: Sangbad, 1995, p. 40, Song No. 115. (English translation mine)

[2] Shaktinath Jha, *Bastubadi Baul* (in Bengali), Kolkata: Dey's Publishing, Refurbished Dey's 1st Edition, 2010, p. 86.

[3] John Gregory Bourke, *Scatalogic Rites of All Nations*, Connecticut: Martino Fine Books, Refurbished Edition 2009.

[4] Robert Keith Wallace PhD and Samantha Wallace, *Gut Crisis: How Diet, Probiotics, and Friendly Bacteria Help You Lose Weight and Heal Your Body and Mind*, Fairfield, IA: Dharma Publications, 2017, p. xii.

[5] Shaktinath Jha, *Fakir Lalon Sai: Desh, Kal ebong Shilpa* (in Bengali), Kolkata: Sangbad, 1995, pp. 409-410.

[6] Sasha Warren, "How the Earth and Moon formed, explained", uchicago news.

[7] Kerry Lotzof, "How did the Moon form?" Natural History Museum.

[8] *Origin of the Moon*—Wikipedia.

[9] "There's A Moon Inside My Body"—Poem by Kabir, PoemHunter.com

[10] Shaktinath Jha, *Bastubadi Baul*, Kolkata: Dey's Publishing, First Modified and Enlarged Dey's Edition, 2010, p. 313.

[11] 'Bristol Stool Scale'—Wikipedia.

[12] Sudhir Chakrabarti (edited): *Bangla Dehatattver Gan*, Kolkata: Pustak Bipani, 3rd Impression, April 2017, p. 129.

[13] Sudhir Chakrabarti (edited): *Bangla Dehatattver Gan*, Kolkata: Pustak Bipani, 3rd Impression. April 2017, pp. 129-130.

[14] Natalie Angier, *Woman: An Intimate Geography*, New York: Houghton Mifflin, 1999, p. 107.

[15] *Kosha*—Wikipedia.

[16] Abdel Mannan, *Lalon Darshan* (in Bengali), Dhaka: Rodella Prakashani, 4th Impression, 2021.

[17] Abdel Mannan (Editor), *Akhanda Lalon Sangeet* (in Bengali), Dhaka: Rodella Prakashani, 3rd Edition, 2013.

[18] Shaktinath Jha, *Fakir Lalon Sai: Desh, Kal ebong Shilpa* (in Bengali), Kolkata: Sangbad, 1995, p. 41, Song No. 119/120. (Bengali translation mine)

[19] Robert Keith Wallace PhD and Samantha Wallace, *Gut Crisis: How Diet, Probiotics And Friendly Bacteria Help You Lose Weight and Heal Your Body and Mind*, Fairfield, IA: Dharma Publications, 2017, pp. 2-3.

[20] *Vaishnava Sahajiya*—Wikipedia.

Contents

CHAPTER 1

Into the Portal of World's 'Baulsphere'

The 'Baulsphere': Past and Present

I have used the term 'Baulsphere' to denote the spread of the domain of the Bauls of Bengal. Yesterday and the day before, the 'Baulsphere' was restricted to the undivided Bengal and, later, the State of West Bengal in India and Bangladesh, inhabited by the Bengali-speaking people. There are so many folk cults in India, but the Bauls constituted one of the front-ranking ones. Today, it has left its footprints in the West also—especially in the US, Europe and Australia and also in the Far East—especially in Japan—although not in a very organised way. It has not been so for all other folk cults of India, except for the Bhangra dance form of Punjab.

An Indian art form can either be exported from India or imported by a foreign country. We have found stray cases of import of Indian music by a foreign country like Britain during the British Raj on some very special occasion like some celebration of the Royalty. Pandit Ravi Shankar was the first ambassador of Indian music to the western world. He was an out-and-out explorer and exporter. A few more Indian musicians, who were not so outgoing or entrepreneurial, followed his tail. Just about the time he was carrying the flag but had not hoisted it, I had spent three nights and four days with him in an apartment on Finsbury Park in London N4. The year was 1962, and the month was August. He was like a pilot car clearing the route to the West for all other Indian musicians from the North and the South of our sub-continent.

He was preceded by another art ambassador who introduced emotion-packed Indian cinema to the logical-rational West, with great success—a person no less than the Oscar-winning Satyajit Ray. I had breakfast with him, at his Mudiyali-South Calcutta residence, in August 1955—

with an overwhelmed heart the weekend after I watched his immortal creation 'Pather Panchali' at the Basusree Cinema in South Calcutta. I didn't have a clue that I'd be having a soul-to-soul talk with Maestro Ravi Shankar who had scored the value-adding music for the Ray movie, exactly after 7 years.

In 1962, I had the occasion to meet another Indian art ambassador, Ustad Alla Rakha who had accompanied Ravi on the double drum percussion during his exploratory trip to the West. In most recent times, Ustad Ji's son Zakir Hussain has been championing his late father's cause. I've never met him but I get to taste his glory from his elder sister's husband Md Ayub Walia of London who is a great friend of mine.

In the domain of country music, the Bauls of Bengal are unparalleled in their lifestyle as well as philosophy and musical art. As their world started unfolding before my eyes, I came to know that the first exporter of the songs of the Baul to the West was Purna Das Baul, the accomplished son of Late Nabani Das Baul who was a close associate of Nobel Laureate Rabindranath Tagore. Tagore, I'm told, used to regard Nabani as his 'Baul Guru'. He motivated Nabani to teach Baul songs to the then students of music at the Viswa Bharati University. Nabani had taught a few Baul numbers to the former Indian PM Late Indira Gandhi also.

Purna Das was taken on a long trip to the US in 1967 by Albert Grossman, former manager of Bob Dylan, the 2016 Literature Nobel awardee. Time then was just ripe for the 'twilight language'-based Baul songs to be presented to the Western youth who were getting disgruntled with the religious doctrines followed in their culture and attempting to break away by unfettering the chains of customs and habits. They were looking for liberation in sex, drugs and hippie lifestyle—which somewhat resembled the philosophy and practices of Baul fakirs, although Purna Das did not represent the typical fakiri class and culture. Purna Das was thus not an exporter of Indian art and culture to the West, rather his sponsor Albert Grossman was an importer.

Bauls, in every respect, have been studied thoroughly by the local intellectuals in West Bengal, India and Bangladesh over the last few decades. Now, I find, scholars in UK, USA, Europe, Australia and New Zealand have undertaken exhaustive researches on the Bauls. Most notable amongst them are: Prof. Dr Rahul Peter Das, MD PhD of Germany and Dr Manjita Mukherjee, formerly of SOAS, University of London and currently of the University of Pennsylvania, USA. However, none of the scholars from the Bengali- and English-speaking worlds have gone deep into the biological and medical aspects of the songs and lifestyle and culture of the Bauls—which I discovered was a virgin land for me to tread on to with my background in biomedical and human sciences. Thus, my 'BaulOlogy' was born.

I was surprised that while UNESCO, Paris had declared Baul songs in 2008 as 'Intangible Cultural Heritage of Humanity', the decision-makers of the world body have not been able to go beyond a purely myopic vision. *(Reference 1)*

The MAGIC of the Baulsphere

I am counting out the hundreds of Westerners and Non-Resident-Indians, who have taken lessons in 'Indian Classical Music' ('ICM') on the Western soil, like the UK, Europe and USA, and performed par excellence. They are not the ones who have taken pains and faced hazards to come to India on the magic call of ICM.

I closely know only four persons of Western origin on whom 'ICM' worked like magnet and pulled them out to the Indian shores. They had adapted to the Indian culture to learn 'ICM' in the traditional Guru-Shishya Parampara style, and have earned accolades in India and in their own and other western lands. They are Amie Maciszewski (sitar) from USA, Clem Alford (sitar) from UK, Lester Silver (sitar) from New Zealand, and Carsten Wicke (rudra veena) from Germany. For the first trip to his Gurukul in Midnapore in West Bengal, India, Clem Alford had trekked all the way from London travelling through Europe, the Middle East, Afghanistan, and Pakistan. Carsten Wicke has made Kolkata his second home where he spends a good bit of time every year. Both he and Lester Silver have also mastered the art and science of musical instrument making. This is the MAGIC of 'Indian Classical Music' ('ICM').

The Baulsphere of Bengal has welcomed Westerners to spend months and years in West Bengal, India and Bangladesh to get to know their music, culture and lifestyle closely; and, I have come to know of some of them. Many Westerners continue to visit the Baul 'akhras', 'melas' and festivals in both these places. Some of them also take interest to learn Baul songs, make documentaries, or write stories about them. But I was so much struck by the case of Deborah that I'm tempted to share her story with you.

Who is this Deborah that I'm talking about? Deborah Cukirman is a Frenchwoman who has transformed herself into a dedicated devotee of the mystic legendary Baul Lalon Fakir Shah and has also started living in Daulatpur, Kusthia, Bangladesh. This I call the MAGIC of the Baulsphere.

She had a feeling, when she was very young, of only 14-15 years age, that her place was somewhere else—not in the materialistic modern French society. Her outlook was somewhat different. She never wanted to have a commonplace life. However, she hardly knew that her call will come from the distant East—from the tropical plains, from a simple rural farmland.

In the past, Deborah had worked as a translator and yoga teacher in France. She also had some connection with the French film industry and had a role to play amongst the organisers of the Cannes International Film Festival. As a part of her post-Master's programme in philosophy in a French University, she had to spend some time in South India to study the philosophy of comparative religions. There, she came across the name of the Bauls of Bengal and was fascinated by the philosophy of Lalon Fakir and cherished a dream to visit Kusthia in Bangladesh where Lalon had lived. She came to Bangladesh in February 2016 for researching on the life and philosophy of Fakir Lalon Shah, and got intrigued by what she learnt and heard. She did return to France but failed to stay there for long—the attraction of the Lalon MAGNET was so strong.

She not only returned to Bangladesh but became the disciple of the renowned Baul Fakir Nahir Shaha who belongs to the Lalon lineage.

Whatever little I've studied about the Bauls of Bengal, if I look at them in the light of the Vedic (Ref: Taittiriya Upanishad) 'Pancha Kosha' concept, I can easily classify them into two very broad categories. The one with an ordinary or normal consciousness, trying to fulfil the 'Biological and Social Imperatives' (BSI) driven by the lower order human bodily needs of 'Tamasic Food and Sex', they are driven by the 'Annamaya Kosha', 'Pranamaya Kosha' and 'Monomaya Kosha' levels. The other one with a higher (beyond 'physical'—shall we say, 'spiritual' needs satisfaction) consciousness is related to the 'Vijnanamaya' and 'Anandamaya' Koshas. Kangal Harinath, Bhaba Pagla, and Lalon Fakir and his direct disciple lineage belong to this second category. They are vegetarians, they don't smoke hemp (ganja), nor do they have many sadhan-sanginis to indulge in 'tantric sex'. They are 'Sattvic' by nature and temperament, displaying love and compassion for all. They believe that God is within you—in every human being. That is why they sing: "*Manush bhojle sonar manush hobi*" ("*If you care for the humankind, you'll become a precious golden man*"). Fakir Nahir Shaha, Deborah's Guru, belongs to this category. Deborah finds life in the Guru's 'ashram' extremely serene and peaceful. She has not only picked up Bengali, she can now speak the language fluently and can also sing Baul songs without much hassle.

Under the tutelage of Nahir Shaha, Deborah now is married not only spiritually to Lalon's philosophy but also to her physical life partner, Nahir's pupil Rajon—who is a very nice, soft-spoken young Baul. Together, they have made a most decent 'made-for-each-other' Baul couple, much sought-after in their local society.

Baul Philosophy: Local or Global (?)

Richard Alpert (1931-2019) was a Harvard psychology professor. As he used to conduct researches on 'Altered Consciousness' which required the use of addictive narcotics, he had to leave his tenured professorship. The University of Harvard did not approve of his weird research activities. He decided to leave the US and make a trip to India in search of sadhus and yogis from whom he could learn the routes to reach 'Altered Consciousness'. He finally located a 'real' spiritual master 'Neem Karoli Baba' in North India and became his protégé. The Guru re-christened him as 'Baba Ram Das' and showered spiritual wisdom on him. Ram Das returned to the US, wrote many books, delivered deeply thought-out lectures, and had a very big following in the US. Ram Das, thus, was an 'importer' of Hindu spiritual doctrines to the West.

At the instance of Baba Ram Das, another American youth Jeffrey Kagel (1947- New York born), travelled to Uttarakhand in India to be at the feet of the same great Guru. Living with him in his ashram for months and years, Jeffrey got really transformed in his outlook. He realised that the cushy life of pomp and splendour that he had in New York was all 'maya' (= an illusion). The materialism in him gave way to a spiritual thought-process. From Jeffrey Kagel, he became 'Krishna Das' and became almost the right-hand 'shishya' of the Guru.

He had a baritone voice and started participating in the 'kirtan' singing sessions in the Baba's ashram—eventually earning the lead role, once he overcame the language problem. One day, suddenly his 'Master' told him to leave India (using only hand gesture and verbal 'bhago' meaning 'go away') and return to his homeland—where he really belonged. Today, Krishna Das and his 'kirtan' troupe is the most sought-after Hindu devotional band in the Western world. I had requested for a WhatsApp appointment with him, through his Secretary Ms Nina Rao, but still waiting on the queue; he is so busy.

This is the case of a Westerner who has imported Indian devotional genre 'kirtan'—in my definition 'sacred music', into the materialistic western world with great success, helping the western audience earn not only happiness but also mental peace and spiritual bliss for an hour or two which help them carry on with poise for a few more hours, before they go for the next dose from Krishna Das's professional recordings. I have used Krishna Das's 'kirtan' to provide solace to a local patient of chronic depression with astonishing result.

So, my question is: if the American man Jeffrey Kagel (alias Krishna Das) could do it, why not the Frenchwoman Deborah Cukirman (alias Deborah Jannat)? I mean, exporting Baul songs and Lalon philosophy to France, the country of her origin—to her part of the world. If you would recall, that earlier, I had written that the credit of taking the Baul Songs and Baul spirit must go to Purna Das Baul who was taken on a long trip to the US by the former manager of Bob Dylan. Purna Das had stayed for long and got the opportunity of interacting closely with the art world luminaries like Bob Dylan, Pete Seeger, Alan Ginsberg, Mick Jagger and Bob Marley. That was a golden era. Subsequently, nothing much has happened by way of musical journeys of Bengali Bauls to the West barring a few stray cases.

I recently got to know through my German lady friend Ursula Hasenbusch, resident in France, that a Bengali couple, Mimlu Sen, translator-musician-composer-author-producer (read her most absorbing treatise '*The Honey Gatherers*', London: Rider, 2010) and her husband Paban Das Baul have settled in Paris, France, for nearly three decades now. I understand that Paban, who has been presenting Baul songs in a westernised package is quite a star in Europe. Paban had first visited France long ago with the legendary Baul Gour Kheypa, when Mimlu Sen had first met them. Gour Khyepa, although sparsely educated, was a Baul philosopher and subsequently he had visited the West more than once not only to perform but to deliver discourses at a few Universities.

This is the age of globalisation. Like the cuisine and confectioneries of Bengal (for example: K.C. Das's 'Rosogollas') which have gained popularity in the Western world, Bengali art, craft, literature, music, dancing, cinema and theatre must find a market there. I feel proud about Parvathy Baul, the superstar Bengali Baul singer who has been so successful in presenting her well-designed Baul song-and-dance packages to the elite western audience at venues like the British Museum in London.

The lack of outgoingness on the part of Deborah, is it because her Guru Fakir Nahir Shaha has preferred her to remain secretive—entirely to herself lest she will be misunderstood by her folks in France, the Lalon songs are so much shrouded in mysticism? Or, is it because she has not graduated from her Lalon school as yet—she is still incomplete—may not be able to answer tricky questions to the questioners' satisfaction? Or is it because the philosophy of the Baul community is to remain content with basics?

'Indian Classical Music' ('ICM') and 'kirtan' have medicinal values. What medicinal values do Baul songs have? Do they have any therapeutic applications at all?

I am told, that many Baul songs have educational value. What exactly do they mean—I will slowly move into that realm. Please bear with me.

Sharing Observations

Before I take a dive into the depths of Baul culture and philosophy, I'm attempting to write a 'Prologue', sharing a few of my general observations with you. [Again, I'm telling you that these are not borrowed from any published documents like an article, a scientific paper, a book, a documentary movie or a feature film which I've read and viewed quite a bit of late. These are based on my own biomedical, neuro-scientific, socio-psychological and management knowledge and decades of experience. Questions and comments would be most welcome.]

Observation 1

Miyan Tansen, the King of Hindustani Classical Music was born a Hindu (Ramtanu Pandey), then converted to Islam. Sant Kabir, the King of 'Nirguna Bhajans' was born a Hindu, but brought up by Muslims. Lalon Shah Fakir, the King of the Bauls was born in a 'kayastha' Hindu family (according to most authoritative scholars) but, post-adolescence groomed by a Muslim couple and indoctrinated by a Muslim 'Murshid' (Arabic for 'guide' or 'teacher'). Bob Dylan, the King of American folk-singing (who calls himself the Baul of America - *Reference 8*) had suffered from 'ADHD' ('Attention Deficit Hyperactivity Disorder') which deterred his concentration and made him restless—really like a 'Baul'. What I want to say is that all these doyens of music had a 'kink' in the lineage or in 'brain health'.

Observation 2

If you're born in a Baul family and pursue 'Baulship' as your career, you don't have to utilise much of the power installed in your cranial brain (the tissue between your two ears) since you have already inherited a 'Baul brain circuitry' from your ancestry. Much more creditworthy is a Baul who was born in a non-musical family and became a 'Baul', took up 'Baulship' as his career. The best example is 'Lalon Fakir' as for pursuing his career he had to plant and grow new types of circuits in his brain.

In Hindustani Classical Music, Late Ustads Ali Akbar and Vilayat Khans will come in my first category whereas Late Pandits Ravi Shankar and Nikhil Banerjee would feature in my second group.

Observation 3

If, as a Baul, you compose the lyric, provide the tune, play the instruments (ektara or dotara, and duggie or khamak) while performing and go for freestyle, improvised, whirling dance like a Sufi Darbesh, you are utilising the bulk of your head brain (which has anything between 8,500 to 10,000 million brain cells or 'neurons') whereas if you're singing a Baul song composed and tuned by your Guru or somebody else, playing an ektara or dotara and accompanied by a jazzy band, then you're using a much smaller percentage of your installed brainpower (may be only 10 to 15 percent as the common saying goes). As a senior Brain Scientist, I'm reminding you about a confirmed biological law that all our body and brain cells follow, and that Is: 'Use Me or Lose Me'.

Observation 4

My years of in-depth research in human brain and behaviour has prompted me to classify 'Human Consciousness' ('HC') into 3 (three) different categories in terms of physical relationships with the opposite sex.

These are:

1. **Pre-Human:** Applicable to people who are promiscuous, not hesitant to having intimate physical relationship with more than one member of the opposite sex. Here the 'drive' comes from the creaturely 'hind' and 'mid-brains' which are respectively predominant in 'Reptilian' and 'Paleo-mammalians' portions of the brain.
2. **Human:** Applicable to those who are happy with only one partner of the opposite sex. This 'drive' comes from the 'Neo-mammalian' portion of the brain which is largest in thickness in humans.
3. **Post-human:** Where the individual does not need any physical relationship with any member of the opposite sex—he/she can handle both the male and female sex hormones present inside his/her body (that is, 'Testosterone – T' and 'Estrogen – E' and 'Progesterone – P') in a way by using some special yogic breathing techniques (in Bengali Baul language—'DAMER KHELA', to facilitate male-female union (in Bengali language—'JUGAL SADHANA'). All prophets and high-level Yogis, like Neem Karoli Baba—the Guru of 'Baba Ram Dass' and 'Krishna Das' about whom I had mentioned earlier, belong to the 'Post-human' category.

Observation 5

I now classify lyrics of songs according to these 3 (three) levels of consciousness. Those Baul Songs that deal with 'Deha Tattva' (the 'Doctrine of the Body' related to conception, contraception, retention of semen and vaginal fluid and allied sexual practices belong to the 'Pre-human' level whereas a typical Baul Song as sung by renowned singers like the Purna Das Baul *(Reference 8)* relate to the 'Human' level of 'Consciousness'. I've a feeling that Baul Songs related to the 'Post-human' level of 'Consciousness' are really rare. It is really amazing that Lalon Fakir (who had only one female companion who was his 'sebadasi' and no offspring) had travelled freely, most comfortably and conveniently at all the 3 (three) levels of 'Consciousness'.

The 'Western Baul' Movement

The 'Eastern Baul' movement had its roots planted in the soil of Bengal in the !4th Century. The Baul Philosophy had developed by drawing ideas from different religious domains, like Hinduism, Sufism, Tantric Buddhism, and Taoism. Lee Lozowick (1943–2010) was an Ukranian-American who had founded the 'Western Baul' movement by being inspired by Bengal's Baul philosophy.

Lee's father was an Ukranian-American artist Louis Lozowick and mother, Adele Turner. Tying the wedlock in 1933, Louis and Adele settled down in South Orange of New Jersey in USA. Lee was always interested in the religions of the East, particularly Hinduism.

In 1975, there was sudden transformation in Lee's spiritual thoughts on getting exposed to the underlying philosophy of 'humanism' of the Bauls of Bengal. He had the opportunity to interact with some of the Bauls of Bengal and the realisation dawned on him that the Bauls were his close kins spiritually. In course of the next few months a few American young intellectuals became his close followers and they started regular group discussions, workshops and discourses on the humanistic aspects of spirituality. Eventually, this movement became known as 'The Western Bauls'. It is certainly a feather in the cap of the Bauls of Bengal.

In 1977, while in India on a religious mission, Lee met the Holy Yogi Ramsuratkumar in South India. In 1979, Lee came back to India to meet the Holy Man again, so much was the magnetic attraction between them. Yogi Ramsuratkumar had once said that Lee and he had been very close to each other for many births. After 1979, Lee started sending from the US to Yogi Maharaj his specially composed poems. He would also visit Yogi Maharaj every year with a bunch of his devoted students who were spiritually inclined, to collect Yogi Ji's blessings. Now that Yogi Maharaj and his close protégé Lee, both have left this planet, Lee's followers and devotees still visit Yogi Maharaj's ashram every year to get a feel of his vibrations in the air of the ashram and its surroundings.

The 'Western Baul Movement' recommends moving in a western Baul path whose mission includes:

- To provide some special inputs for realistic and most practical (and not abstract) spiritual advancement.
- To remind about some good spiritual habits and practices.
- To organise special discourses and podcasts and publish newsletters as to how humanism can be practised in modern times.
- To share with the public, in general, Western Baul practices.

Lee Lozowick was a very versatile person. He was a spiritual teacher, poet, songwriter, playwright, singer and author of books packed with spiritual wisdom.

Read more about the 'Western Baul Movement' in the last portion of this volume under the 'Essence of Baulsphere'.

References

[1] "Baul Songs" UNESCO: Intangible Cultural Heritage (Nomination File No. 00107).

[2] UNB, Kushtia, "Love for Lalon brings Frenchwoman to Kushtia", *Prothom Alo English*, 18th October 2018.

[3] "Deborah, a citizen of France, in practice of Lalon", Desh Darpan TV.

[4] *The 'Pancha Kosha' Concept*—Wikipedia.

[5] Saheb Khandare, "Baul Songs of Bengal", academia.edu. https://www.academia.edu

[6] Paban and Mimlu, "West calling: Bengali Baul singers reach foreign shores", *India Writer Network*, 10th September 2015.

[7] Chandrani Banerjee, "Baul Music and the Lure of the West", *TUCK Magazine*; 15th November, 2017.

[8] *E Gari Cholche Aaajab Koley*—Documentary on Purna Das Baul—Unlisted, not for public viewing, specially shared with me by the Filmmaker exclusively for my research purposes.

[9] 'Western Baul' – https://westernbaul.org

[10] 'Western Baul Podcast Series' – https://www.hohmpress.com

[11] 'Western Baul Podcast Series'.

CHAPTER 2

Keynotes

Madcap Making Home in the Hempland

Gour Kheypa (1947-2013) was one of the last living Baul philosophers. He sang in the traditional Baul style with an ektara, a khamak and ghungroo tied around his ankle or to his toes, at times. He was a guest lecturer at the Brown University and the Vassar College. Yet, he was one who followed the tradition of the Bauls and had made his home in the hempland. In other words, he could not live without smoking ganja. He lived life on his own terms. Even in the documentary film 'Kheypar Mon Brindaban' made on him by film-maker Ladly Mukhopadhyay, he is seen smoking ganja and his bidis throughout the film. He turned down an offer to act in Peter Brook's 'Mahabharat' as Brook said he would not be allowed to carry hemp to the US. He, who passed away tragically in a car crash in January 2013, was perhaps the last of the genuine Bauls who lived, thought and ideologised the principles of Baul philosophy and was proud to be a Baul. One keynote of his philosophy was his thrust on how and why the philosophy of the body must transcend into the philosophy of the mind and soul.

He would emphasize again and again that Baul was not just a folk performance but an entire philosophy—a way of life, an ideology of all genuine Bauls live up to and music was just a part of that. He was an advocate for 'natural' against 'artificial'—'expressed' instead of 'suppressed' or 'repressed'—the 'Sahaj Manush' model so much discussed in the Baulsphere.

Let me elaborate on this 'Sahaj Manush' concept from my 'Neuro-management' ('NM') point of view. There are two invisible enemies of our mind which are apparently perceptible to us as most of us are chasing the chimera of 'Success' in life. These two enemies are: number one, our 'Sub-conscious Mind' which stores all our memories of the past; and, number two, our brain's 'Default Mode Network' ('DMN') which gets activated when we are not engaged in any meaningful task—our 'Task Mode Network' is not active. Most of us, in a small, medium, or big way, express our positive experiences but suppress (forcibly put an end or stop) or repress (inhibit a feeling not allowing it to come to the surface) our negative emotions which are potent with negative vibrations. These negative vibrations are invisible to the naked human eyes, and they make our 'aura' negatively charged and affect our relationships with others adversely—even affect our own physical and mental health. *(Reference 2)* Such circumstances make us 'Complex Humans' ('Jatil Manush' in Bengali) instead of 'Simple Humans' ('Sahaj Manush' in Bengali). Does that mean that it would be advisable to be straightforward in our communication—we ought to express all our feelings and emotions—both positive and negative, as Gour Kheypa did. To tell you frankly, such people who have no restraint in their communication, they speak out whatever they feel—are called 'KHEYPA' which means 'mad', 'out of their mind'.

If I have to explain using neuro-science, I'll have to mention that for any stimulation/excitement for action or activation of a brain cell (or 'neuron') to act, the neuro-transmitter 'Glutamate' ('G') is responsible. Its source tissues are present in every part of the nervous system. Its reverse function—that is, of 'restraint' is performed by another neuro-transmitter known as 'GABA'. Imagine, you have some delicious sweets kept in a dish on the table in front of you. When you're tempted and eager to have one, the anticipatory 'feel good' chemical 'Dopamine' ('D') is released from your brain's 'Reward Circuit'—which makes you extend your hand and activates your fingers to pick up a sweet, that is the job of 'G'. But, then the 'Executive Control Centre' of your Pre-Frontal Cortex says you've already had some sweets so you must restrict and restrain yourself—you automatically withdraw your hand without touching the dish. This is the action of 'GABA'. So, I suppose Kheypa Bauls lack in the 'GABA' release in their brains as they are straightforward in their expressions—both verbal and non-verbal. Theoretically, this is supposed to lead to inflammatory conditions which are also hallmarks of mental disturbance and lack of emotional balance—which may prompt the person to be addicted to cannabis, marijuana, or hemp. The victims may have inflammatory bowel disease, depression and anxiety. Both the vagus nerve and gut microbiota are likely involved in this. Stimulation of the vagus nerve has been shown to reduce inflammation and stress, and some researchers are even suggesting that vagus stimulation could be a new drug-free anti-depressant. Certain healthy gut bugs like the probiotic *'Lactobaccilus rhamnosus'*, can even send signals to neurons to release 'GABA' to promote calmness. Research studies need to be conducted to find out whether consumption of faeces in the 'Chari Chandra Ved' ritual has got anything to help solving this problem. *(Reference 3)*

When an innocent child speaks in a straightforward manner, without considering what the impact would be of the communication on the listener(s), when it calls a spade a spade, it is not considered mad; instead, it is 'child-like' behaviour. Mad man, in the Baul-Fakir parlance, does not mean insane. He is branded as 'child-like'. It indicates someone who is free from the bondage of home, family, caste, community, and religion. A mad man has none of these attachments. Like a little child is attached only to its mother, Ramakrishna Paramhansa—who was regarded as a 'mad man' was attached only to the Mother Goddess Kali. There is this famous song composed by Sadhak Ramprasad: *"Oh, Mother! Make me mad"* (In Bengali: *"Amay de Ma pagol kore"*)! Insanity was one of the phases of Sri Radhika's evolving consciousness.

To quote from a Baul song by Gossain Gopal:

> *"Lord Brahma is mad, Lord Bishnu is mad,*
> *another mad man is out of reach,*
>
> *In mountain Kailash, Lord Shiva has become mad*
> *by consuming hemp (ganja) & dhatura." (Reference 4)*

The mad man, that we're concerned here, in my perception is totally 'focussed'. In the language of 'Neuro-management' ('NM'), it is the 'Flow Brain State' when you lose track of time, place, space, the environment (both external and internal), and 'self' (the 'Stupid Ego'). *(Reference 5)*

A true sadhak or worshipper of God is a mad man. The symptoms (not in all cases though) may include: lack of decency, incoherent dialogue, self-talk (at times), consumption of food which are generally considered most disgusting. In social sense, his outfit, behaviour, thought process, habits and rituals—everything appears to be arising out of the abnormal part of mental consciousness. Sometimes, such persons are endowed with mystical powers.

In Baul ritualistic practices, some Baul interns lose their balance during their training period. By smoking cannabis, by trying to pierce the four moons, many Bauls land up in madness, suffering from a suppressed internal conflict between socially acceptable and socially unacceptable practices.

I've bumped on to a most relevant beautiful Baul lyric which I am sharing with you below: *(Reference 6)*

"I come across fake, non-genuine madcaps everywhere
fake, non-genuine madcaps everywhere!
How many are real mad men & eccentrics?
Couldn't get a mad man of my choice,
Oh, dear! Couldn't get a mad man of my liking.

I've found some men are mad in love,
Some are mad about property, wealth, name and fame!
Oh, Kheypa! There are people who are mad for wealth,
name & fame in our land!
Their minds are ridden with desires and attachments,
They don't realise the truth!
I'm so frustrated that I've not been able to find a madcap
whom I could love!

It is really hard to find a madcap like Lord Shiva,
Who drinks poison as if it is nectar,
He rides on the bull, sits on the hide, wears a snake as his necklace,

Oh, Kheypa! He rides on the bull, sits on the hide and wears a snake around his neck!!

Why does he carry a begging bowl,

Who has Goddess Annapurna as his home maker,

Oh, Kheypa! I've not been able to find a mad man of my liking!

There is a madcap above everyone,

Who has nurtured this cosmos,

Who has left this planet being mad in Radha's love!

Oh, The melody of whose flute makes the Yamuna river flow in full stream,

Oh, I haven't got a madcap of my choice.

Oh, I haven't got a mad man of my liking!

Oh, Kheypa! That is why I have not become mad

I'm still far from madness....

As I've not yet found a mad man whom I can love and give everything!!

I haven't got a mad man, an eccentric of my choice!!"

Simply wonderful!!

If I've to look at this verse from my angle, I'd say that the 'mad man of my choice' would be my 'True Passion' which is the result of the convergence of 3-D's: Dream, Drive and Domain. What has been your 'Dream' (you're simply 'mad' for fulfilment of that 'Dream')? What is the fountainhead of your 'Drive'—wherefrom your 'Drive' arises? 'Drive' is the motivating force that makes you act, makes you take bold steps. Have you been able to identify the 'Domain' of your choice—the field where you'll be driven to fulfil your dream? *(Reference 7)*

Let us see how the King of Fakirs, Lalon Shah expresses his wish poetically to win over the mind of the Madman: *(Reference 8)*

"With what wealth can I win over the mind of the Madman?

What wealth do I have, what wealth do I have—I always brood in my mind!"

Lalon's 'Madman' here is most likely his 'Guru'. He is most eager to earn his blessings.

> *"I've my body and mind which certainly represent wealth*
> *but those are not mine—those belong to him only."*

In Baul-Fakir culture, the disciple has to practice total surrender to his Guru. So his personal resources do not remain as his wealth—those would have been surrendered to the Madman.

Lalon says:

> *"I'm just a porter. I carry load for others.*
> *And when I try to think who I am, I can't figure it out, I get lost!"*

> *"Oh! The Madcap is no simple.*
> *What special thought can I mix with my ordinary wealth to make it special for him so that he accepts it readily and happily.*
> *If he does not like what I offer to him, he may run to the cremation ground and smear ashes on his whole body to tone down his frustration so that others avoid him, he appearing eccentric."*

All such wandering thoughts fill the great songwriter's brain's 'Default Mode Network' ('DMN') circuit and he writes:

> *"By having such random thoughts, I've become mad myself, as I cannot stop the thought wave."*

However, Lalon feels that he is still sane and not totally lost like the Madcap.

> *"But, compared to him I'm still OK as I can make out who is close to me and who is distant."*

Finally, Lalon reflects:

> *"This describes the thought process of a man, mad for simple attention and affection from his Guru—when he forgets his own selfish self".*

Worldly sense of self and value system develops 'Practical Intelligence' ('PI'), 'PI' builds the 'I'—the i-identity which brings, in its tail, the 'Six Enemies of the Mind'; Desire ('kam'), Anger ('krodh'),

Greed ('Lobh'), Infatuation ('Moh'), Ego/False Vanity ('Mad') and Jealousy ('Matsarya'). Opposite of 'FI' is 'Innocence'—'madness'. That is why, Sadhak Ramprasad sings: "Oh, Mother! Make me 'mad'". 'Madness' is 'Egolessness' and 'Egolessness' means 'Alive yet dead' (in Bengali: 'Jyante Mara'.)

Poet Gobinda Gossain writes:

> *"Gossain Gobinda says that you will get his feet*
> *provided you are 'alive or living yet dead'"*

The Minstrels Amidst Nature

We are auto-piloted healing machines. When we have a cut, it heals automatically. When we have a bone fracture, a callous is formed automatically at the site of the fracture, even if the injury is not clinically managed. This auto-healing power was very strong and effective in our forest-dwelling hunter-gatherer ancestors as they were living in the midst of Nature and its vast resources. They would drink and bathe in spring water, eat fresh fruits and vegetables and consume fish, birds and animal flesh captured and killed by them. They had a very strong immunity system. And, moreover, they used to hear Nature's beautiful music all the time around them, which served them as 'medicine' and healing sound vibrations for the trillions of microbial guests living on the surface and inside the body.

For the metro, urban and semi-urban people like you and me, the food that we eat are products of 'trauma' caused by pesticides and herbicides, as well as long storage in refrigerators, ice boxes and chemical processing. The water that we drink is delivered to us through miles long pipelines which have sediment-thick inner wall, after treatment at water treatment plants. We swim in swimming pools which have chlorinated water. We use fluoride toothpastes, chemical-rich soaps, hair oils, shampoo, after shave lotion, face cream, and body spray. The make-up that ladies go for are all extra-artificial.

Each of us, modern men and women, young-middle-aged and old, is living inside an artificial bubble. The trillions of microbes that are our guests on the surface and inside our bodies who are the successors of the invisible creatures that our pre-historic ancestors had nurtured on and in their bodies are not at all happy. They are sufferers of multi-faceted trauma which we are not consciously aware of as we are so much involved in the rat race for success and material acquisitions. Some of us are becoming materially rich but physically and mentally we are falling apart, failing to enjoy the wealth that we have accumulated. Most of us are suffering from some minor, mediocre, and major health problems. As a remedy, the allopathic doctors practising western medicine are prescribing antibiotics which upset our gut's microbial diversity, damaging our gut health.

There is a very interesting research study that I would like to share. A team of medical missionaries gifted a few boxes of antibiotics to a group of African forest-dwelling tribals, and asked them to consume at the sign of any illness. The tribals were thrilled to see the aluminium foil packaging and ate up all those tablets and capsules merrily and, on the next day, when their stool samples were tested—to the utter surprise of the researchers, it was observed that the gut microbiota of the tribals had remained almost unaffected because of their extra-strong immunity. Apart from their existence in the midst of Mother Nature, one main reason was—they were listening to the MUSIC of the Nature all the time. It is a real case study. *(References 9 & 10)*

The Bauls and Fakirs of Bengal are wandering minstrels living mostly on alms which consist of grains, fruits and vegetables—all fresh, grown in the backyard of the villagers. They are in regular touch with the rural soil from where they acquire fresh microbes of different genres. They drink water from rivers, streams and springs where they also go for having a wash. They listen to the MUSIC of the NATURE—including bird songs which are often referred in the lyrics of their songs. They breathe fresh air, play in the dirt and dust. So, madcap Bauls and Fakirs are dirty, they have filthy habits like 'tantric sex' and 'Chari Chandra Bhed', but they are much more resilient than the non-madcaps of the rural society.

Search for the Soul

In the 'Pancha Kosha' model of 'Taittiriya Upanishad' *(Reference 11)*, the 'Soul' or the 'Jivatma' is hidden under five sheaths that represent the 'Gross Body' ('Sthula Sarira') and the 'Subtle Body' ('Sukshma Sarira'). The 'Gross Body' is the visible 'Annamaya Kosha' that represents everything grossly physical and materialistic providing pleasure and comfort to the body, starting with food, clothes and shelter, and sex. I describe it as the 'Dietary Energy' ('E-D'). 'E-D' covers sexual satisfaction also as sex is the food for our genital organs. The 'Subtle Body' starts with the 'Pranamaya Kosha'—the life force—the 'Breath Energy' ('E-B'). The sheath next to the 'Pranamaya' is the 'Monomaya Kosha' which represents the 'Emotional Energy' ('E-E'). It involves interaction and exchange of ideas and feelings with others, the ultimate aim being 'Relationship Building'. It includes sexual relationship based on 'love' (or 'prem') and not just 'kam', which comes under 'Annamaya Kosha'.

In the Baulsphere, the Bauls and Fakirs are associated with these three 'Koshas'. They talk about 'kam rati' which is related to 'E-D'. They talk about 'Damer Khela', 'Haoa', 'Bad Haoa' which are all related to 'E-B'. They talk about 'prem rati', 'sahaj manush', 'moner manush', 'manush tattva' and so on—which are all related to 'E-E'.

The sheath next to the 'Monomaya' is 'Vijnanamaya'—which is 'Intellectual Energy' ('E-I'). I have recently come to know closely a young Bangladeshi who, I presume, would fit into this 'E-I' group. His name is Sudam Sadhu; he is a Hindu Lalonpanthi, specialising in the 'Tattva's of philosophical nature rather than those linked with the 'Gross Body' like Deha Tattva, Janma Tattva, Prajanan Tattva, and such other physical aspects. Sudam would be around 35 in age; dressed entirely in white, he lives the life of a recluse in a small earthen hut near the Lalon's majar in Kusthia. He has got a very powerful voice which he uses with ease to render beautiful Baul songs. He also gives lectures and discourses with equal ease using his soft yet most confident vocal tool.

The innermost sheath protecting the Jivatma is the 'Anandamaya Kosha' which is the source of creative energy 'E-C'. 'E-C' was/is very strong in all the Fakirs and Bauls who create songs, Fakir Lalon Shah being the most prominent amongst them. Through their creations, they get united with the 'Paramatma'.

Bauls believe that 'atma' (or the 'soul') is in the 'sukranu'. Each 'sukranu' has its own typical 'atma'. Scientifically speaking the 'sperm' (or 'sukranu') is a storehouse of 'Creative Energy' and I would be tempted to look at it in terms of the 'Pancha Kosha' model as it would have all those propensities of the five koshas in it, in differing quantities from one 'sukranu' to another.

There is a Baul verse:

> *"This body is a bundle of soil*
> *Filled only with 'air'." (Reference 12)*

Read what Fakir Lalon Shah's direct disciple Duddu Shah writes:

> *"Soul is nothing mystifying,*
> *Nor it is an object of mystery.*
> *Being a combination of different ingredients,*
> *The Soul emerges and manifests itself,*
> *In a living creature and remains there until it breathes its last."*
> *(Reference 13)*

Real 'life force' or 'soul' is in the 'menstrual blood carrying the ova' and 'semen carrying the sperms'. But, both the 'ovum' and the 'sperm' move out of the body, being driven by 'vayu' or 'air'. Again, the 'sperms' contained in the semen are brought back with the help of 'vayu' or 'air'. If we believe that our 'soul' is nested in the 'semen' then with every ejaculation, the soul is becoming broken into pieces, its integrated wholeness is disturbed. Therefore, 'vayu' or 'air' has tremendous significance. A Baul sadhak attaches value to good air and bad air. The main thing is—the 'semen' is always moved or driven by 'air'.

> *"Those who deal with the yoga related to 'breathing in & breathing out', all of them are called 'Bauls'." (Reference 14)*

There is a 'nadi' inside the 'Sushumna Nadi', which is called the 'Vajra Nadi'. This 'nadi' is the carrier of 'semen' and it controls the sexual energy within us. With the help of some 'mudras', one can control the 'Vajra Nadi' as well as the flow of 'semen'.

'Sadhanas' are related to different levels of consciousness. Most Bauls and Fakirs go for body-based sadhanas, which is also common amongst the Tantriks. One of the goddesses that the Tantra-adoring Buddhists used to worship was 'Vajreswari' (has it got anything to do with the 'Vajra Nadi' inside the 'Sushumna', I don't know). However, the Vaishnavas talk about one goddess Basuli who is linked with Tantra, Vajrajan and Sahajjani Vaishnava cult. Goddess Basuli was supposed to be a very pious lady. Some of the New Age Bauls used to perform their 'sadhana' centering around the thought of this Goddess.

In body-based 'sadhana', the woman of piety, is regarded as the 'Guru of Consciousness' or the 'Guru of Love'! This Guru remains unexposed and unintroduced. She helps the male to be self-aware—to be aware of what powers he has for pro-creation (aka 'creation' of new life)—which he can use for procreation or restrict/control for 'creations' of a higher order which is impossible for other creatures. This woman is the person the sadhak has been looking for and 'Tribeni' is the place for her worship.

'Tribeni' is the female genital organ where the three 'nadis'—Ida, Pingala and Sushumna are originating from and it is the place from where the menstrual blood, the vaginal discharge as well as urine are released. 'Urine' is the fluidic waste of the body which is of great value in preventing diseases when consumed. In men also, the path through which semen and urine are released is the same. There is a study that circulates in the Baul society is that the urine of Prophet Muhammad had never touched the ground of Mecca. When the prophet was in his death bed, his attendant, instead of throwing out his urine, used to drink it himself.

Unless you have attained satisfaction by fulfilment of your sexual desire, you cannot be a 'liberated' person. Whenever, you are not task-engaged, your brain's 'Default Mode Network' ('DMN') would have disturbing sex-related thoughts.

You must practically realise what power you have inside your own body to 'create' another human being, where the male provides the seed ('bij/ bastu') and the female provides the fertile land. This is the mundane, lower level of 'creation'. Once you've experienced it practically, you now have the opportunity for utilising the same resource for the higher level of 'creation': creating a piece of music or dance, a work of art or culture, some literature, or even a scientific theory, or a technical innovation. The same resource or power having two altogether opposite ends of application.

There is a Baul proverb:

> *"Where I've been born, that is my place of work;*
> *That is from where I can earn something higher!"*

Those who belong to the 'Annamaya', 'Pranamaya' and 'Monomaya' Koshas of the 'Pancha Kosha' model, they are most active on 'body consciousness' ('Dehabad'). They know that mantra, offering worship, meditation and such other strategies which are normally recommended, do not help in toning down the charge in the whole body and stilling the mind. Mind cannot be stilled unless the body is totally relaxed. The 'ParaSympathetic Nervous System' ('PSNS') state has to be attained, which happens when you connect your body with that of the 'Person of Your Heart' ('Moner Manush' in Bengali). During such long-lasting physical connection when ejaculation is controlled, all thoughts, worries and anxieties disappear. Baul's 'DMN' has got engaged in a 'Task' that he enjoys most, he is deeply in love with….!!

References

[1] Shoma Chatterji, "The wandering minstrel who turned down Peter Brooks' Mahabharat", *indiatogether*, 29 October 2014.

[2] Rupert Sheldrake, *Morphic Resonance: The Nature of Formative Causation*, New York: Simon & Schuster, 2009.

[3] Heather Gerrie, "Our second brain: More than a gut feeling", The University of British Columbia, Faculty of Medicine: Graduate Programme in Neuroscience.

[4] Shaktinath Jha, *Bastubadi Baul* (in Bengali), Kolkata, Dey's Publishing, 1st Dey's Refurbished Edition, 2010, pp. 92-93. English translation of the verse is mine.

[5] Mihalyi Csikszentmihalyi, *FLOW: The Psychology of Optimal Experience*, New York: Harper Perennial Modern Classics, 2008.

[6] "Moner moto pagol khunje pelam na". Bengali Lyrics. (English translation mine)

[7] Siddhartha Ganguli, *SMART Leading & Parenting of Teenage Kids in the Digital Era: A Neuro-managed Way*, New Delhi: Allied Publishers, 2021.

[8] Shaktinath Jha, *Fakir Lalon Sai: Desh, Kale ebong Shilpa* (in Bengali), Kolkata: Sangbad, 1995, p. 38, Song No. 26. English translation mine.

[9] Zach Bush, "The Root Cause of Disease and How to Prevent it", Video presentation.

[10] Jack Gilbert and Rob Knight, *Dirt is Good: The Advantage of Germs for Your Child's Developing Immune System.*, New York: St. Martin's Press, 2017.

[11] *Kosha*—Wikipedia.

[12] Shaktinath Jha, *Bastubadi Baul*, (in Bengali), Kolkata: Dey's Publishing, Refurbished First Dey's Edition, 2010, p. 91.

[13] Upendranath Bhattacharys, *Banglar Baul o Baul Gan* (in Bengali), Kolkata: Orient Book Co., 5th Edition. Bengali Year 1426, English 2019-2020, pp. 810-811.

[14] Upendranath Bhattacharya, *Banglar Baul o Baul Gan* (in Bengali), Kolkata: Orient Book Co., 5th Edition, Bengali Year 1426, English 2019-2020, p. 47.

CHAPTER 3

The Baul Alchemistry

Bid Goodbye to 'LUST' (In Bengali: "Kam Ke Dao Biday")

In Hinduism, Islam or Buddhism, if one has to follow the rigid rituals due to social pressure, it is not unlikely that the average follower will tend to suffer from boredom, irritability and stress. Religious history would reveal that orthodox protagonists of religions used to compel innocent people by showing them the 'virtue'-and-'sin' ('carrot-and-stick') bait. In reality, none of these rules and rituals are God-made; they are all man-made. There was thus an imminent need felt by a non-God-fearing class of people to make things much simpler. Thus was the emergence of the 'sahaja' or 'sahajiya' concept which, if I translate into English turns out as one would have it: 'Keep It Simple Stupid' ('KISS').

A cursory glance at the history of Bengal shows that a time came when the deep philosophies of Hinduism, Islam (the Sufi doctrines) and Buddhism were beyond the reach of common people who had to earn their living using their BODY (not so much the BRAIN)—the farmers and agricultural workers, the wood-cutters and wood-gatherers, the boatmen, fishermen, hunters, fruit-gatherers, the carpenters, blacksmiths and goldsmiths, the bricklayers, masons and their helpers. They were behind the emergence of the 'KISS' group.

Being a born Hindu myself, I do not know how many Hindus of that strata of the society would have understood the concept of 'Para Brahma'—the 'Supreme Energy' of the 'Cosmos' that can be regarded as GOD. Most people in any society and in any religion cannot extend their sensory powers, beyond what they can directly see, hear, smell, taste or touch.

Thinking deeply, one would be able to figure out that GOD has two main aspects within His Divine Self. The 'masculine' form of 'Para

Brahma' is Lord Shiva ('Purusha') and the feminine form: Adi Para Shakti ('Prakriti'). Their union in the form of 'Ardhanarishwara' roop ('morph') is indeed a complex form of 'Para Brahma'. It is only now when I am at a higher intellectual plane than an average Hindu that I can conceptualise that 'Para Brahma' is beyond all descriptions—that it is formless—that it eternally pervades everything everywhere in the universe, and whatever is beyond.

As a biomedical scientist, I'm also aware that, irrespective of whether you are a man or a woman, you do contain both the male and female sex hormones—'Testosterone' ('T') and 'Estrogen' ('E') and also that you're an effective person if you can manage to balance these two sex chemicals in ideal proportions according to the demands of the situation. [This is an extremely important section of the totally new and novel multi-disciplinary domain that I'm in the midst of developing—'Neuro-management' ('NM').] 'Brahma' is the spirit—the SOUL inside us. It is a part of the 'Para Brahma'.

Whether they understand this core metaphysical philosophy or not, in the Hindu Baul sect, those who are from the 'Shaiva' or 'Shakta' background, they arrange their hair like 'bun' (even women), put on a loose robe; and the 'Vaishnavas' put on a headgear ('pagri') and the Muslim Bauls dress like a fakir. They are taught by their Gurus/'Murshids'/'Sais' that the God is not in a temple, mosque, church or monastery, He is inside you. In fact, the entire cosmos ('Brahmanda') is inside your body ('Dehabhanda') [On this, I will reflect later.] You need not worship. Worshipping is a dualistic concept. 'Dualism' separates between the 'Creator' (God) and the 'Created' ('You') and, thus, worshipping is customary. If the seat of 'God' is within or inside you, then why should you worship.

They are also taught that since the entire world is a balance of 'Purusha' and 'Prakriti'—the masculine and feminine energy, a Baul has to master his sadhana to achieve this balance with one or more than one female consorts.

It is simple physics. Every battery has two terminals: positive and negative. Without the two terminals being connected, energy cannot flow at all. It is also simple mechanics. Every 'lock' has a hole. Once it is locked, you need the right 'key' to open it. Most interestingly, the male Baul has a 'key' which fits the 'hole' in every female 'lock'—but may not be snugly. Such lack of snug 'lock-and-key fit' is a product of LUST (in Indian language 'KAM'). Those who are blinded by LUST, they go for such forcible wrong fitting. Snug, perfect fitting requires the production of the neuro-transmitter 'Oxytocin' ('O') in both the male and female partners' brains. 'Oxytocin' is the LOVE HORMONE (in Indian language, 'PREM RASA'). This 'Love' is not the 'erotic' or simple 'romantic' love. 'O' is the 'bonding-compassion-trust' molecule which functions like the 'Dendrite' or 'Araldite' adhesive. Satisfaction of LUST generates the brain's reward molecule 'Dopamine' ('D')—the pleasure from which is transient, temporary. 'O' has the potential to give you 'Sustained Happiness'.

'O' used to be known only to gynaecologists, obstetricians and veterinary surgeons. 'O''s function is to make the birth canal, the vaginal passage, slippery so that the baby inside the womb can be pulled out without discomfort to the mother. It was Dr Paul Zak, economist and neuroscientist, who has brought it out from the dark vaginal canal into broad daylight and given it a most coveted place in the domain of human relationships.

Bauls are taught such complex 'Bio-philosophy' based on 'Brain Science' by using simple body-based analogies. They are really a remarkable lot, that way.

Let me share a classical Greek scientific thought from Hippocrates, who is considered one of the most outstanding figures in the history of medicine. Hippocrates thought that the female womb wandered... took a trans-corporeal journey up to the breastbone, even to the throat, becoming particularly frantic, when it wasn't fed on a regular basis with semen. Women, especially virgins and unmarried women are sexually more driven than men, but I do not know what special discipline the Bauls and Fakirs recommend for their female companions. Do they expect the female consorts' role is only to arouse the sadhak Bauls for performing their typical sadhana?

Lesson: 'Pre-humans', under stress, go for lustful sex. Be 'human', "Bid Good Bye to Lust, Make Love Your Companion" (In Bengali: "'Manush Hoo, Kam Ke Dao Biday, Prem Ke Karo Sathi")

The Baul Alchemy

I am a simple Brain Scientist. I do not want to overload my brain. I always try to keep the load on my own and my readers' brains light. So, my perception of 'Sahajiya' is very simple. Those who wish to indulge into the complexities of 'Indology' can read Paritosh Das and Edward C. Dimock, Jr. *(References 11 & 12)*

Through my years of study, research and clinical work on the human body, brain and behaviour, it is very clear to me that we have everything available inside us, as the Bauls say, "Brahmanda royeche Dehabhande" (In English: "Whatever is there in the 'cosmos', we've within the container of our body").

You and I don't have to take 'ganja' and 'charas' to access the 'Altered State of Consciousness' ('ASC'). 'Ganja', 'Charas', 'Cannabis' are externally available 'Phyto-cannabinoids'. We've got inside our body 'Endo-cannabinoids' which produce the same 'ASC' effect, by being released from inside our brain and body itself. I've got to know the entire team of Israeli scientists at the Hebrew University of Jerusalem, led by Late Prof Raphael Mechoulam, who had discovered the 'Endo-cannabinoid' 'Anandamide' in 1992 which we can get released from our 'Pituitary Glands'. It is also known as the 'Bliss Molecule'. The Czech scientist Prof. Lumir Hanus working at the Hebrew University and his co-researchers who discovered this first 'endocannabinoid' gave it a Sanskrit name 'Anandamide' as it provides BLISS. *(References 13 & 14)*

Then we have Professor Rick Strassman MD of the University of New Mexico School of Medicine who has spent his entire life researching on another rare neuro-chemical 'Di-Methyl-Tryptomine' also known as 'The Spirit Molecule', which—as it is claimed, can erase all your negative memories and charge the entire brain with the glow of positivity, which sadhus and yogis long and meditate for in the wild.

While it is available inside our brain, it is also possible to brew it in a beverage form from 'Ayahusca' leaves available in the Amazon Valley in South America. *(Reference 15)* DMT is released, Prof Strassman's pioneering research has shown, from the 'Pineal Gland'.

The 'Pituitary' and the 'Pineal' glands are both located inside our brain in the proximity of the 'Ajna' and 'Sahasrar' chakras—which are the two much discussed energy centres inside the brain according to the Tantric and Yogic Sciences. How can one get access to these two very precious and powerful brain chemicals is the subject of study in my domain of 'Neuro-management' ('NM') which I'm in the process of developing.

Like the tribes of the Amazonian rainforests (Awa, Guarani, Kawahiva and Yanomami of Brazil and Ayoreo of Paraguay), the Maoris of New Zealand, the 312 varieties of aborigines of Papua New Guinea, and the Jarwa and other tribal inhabitants of the Andaman and Nicobar Islands, the originators of today's Bengal Baul Sect, have been familiar with the alchemy of the human body. However, they are the only people who have been expressing their knowledge through the lyrics and poetry of their songs. That our body possesses all the special ingredients for the fulfilment of what I call the 'Biological Imperatives' (survival and replication) had been known to them.

The following quote from a recent well-researched volume indicates that the Bauls of Bengal might had adopted some aboriginal rituals and practices: "...the 'Baul' is a 'wealth of nation'. It turns out to be a rich heritage of Bengal. But the research traces the root of such great tradition. It stems from the culture of 'aboriginals'." *(Reference 16)*

Coming back to the 'Love' hormone 'Oxytocin' ('O') which I had introduced a little while earlier, you need not wait for your lover's hug, take it through a special nasal spray (commercially available), or get the 'O' chemical injected into your body.

'O' is available in the male 'semen'. Read the following quote from a scientific, peer-reviewed paper: "In several species, a pulse of systemic Oxytocin, presumably of hypothalamic origin, appears to be associated with ejaculation. In addition to systemic Oxytocin, the peptide is also made locally in the testes, and presumably also in the epididymis and prostrate." *(Reference 17)* 'Epididymis', a new term for many of us, is a highly convoluted duct behind the male testis, along which 'sperm' passes to the vas deferens.

Sex, even virtual sex, has been found to stimulate the release of 'Oxytocin' ('O') which appears to intensify erection and ejaculation. Read another quote from a published scientific paper:

"At ejaculation, a burst of 'Oxytocin' is released from the neurohypophysis into the systemic circulation and stimulates contraction of the reproductive tract aiding 'sperm' release." *(Reference 18)* 'Neurohypophysis' is the centre inside the brain for the hormonal secretion of 'Oxytocin'. It is regulated by brain cells that project from the 'Hypothalamus'.

Therefore, it will not be unjustified to conclude that drinking freshly ejaculated 'semen' will provide one with a gulp of 'Oxytocin' ('O'). Is it not practiced by the Bauls, who do their 'sadhana'? 'Oxytocin' ('O') is also present in urine. (Although more search is called for). If that be so, then drinking fresh 'urine' which is also a part of 'Baul Sadhana' will provide a supply of 'O' from internal sources. The logic behind the presence of 'O' in urine is this: 'O' stimulates the uterine muscles to contract and also increases production of 'prostaglandins'—a hormone-like substance, which increase the contractions further. This fact may be extended further to guess that 'O' may also be present in 'menstrual fluid' and 'vaginal white discharge' which are also supposed to be drunk as a part of 'Baul Sadhana'.

The last point that I'd like to highlight is this. Each organ of our body generates a unique resonance frequency (RF). Higher frequency in the body means greater energy availability which results in better health. Abdomen which is in the centre of the digestive system has a resonant frequency of only 4 to 8 Hz, compared to the head, containing the brain, for which the energy frequency range is 20 to 40 Hz. Since the digestive system has slow-acting organs, eating 'tamasic' food (like red meat, poultry etc.) which take longer to digest than fibrous fruits and vegetables, fish and eggs, would make the digestive department operate at a still lower frequency. So, the wisest amongst the Bauls go for vegetarian diet. *(References 19 & 20)*

The other point is the private genitals (which are normally low resonance frequency organs when not excited) of both the male and the female lose a lot of precious biological energy while being guided by LUST (in Indian language: 'kam'). It is only LOVE (in Indian language: 'prem') that would make them operate at a balanced to high resonant frequency range (as affecting 'bonding' is the primary objective, earning 'Dopamine' through the lustful physical act is secondary) thus helping the human system to conserve energy. This is why, the wisest of the Bauls highlight 'Prem Rasa' in their songs. This is one example of the fact that many Baul songs are of great educational value.

The Human Sexuality and Reproductive System

The 'World Health Organisation' ('WHO') recognizes that sexuality is a central aspect of being human and encompasses sex, gender identities and roles, sexual orientation, eroticism, pleasure, intimacy and reproduction. There is robust research evidence that sexual health positively correlates with mental health and life quality.

Sexual drive is a basic physiological urge like hunger, thirst, need for oxygen and sleep. It is linked with the Basic Biological Imperative that we, all living beings, have to fulfil: Survival and Replication. Satisfaction of each basic physiological urge leads to the release of the 'feel good' neuro-chemical 'Dopamine' ('D') from the brain's reward circuit. Therefore, the system that produces the reward chemical 'Dopamine' ('D') plays a central role in the control of its appetitive component (including the drive to engage in copulation). Copulation activates the 'D' neurons and repeated copulation produces continuous activation of the dopaminergic system.

Having studied 'Happiness' for decades, I've come to classify 'happiness' into three categories:

1. 'Smart' Happiness which is momentary, transient—it comes and goes 'smartly'; it is fleeting 'Happiness';

2. 'Short-lived' or 'Short'-Happiness, where the trace of the happy experience lingers for a little longer time and then the experience gets stored in the memory with the potential for retrieval on demand; and, finally,
3. 'Sustained' Happiness which is long-lasting.

Copulation provides only 'Smart' and 'Short-lived/Short' Happiness, unless the sexual partners have a tight bonded relationship with the neuro-chemical 'Oxytocin' ('O') flooding both the brains steadily without any break thus providing 'Sustained' Happiness.

However, the Baul and Fakir philosophy looks at human sexuality from a different perspective and follows an altogether reverse route. I have already provided some exposure to it earlier and there is more to come later. Here, let me brief you about something you may not be aware of. It is about what very special chemicals are produced in the human reproductive system.

"The womb fabricates drugs that, in other contexts, would be considered illegal. It synthesizes and secretes 'beta-endorphins' and 'dynorphins'—two of the body's natural opiates and chemical cousins to 'morphine' and 'heroin'." *(Reference 21)*

The uterus also makes 'Anandamide' ('AEA') which, until a couple of decades ago, was thought to be the exclusive property of the 'Central Nervous System' ('CNS')—the brain and the spinal cord. The brain was thought to make this compound endogenously because it sometimes needed to ease pain as a part of its anodyne (pain-killing) function and to produce 'bliss' which is equivalent to 'Sustained Happiness', the dictionary meaning of 'bliss' being 'Perfect Happiness' or 'Great Joy'. *(Reference 22)* Most amazingly, the uterus produces at least as much opiate material as the brain tissue does and perhaps two times more of the cannabis equivalent than any other organ of the body does.

I am elaborating below such special chemical functional activities of the human reproductive system—both male and female.

Cannabinoids are several structural classes of compounds. Phyto- or Exo-cannabinoids are found primarily in the cannabis plant. Endocannabinoids are found in most animal organisms including humans. Cannabinoids could also be made synthetically. The endocannabinoid system plays a key neuro-modulatory role in the brain. The main feature of endocannabinoids is that they are produced on demand, in response to the requirement for enhancing neural activity, such as to produce 'Sustained Happiness' and to contribute in the brain's plasticity process. In other words, endocannabinoids play a very crucial supportive role.

'Ganja' is a highly potent form of cannabis, a phyto- or exo-cannabinoid, generally used for smoking. 'Ganja' is the most common term for marijuana in West Indies.

THC (Tetra-Hydro-Cannabinol) is one of the many cannabinoids, or chemicals found in the cannabis plant. It's the primary psychoactive compound and is the one that's primarily responsible for the 'high' associated with cannabis. Both hemp and marijuana plants are the same species. The main difference lies in how much of THC each contains. The term 'hemp' is used to mean cannabis that contains 0.3 percent or less THC content by dry weight. In 'hemp', the THC level is so low, that it's unlikely to get you 'high'.

When people say 'marijuana', they're talking about cannabis that can get you 'high'. 'Marijuana' thus refers to cannabis that has more than 0.3 percent THC by dry weight. THC content can vary among cannabis plants.

Cannabidiol (CBD) is a cannabinoid that has numerous health benefits. CBD is found in some amount in all cannabis plants. That means it can be derived from either hemp or marijuana. But CBD products derived from hemp containing less than 0.3 percent THC are approved for use. *(Reference 23)*

'Anandamide' ('AEA') is a cannabinoid-like molecule normally produced in the brain and the body, that may regulate sperm functions required for fertilisation in humans, a study headed by scientists from the University of Buffalo in USA has found. The natural endocannabinoid signalling system regulates sperm structure, vigour and fertility. The study presents the first evidence that 'Anandamide'

('AEA') exists in the male semen (seminal plasma), female oviductal fluid and follicular fluid, and can regulate directly the human sperm's ability to fertilise an egg. Herbert Schuel, PhD, University at Buffalo professor of anatomy and cell biology and his collaborators were the first to report cannabinoid receptors in sperm, using sea urchins as a model, and that 'Anandamide' ('AEA') also activated these receptors. *(Reference 24)*

Cannabinoid receptor type 1 (CB1) is widely distributed in neurons (that is, brain cells) and non-neuronal cells in brain and peripheral organs including sperm, eggs, and pre-implantation embryos, highlighting the significance that Mother Nature assigns to our reproductive system. The cannabinoid receptor found in the human brain is expressed in the human testis, and 'Anandamide' ('AEA') is produced in the testis and uterus of mammals. Human sperms are bathed in male reproductive tract secretions when they are ejaculated into the female's vagina. But they are not immediately capable of fertilising eggs. However, once removed from the seminal plasma where they were bathed in 'Anandamide' ('AEA') and exposed for several hours to secretions within the female reproductive tract, sperms become 'capacitated' and can fertilise eggs. Within the uterus, 'Anandamide' ('AEA') regulates early development of the fertilised egg and determines where the embryo will implant to initiate pregnancy.

Marijuana, the commonest recreational drug of abuse, is known to have adverse effects on multiple aspects of male reproductive physiology. Its use is associated with impotence, decreased testosterone production, impairment of spermatogenesis, production of sperms with abnormal morphology and decreased sperm motility and viability. It does not allow an appropriate 'Anandamide tone' that is required for normal embryo development, oviductal transport, implantation, and pregnancy.

In heavy marijuana users, there is a strong possibility that they are jeopardizing fertility by OVERLOADING the signalling system. Cannabinoid receptors are fixed. "Anandamide' ('AEA'), an endocannabinoid may signal through cannabinoid receptors (CB1 & CB2) to regulate human sperm functions and male reproduction by modulating sperm motility, capacitation and acrosome reaction in vitro. As the regulation of the endocannabinoid system appears to be necessary for the preservation of normal sperm function and male fertility, there may be implications for the adverse reproductive consequences of the use of marijuana/ganja. Exocannabinoids/ phytocannabinoids are likely to compete with endocannabinoids at the cannabinoid receptors, upsetting the finely balanced endocannabinoid signalling system. *(References 25–27)*

Bauls have moved the reproductive system to a back seat as they are not in favour of creating any future progeny or successors as the responsibility that would arise would go against and interfere with their simple and almost nomadic lifestyle. They, barring a few very rare exceptions, are ganja smokers as they desire to enjoy the esoteric 'high' experience that 'ganja' smoking provides. That would, I presume, leave them with an adversely affected sperm population in all respects. Now, if they do not want to go for ejaculation during the intercourse with a female partner who has her period, instead go for semen retention—whether this strategy of theirs is to prevent procreation of inferior quality zygotes and eventually kids, or whether it is merely for preservation of the precious seed and build up a stock of 'pitridhan', is not clear. Whether the devotee Bauls are aware of the scientific facts that I've shared, I'm not aware!!

The Baul Devotee's Female Partner and Her Body Magnetics

Men look at the female bodies and they can't readily see the females' external genitals—the handy triangular-shaped crevice (which has often been described most poetically in Baul lyrics) covered by a leaf of pubic fur. "At the same time, men hunger to breach the portal of the fur and the outer pleats, to reach the even more concealed internal genitalia, the sacred nave of the vagina. No wonder, then that woman becomes conflated with interiority. Men want what they cannot see…" *(Reference 28)*

Men can feel the sexuality of women when they menstruate. Menstruation is a phase of menstrual cycle in which the lining of the uterus (known as 'endometrium') is shed. The physiological functions of the uterine endometrium are preparation for implantation, maintenance of pregnancy if implantation occurs, and menstruation in the absence of pregnancy.

Menstruation, known as 'period', lasts for a few days (normally 3 to 5 days, but anywhere from 2 to 7 days is considered normal). The menstruating female may notice the shedding of the endometrium lining that appears as tissue mixed with the blood. Because of the blood loss, females have higher dietary requirements for iron than do males to prevent iron deficiency.

The ancient physician Hippocrates considered that menstruation was intended to cleanse the body of "evil humours" and modern evolutionary biologist Margie Profet contends that the primary function of menstruation is to remove sperm-borne pathogens from the uterus. In support of this theory, she has pointed to the relatively high levels of macrophages in menstrual blood. Macrophages represent a type of white blood cells that surrounds and kills microorganisms, removes dead cells, and stimulates the action of other immune system cells.

In pre-historic, pre-human hunter-gatherer societies, males would go on hunting journeys whilst the females of the tribe were menstruating, speculating that the females would not have been as receptive to sexual relations while menstruating. It was safe to leave them behind for just a few days as no promiscuous behaviour could be anticipated. *(Reference 29)*

However, the Bauls get magnetically charged and go for sex with their female partners while they are menstruating to fulfil twin objectives: (i) they do not want their partners to become pregnant as they are against the practice of having any progeny; and, (ii) they use special breathing techniques to prevent their semen to be released in the vagina of their partners, instead they suck some menstrual blood into their penis, mix it with semen and move the mix upward, against gravity.

Moon's Kin

In our Indian culture, the mother or grandmother or any senior female in the family introduces the moon as an uncle. He is introduced as 'Chanda Mama'—the 'Moon Uncle'. And hillocks on the moon land, which appear hazy and blurred from our planet, together resemble an elderly woman and she is introduced to a kid as 'Chander Buri' or 'Chander Mashi'. We're brought up in our culture to imagine that we are related to the Moon—that we are Moon's kin.

The female's menstrual cycle has some link with the waxing and waning of the moon. Men also undergo hormonal changes which, I suppose, has some link with the lunar cycle—but they don't menstruate—so it is not that tangible.

Ever since I came to know of Diana Fabianova, a young film maker from Bratislava, Slovakia, I've been following her. Being a pioneer of some sort, I like and adore pioneers. I've great regard for Diana as she has made the world's first documentary on 'Menstruation'. *(Reference 30)*

Diana says, menstruation is not just a physiological process, it is a symbol of femininity. *(Reference 31)* I would add that it is not only a symbol of femininity but also of fertility and the female carries this symbol throughout her life until menopause. For women, menstruation is a great health barometer. And I must say that in the Baul culture this biological feature of the female is not only held in high esteem but the Bauls also go for physical co-habitation and sexual intercourse only when their female partners are menstruating; whereas in some non-Baul cultures, menstruating women are treated as almost untouchables. Among the ancient tribals of Australia, Amazon Valley, Alaska, Papua and New Guinea, menstruating young girls have to undergo a very tortuous time. The opposites are seen also. In some cultures, there is a belief that the first-time menstruating girl has supernatural and magical powers—she radiates a very special aura. In Hinduism, we have the tradition of 'Kumari Puja' where the menstruating damsel is worshipped. In Baul culture, devotee Bauls queue up to drink the first-time menstruating girl's vaginal blood.

Diana Fabianova's excellent documentary the 'Moon Inside You' could not be shown in any of the TV Channels in USA as she faced a lot of resistance. One reputed TV producer told her we can broadcast videos showing blood oozing out of accident victim's injured body part even battlefield blood or a murder scene blood, but we cannot project a movie on menstruation as menstrual blood is impure.

In fact, there is a popular belief that menstrual blood is impure. My question is most fundamental. Every person's organs and body fluids have their own vibrational frequencies. The purer you are, the higher will be those frequencies. If you are influenced by any one or more of the 'Six Enemies of the Mind' ('Shadripu') *(Reference 32)*, automatically the vibrations of your organs and blood become lower because of the impurity. That is why in the Baul culture, a trainee Baul has to practise total surrender to his Guru along with his wife (in case he is married) and allow the Guru to have physical relationship with her if he so desired. Besides, it would be desirable if they left their home and lived in the akhara or ashram to imbibe the local vibrations by consuming the same food, participating in the same rituals (like going round on 'Madhukaris' seeking alms), sharing the same mat or chatai. The whole idea is to develop a 'synchrony' which is essential for any sadhana or worship.

The Sadhak Baul has to have physical relations with many female partners ('sadhan sanginis'), who are all residents in the same campus, while they are menstruating without any feeling of 'disgust' (instead having feeling of 'love' and enjoying orgasm).

I wonder if the female akhara residents also have 'menstrual synchrony'. Martha McClintock (who was Professor of Psychology at the University of Chicago), while she was still a graduate student, did a pioneering study on college students living together in hostel dormitories which revealed 'women who live together menstruate together'. *(References 33-35)* If that be so in the case of Bauls, then they have been following certain practices in their very special culture, which modern scientific studies are finding to be not only scientifically valid but also more convenient and less messy from the health and hygiene points of view.

Diana Fabianova had observed, during her research, that many women felt that they would need to hide their menstruation from their partners, because they thought their partners would feel averse and would avoid close physical contact. However, she had also observed that when the male partner had accepted it as a natural feature of female biology and if he had truly loved the female then he would be full of empathy for her. In fact, in effective Baul akharas, the experienced Baul Gurus take pains to counsel the Sadhak Bauls and their Sadhan Sanginis to develop that kind of an understanding and a well-bonded relationship.

How to check whether the male-female partnership is well-bonded? The female is most likely to go through a 'Pre-Menstrual Syndrome' ('PMS'). She will be in a bad mood or feel a deep sadness but unable to explain why. It is a very important signal for the partner. And a genuinely loving partner will not only understand the female's predicament but also extend empathy to provide her with all kinds of support. I am sure this does happen in well-managed Baul akharas. In such a case, the male partner for the female is no less than why 'half', but a 'full' God. Bauls and Fakirs rightly believe that God is inside every human. A male with Oxytocin-rich blood is certainly a godly creature!!

The legendary Fakir Lalon Shah had penned a beautiful 'Moon Song'. *(Reference 36)* The song carrying a deep meaning is meant for special listeners. My perception is that, in this lyric, by 'moon' Lalon means the female genital and 'moonshine' is the menstrual blood or the vaginal discharge. The 'golden hillock' and the 'golden palace' represent the female 'clitoris'. My perception is entirely my own; yours may be entirely different—and I do not want to impose anything on anyone.

"If you're too lucky, you will get to see that moon!!
It is a special moon that never disappears,
Its rays shine all the time!!
It's an ocean in the midst of a point
There is a golden hillock in the middle.
In too little a space
There is the golden palace of the uncatchable moon.
All your pains & sorrows disappear at the sight of the moon.

You get lost when the moonshine touches you, embraces your body,
Such is the moon's glory and aura.
Fakir Lalon gets almost drowned
But then he saves himself such is the such is the
magical spell of the moon."

Carnal Control

What a serendipitous encounter! I was highly appreciating Lalon Fakir's musical endeavour to provide sex education to his fellow illiterate villagers when the Times of India (Kolkata edition, 6th December 2022) headline on the inside flap flashed in front of my two elderly eyes. It read as:

> *"I could feel them cutting me up and sewing me back. Survivors Recall Horror of Tubectomy without Anaesthesia".*

The text went on: "Alauli (Bihar): For Dayamani Devi, the pain of a tubectomy surgery without anaesthesia as she felt the blades of a novice slice through her body and wailed, will go away. Not the 'pain of children doing nothing... I don't want my sons to become labourers', says the 30-year old, adjusting her sari's pallu as she holds her 2-month old on a cot at her parent's home. Her husband Dheeraj Patel works as a labourer in Haryana earning Rs. 15,000/- a month."

Dayamanti is among 24 rural women who underwent tubectomy without anaesthesia at Alauli block in Bihar's Khagaria district, remaining conscious and crying out in pain on the operating table. Most had 3 to 5 children already. *(Reference 37)* This is a gory example of birth control and family planning in modern digitalised India, which was the venue of the last G20 Summit, by INFLICTING PAIN on innocent rural wives.

Almost 150 years ago, the great philosopher and social reformer Lalon Shah Fakir had endeavoured to educate the illiterate rural population of undivided Bengal of his neighbourhood, regarding birth control, WITHOUT INFLICTING ANY PAIN on them. He was against producing any kids as he possibly felt the same way as I feel.

I have always classified children into 2 (two) categories—children of LUST (in Indian language, 'KAM') and children of LOVE (in Indian language, 'PREM'). When the libido or sexual drive is filled with LUST, the quality of the 'sperms' and the 'ova' are both inferior just the same way as the quality of an artwork gets negatively affected when the artist has a negative mind-set (angry, afraid or sad)—for whatever the reason may be. Under such circumstances, the fertilised egg is certainly not of the best quality as it would happen when the libido or sexual drive is brimming with LOVE, in the case of both the sexual partners. When I used to run my most popular clinic on 'The Winning Child'—based at Kolkata but roving with me wherever I went on tour to Mumbai, Chennai, Delhi, Pune, Bengaluru, Hyderabad, Guwahati, Dibrugarh and Tinsukia, and parents used to bring their problem children for consultation, that was one main question that would bother me and I would ask the parents most politely and tactfully. On the basis of my clinical experience, I wrote my first best-selling Bengali book 'Swapno Santan' ('The Dream Child' in English) which was serialised in the widely circulated Bengali health magazine 'Suswastha' and, in the book format, it has gone into several editions.

In the Baul terminology, there are two types of sexual relationships—'KAM RATI' (relationship of 'LUST') and 'PREM RATI' (relationship of 'LOVE'). In my 'Neuro-management' ('NM') language if both the partners are driven by 'lust' then they will both have a high level of the aggressive hormone 'Adrenaline/Epinephrine' in their blood. On the other hand, the lustful partner will be 'Adrenaline-high' and the stressful partner will be 'Cortisol-high' ('Cortisol' is the stress hormone). If both are driven by 'love' then 'Oxytocin' will be high in both, resulting in 'UNCONDITIONAL LOVE'—trust and tight bonding.

Lalon, although illiterate, had sharp intelligence to understand and feel that his co-villagers who were agricultural labourers, farmers, boatmen, fishermen and had some such occupations, for them 'sex' was the only entertainment (unlike in his case where 'music used to keep his brain free from sexual thoughts') and their typical style was lustful sex (Adrenalin/Epinephrine released in the male partner's blood and Cortisol released in the female partner's blood) leading to poor quality zygote formation. The children so produced could not be better than almost 'pre-human' products. There would be addition to the human resource of his village and its neighbourhood but such human resource could never be converted into 'Human Capital'.

After listening to my logic, one very intelligent follower of mine commented: "Sir, then Lalon Shah must have been a product of 'Prem Rasa'." "Must have been" was my prompt answer. Lalon accepted his wife when she approached him after a gap of quite some time after he had turned into a recluse, on the understanding that she will not be his physical partner but just a care-giver. From time to time, the woman was burning in the fire of her desire but Lalon was like a solid, unmoved, mountain—the restraining brain chemical GABA was so strong in him. Naturally, they had no kid of their own but had brought up a village girl whose mother had died and the poor, helpless father had approached Lalon with the request of taking care of the motherless child.

To quote Carola Lorea, the American researcher who has studied the Baul rituals and lifestyles: "A consistent part of Bauls' lyrics deals with body-centred practices that aim at controlling sexual desire. The esoteric knowledge of conception and contraception is revealed in the lyrics of the songs through an enigmatic language that needs to be decided by the gurus in order to be understood and experienced." *(Reference 38)*

Another reputed researcher from the University of Edinburgh, Scotland, UK, Jeanne Openshaw reflects: "Thus Baul gurus are regarded as the guardians of the secret of both suppression and enhancement of fertility, for knowledge of conception is also knowledge of contraception." *(References 39 & 40)*

Fakir Lalon Shah was the GURU of all Baul and Fakir Gurus. Naturally, therefore, many of his songs and oral teachings talked most strongly about sexual restraints. He was totally against the increase in population by addition of sub-standard humans, which I call 'Pre-humans'.

Celibacy and Baul Sadhana

Swami Sivananda had put his age as 120 in a Hindustan Times press report published on 19th August 2016. *(Reference 42)* The sprightly monk had put his longevity down to a disciplined life of yoga, no sex (celibacy), and a bland food habit. The report said that he was fit without any medical complications, lived independently, and even travelled alone on trains. I've not had a chance to interview him but making an attempt here to speculate some hidden points.

Number One: 'Yoga' is a general term which to my mind is to get connected with the Supreme Being—the Cosmic Consciousness. If I keep the physical 'hatha-yoga' out, the 'mental-yoga' performed through meditation can be of many kinds—resulting in 'very low' ('theta') to almost 'zero' (the lowest level of 'delta' wave) vibration(s) of the brain cells, minimising energy expenditure. If you can regularly practice and attain that level then you will lose 'body consciousness' (that is, feeling of heat, cold, pleasure, pain and so on). If you can live at a minimum energy expenditure level, you can certainly live longer.

Number Two: If you can conquer 'body consciousness', you will not have the normal propensity to respond to any sexual stimulus. So, it is not that you will have to suppress or repress your libido. You will be a 'zero-libido' individual. As a male, you will preserve the 'seed of life' ('semen' which the Bauls call 'bastu' or 'bij') which, being unspent, will multiply energetically inside you, building up high 'reproductive energy' reserve (which Taoists possibly described as the 'Golden Embryo'—the Vedic 'Hiranyagarva', which might be equivalent to the 'Kulakundalini' power of Yogic Sciences). *(References 43–45)* As a female, you will not get affected as your body will follow the typical menstrual and ovulation cycles, remaining unutilised. This is despite the fact that in both the cases of male and female, the genital organs ('penis' and 'clitoris' respectively) will shrink and suffer from 'disuse atrophy' according to the biological law of 'Use It or Lose It'. *(References 46–51)*

Number Three: Living at a minimum energy expenditure level, your need for dietary energy will be minimised so a small quantity of food will be adequate for your living (being a recluse, you don't need to spend energy for any physical work). You will be satisfied with food, which is good enough for living but does not tempt you to become greedy and want more.

To quote Swami Sivananda: "I eat very simply—only boiled food without oil or spices, rice and boiled dal (lentil stew) with a couple of green chillies." He, I am told, would sleep on a mat on the floor and use a wooden slab as a pillow. A typical example of total freedom from 'body consciousness'.

Swami Sivananda received his 'Padma Shri' award from the former Indian President Ram Nath Kovind in March 2022 when he walked barefooted to Rashtrapati Bhavan's Darbar Hall. *(Reference 52)*

Lalon Fakir died on 17th October 1890 at the age of 118 (estimated as his exact date of birth is not known) in the Kusthia district (presently in Bangladesh). He also had a very simple, austere-style, highly disciplined life. Although he had accepted his wife, even after he had become a recluse, it was not as a physical partner but as a mere care-giver. So, he must have had a zero-sex, celibate life, having very ordinary village food. In 2004, Lalon was ranked 12 in BBC's poll of the Greatest Bengalis of all time.

Lalon, a celibate himself (it is entirely my speculation as I've no documentary evidence as yet) had known that he should not expect the same level of understanding and consciousness from all the people around him—the simple and plain villagers. He knew very well that most of them would belong to, in my language', the 'Pre-human' category where sex was the only entertainment for them. For them, he insisted on 'Prem Rati' (physical relationship with 'love' based on the brain chemical 'Oxytocin') instead of the creaturely/animal-like 'Kam Rati' (physical relationship with 'lust' (to earn the easily available reward molecule 'Dopamine').

He never insisted upon his disciples to have a no-sex life, as he knew very well that they would not have attained that level of consciousness where they will not be affected by any sex-related stimulus. He allowed them to have at least one 'sadhan sangini'. So, during his time, having sex was not prohibited in the Baul culture, but it had to be controlled to restrain ejaculation and orgasm. Tantric sex, coitus reservatus, and the Karezza method *(References 53–56)* were the ones they could choose from. However, to learn and achieve proficiency a novice Baul had to have a seasoned Guru who had both the knowledge and experiences of such practices.

To quote Carole Lorea *(Reference 57)*, an American field-researcher on Bauls (especially 'Bhaba Pagla'): "In a substantially tantric conceptual world, where all the macrocosmic realities have their counterpart within the human body, bodily substances responsible for reproduction are the holiest and purest types of substance. Thus, all questions about the Creator, the origin of human life, its aim and its end, are to be answered by looking at the dynamics that take place in the process of human creation."

'Pre-human' sex is where 'fecundation' (the process whereby a new organism is produced by fertilization) is achieved through the secretion of male seed in the female's womb. In the world of Bauls, it is the female secretion which is absorbed and drawn upwards in the body of the male partner by following a secret procedure, learnt from a Guru. It is a reverse (in Bengali, 'ujan') process—as the sadhaka draws a drop of menstrual blood into his sex organ thus uniting blood and semen into his own body. Then using yogic techniques of breath control he takes the fluid upwards into his brain at the 'ajna' or 'sahasrara' chakra level via the 'sushumna' nadi. *(Reference 58)*

The male partner attempts at re-creating the same condition for the development of a foetus in his own body. The foetus is created by the union of the 'bij' and 'raja', and then by the four elements—the 'caricandra'. The male partner knows how to hold 'bij' and 'raja' in his body and nurture the mix with 'caricandra'.

He can produce a 'lingadeha' inside his body and create in the same way as women create. He creates a foetus without giving birth to a child. The idea of a pregnant male and the creation of a 'golden embryo' are well documented in the doctrines and iconography of Taoism. *(References 59–61)*

Acknowledgements

On the biomedical front, to clear certain doubts I had to consult Dr Rakesh Biswas, MB BS, MD, Professor at the Kamineni Institute of Medical Sciences, Hyderabad, India; and, Saptarshi Saha, senior medical student in a Chinese Medical College. On the lifestyle of yogis, I had to consult my friend from Russia—Artem Rogachevskii, scholar on Upanishadic literature. I am indebted to all the three for their very prompt help.

References

[1] Shri Dattaswami, "Difference between Brahman & Parabrahman", Speakingtree.in

[2] *Para Brahman*—Wikipedia.

[3] Paul Zak: *The Moral Molecule: How Trust Works*, London: Bantam Press, 2012.

[4] Stephanie Watson, "Oxytocin: The Love Hormone", *Harvard Health Publishing*, Harvard Medical School, 20th July 2021.

[5] *Oxytocin*—Wikipedia.

[6] Jillian Levy, "Oxytocin (The Love Hormone): Benefits + How to Increase Levels", *Dr Axe*, 14th February 2022.

[7] "Oxytocin"—Cleveland Clinic, USA; last reviewed in 27th March 2022.

[8] *Lalon*—a full-length movie by Tanvir Mokammel, Kino-Eye Films, Bangladesh, 2004 (Initial release).

[9] *Hippocrates*—Wikipedia.

[10] Natalie Angier, *Woman: An Intimate Geography*, New York: Houghton Mifflin, 1999, p. 93.

[11] Paritosh Das, *Sahajiya Cult of Bengal and Pancha-Sakha Cult of Orissa*, Kolkata: Firma KLM Private Limited, 1988.

[12] Edward C. Dimock, Jr. *The Place of the Hidden Moon: Erotic Mysticism in the Vaisnava-Sahajiya Cult of Bengal*, Delhi: Motilal Banarsidass Publishers, First Indian Edition 1991.

[13] *Anandamide*—Wikipedia.

[14] Meet the Experts: Interview with Professor Lumir Hanus—by Yuval Zolotov, Fundacion CANNA.

[15] Rick Strassman, *DMT: The Spirit Molecule: A Doctor's Revolutionary Research into the Biology of Near-Death and Mystical Experiences*, New York: Simon & Schuster, 2000.

[16] Joydeep Mukherjee, *Folk Tradition of Bengal (and Rabindranath Tagore)*, 2018, on-line book. (Chapter 2.2—The Baul Philosophy and Theory of Lalon)

[17] R.Ivell *et al.*, "Oxytocin and male reproductive system", *Advanced Experimental Medical Biology*, 1997.

[18] Hemlata Thackare, Helen D. Nicholson, Kate Whittington, "Oxytocin—its role in male reproduction and new potential therapeutic uses", *Human Reproductive Update*, Vol. 12, Issue 4, July/August 2006, pages 437–448.

[19] J.M. Randall *et al.* "Resonant frequencies of standing humans", *Ergonomics*, September 1997.

[20] "Resonant frequencies of human body organs", Table uploaded by Maria Lucia Machado Duarte, *ResearchGate*, [researchgate.net/figu]

[21] Natalie Angier, *Woman: An Intimate Geography*, New York: Houghton Mifflin, 1999, p. 111.

[22] Meaning of 'Bliss': Dictionary, Oxford Languages.

[23] Sian Ferguson, "Hemp vs. Marijuana: What's the Difference?" *healthline*, February 13, 2023.

[24] Lois Baker, "An Internal Cannabinoid-Signalling System Regulates Human Sperm, Fertilisation Potential, Study Finds", *University at Buffalo, News Center*, December 12, 2000.

[25] Herbert Schuel, "Tuning the oviduct to the anandamide tone", *The Journal of Clinical Investigation*, September 2006, Vol. 116, No. 8, pp. 2087–90.

[26] A.A. Amoako *et al.,* "Anandamide modulates human sperm motility: implications for men with asthenozoospermia and oligoasthenateratozoospermia", *Human Reproduction*, Vol. 28, Issue 8, August 2013, pp. 2058–2066.

[27] Annette Fenner, "Anandamide shows promise for lifelong delayed ejaculation", *Nature Reviews Urology*, Vol. 12, No. 244, 2015.

[28] Natalie Angier, *Woman: An Intimate Geography*, New York: Houghton Mifflin, 1999, p. x.

[29] *Menstruation*, Psychology Wiki.

[30] "Moon Inside You" (a documentary with English sub-titles), by Diana Fabianova, 2009.

[31] "Menstruation Taboo"—a TED Talk by Diana Fabianova at Bratislava, Slovakia.

[32] *Arishadvargas*—Wikipedia.

[33] Natalie Angier, "Scientist at Work: Martha K. McClintock; How Biology Affects Behaviour and Vice Versa", *The New York Times*, May 30, 1995.

[34] Anna Gosline, "Do Women Who Live Together Menstruate Together?", *Scientific American*, December 7, 2007.

[35] Charlotte McDonald, "Is it true that periods synchronise when live together?" *BBC News*, 7 September 2016.

[36] Shaktinath Jha, *Fakir Lalon Sai: Desh, Kal ebong Shilpa* (in Bengali). Kolkata: Sangbad, 1995, p. 89, Song number 360. (Translation is mine)

[37] Manoj Chaurasia, "I could feel them cutting me up & sewing me back", *Times of India*, Kolkata, Tuesday, 6th December 2022, Inside Flap.

[38] Sudhir Chakrabarti, *Bratya Lokayata Lalon* (a book in Bengali), Kolkata: Pustak Bipani, 5th Impression, February 2022.

[39] Carola Lorea, "Why did you go swimming in the river full of algae?—Conception and contraception in Baul's songs and oral teachings", *Folklore and Folkloristics*: Vol. 7, No. 1, June 2014.

[40] Jeanne Openshaw, *Writing the Self: The Life and Philosophy of a Dissenting Bengali Baul Guru*, New Delhi: Oxford University Press, 2004.

[41] Jeanne Openshaw, *Seeking Bauls of Bengal*, London: Cambridge University Press, 2004

[42] "Live longer, healthier like this 120-year-old Varanasi monk in 5 easy steps", *Hindustan Times*, 19th August 2016.

[43] Narayani Ganesh, "The golden womb and the cosmic egg" *The Times of India*, 16th February 2011.

[44] Barclay Powers, "Integral Immortality: The Kundalini/Golden Embryo: Theory of Everything".

[45] Tin Jee, "The Spiritual Embryo in Taoism—Sun Toy", *Tin Yat Dragon*, 25th January 2022.

[46] Jennifer Minchin, "Brahmacharya—practicing moderation" *be Yogi through Restraint*, 13th January *2015*.

[47] Medically Reviewed by Dan Brennan MD, " The Psychological Benefits of Celibacy" *WebMD*, 28th June 2021.

[48] "Celibacy and the Human Body: An Introduction", *Oxford Academic,* November 2007.

[49] "5 Things You can do to Reverse a Shrinking Penis", *Private Gym, Adult Fitness Concepts. LLC,* 2022.

[50] Quispe Lopez, "What happens to your body when you don't have sex for a long time, according to experts", *INSIDER,* 24th June 2020.

[51] Jenna Fletcher, "What is clitoral atrophy? Symptoms, treatment and more", *Medical News Today,* 30th April 2020.

[52] Shikha Salaria, "Disciplined life in single Varanasi room: Legend of 125-yr-old Padma awardee yoga guru Sivananda", *The Print,* 30th March 2022.

[53] Jenn Sinrich, "Tantric Sex for Beginners: It's Not All About the Orgasm", 17th January 2019.

[54] Peter von Ziegesar, "Anti-climax", *Aeon Newsletter.* 27th January 2020.

[55] "*Coitus Reservatus*"—Wikipedia.

[56] Kesiena Boom, "The Karezza Method: 5 Reasons to Try this Spiritual Sexual Practice", *mbg,* 25th June 2020.

[57] Carola Lorea, "Why did you go swimming in the river full of algae?—Conception and contraception in baul's songs and oral teachings", *Folklore and Folkloristics,* Vol. 7, No. 1, June 2014.

[58] Carol Salomon, "The cosmogonic riddles of Lalon Fakir", *WorldCat,* 1991.

CHAPTER 4

The 'AURA' of Lalon

Lalon: Reformer of Human Consciousness

How I wish I were an anthropologist like the great lady Margaret Mead (1901-1978) *(Reference 1)*, moving into the deep forests and wilds, observing the aborigines who still belong to 'pre-history'? Being obsessed with Brain Science, my primary objective would have been to study whether their sex life is based only on 'pleasure' thus releasing the transient molecule 'Dopamine' ('D') in the reward circuits of their brains. (Read the breath-taking book *'The Molecule of More'*). *(Reference 2)* Hunger or thirst for 'Dopamine' would be a basic propensity in a society which is still 'Pre-human' as one can satiate 'D' hunger from consumption of food and consummation of sex.

I would have been curious to know if there was any role of 'Oxytocin' ('O') in the lives of those pre-humans; whether the presence of 'O' was still restricted to the slippery dark alleys of the 'vagina' of pregnant females. My perception is 'O' would not have been promoted to the level of the 'love-compassion-empathy-bonding' molecule in a pre-human society as 'love' would exist only in its 'erotic' form and not the way Dr Paul Zak, the founding father of 'Neuro-economics' has introduced it to us anew. *(Reference 3)*

There would be no 'love' in a society where most people exist at a pre-human level. 'Love' got a foothold when the pre-humans started becoming humans, 'lust' started taking a back seat. 'Sex' is basically a drive at the call of the 'Selfish Genes' *(Reference 4)* for the mere biological purpose of leaving an imprint of the individual's genes in the next generation.

Today, the Baul society's practice of promiscuous relationships (in Bengali, 'parakiya') are much criticised as much as is one Baul's having several 'sadhan-sanginis' (female companions for performing Baul rituals). Such relationships were so common and only natural in pre-human societies, as because of 'Oxytocin's' undiscovered role as the 'love-and-bonding' molecule, there was not even any live-in relationship, forget about customised 'marriage'. Today, in modern society, promiscuous relationships do exist behind the on-stage visible living and because it is looked down upon socially, many promiscuous persons suffer from a feeling of guilt which would tend to make their blood high in 'Cortisol' (stress hormone), thus affecting their physical and/or mental health, with the triggering of the 'Sympathetic Nervous System' ('SNS') tending to keep them in the 'freeze-fight-flight' mode. The Baul society which does not discourage such relationships like in a pre-human society would, hopefully, be free from such problems and would enjoy the 'Shanta Rasa' (peace & poise) of the 'Para-Sympathetic Nervous System' ('PSNS') which activates the 'rest-relax-and-digest' state of biology.

There is another major biological advantage of a male's having physical relationship with a few females. If the male is guided purely by 'Lust' (in Bengali, 'kam') unless he finds 'novelty' in the female with whom he shares the bed, the quality (sperm count, viscosity etc.) of his 'semen' would not be the best as partnership with one female gets stale *(Reference 5)*. Research shows that males reduce their 'investment' in sperm quantity or quality upon repeated mating with the same female and increase such 'investment' when mated to a novel female. In the language of the Bauls, 'semen' is called the 'bij' or 'bastu' and one of the Baul practices is 'bastu dharan'—preserving the 'semen' without ejaculation using special breathing techniques. This 'bastu', the Bauls say, is the 'gift' of the father—it should be considered as an 'asset'—it should not be wasted by ejaculating. So, possibly, the Baul practice of having several 'sadhan sanginis' is to accelerate the libido or sexual drive to its peak to enhance the quality and quantity of the 'semen'. If that happens to be true, then it is really interesting and most scientific. Only 'celibacy' does not lead to a result of this sort. The Bauls are really ingenious in certain respects.

Basically, we have not been able to transcend our 'pre-human' biology. 'Pre-human' propensities drive us most of the time when our brain's 'Default Mode Network' ('DMN') is active if we have not been able to discover our 'True Passion' and are driven by its pursuit. 'Human', or Freud's 'Ego'-level existence is just the outside cloak—inside is the 'pre-human' flame burning all the time—which is the serpentine 'kundalini' power. We suppress or repress the 'pre-human' spirit due to the pressure of Freud's 'Super-Ego' *(Reference 6)* or religious doctrines (like the 'Shariat' of Islam) which are behind the social customs and taboos. This picture was crystal clear to Lalon and he had expressed it through many of his songs. 'Atma-tattva'—'Doctrine of the Self'—knowing yourself—clear biological self-knowledge is at the core of Lalon's philosophy. He would, apparently, compose and sing his songs for 'Pre-human' folks with the idea of educating them to come up to the 'Post-human' level where the concept of 'virtue' (in Bengali, 'Punya') and 'sin' (in Bengali, 'Pap') is not to be seen, heard, felt or experienced anywhere. You invoke the state of 'Bliss', inside your brain, without taking the help of 'Cannabis' or any other drug—as must have been Lalon's regular 'yogic' or 'tantric' habit.

At one time, I was terribly impressed to know about Matsushita's endeavour to turn 'Ordinary' people into 'Extra-ordinary'. Konosuke Matsushita (1894-1989) was the Founder-Chairman of the largest Japanese multi-division consumer electronic company: The National Panasonic Corporation' *(Reference 7)*. He is referred to as the "God of Management" in Japan. I am now equally, if not more, impressed by Lalon Shah's silent war against 'pre-human' existence. Through his songs and oral teaching, he was fulfilling his life's mission to turn 'Pre-humans' into 'Post-humans'. If Matsushita is referred to as the "God of Management" in Japan, will it be too much if we regard Fakir Lalon Shah as the "Reformer of Human Consciousness" in the Bengali-speaking world? Lalon had worked on human attitude, human consciousness.

Lalon's Taoist Link

In one of his biologically overloaded songs (*"Chander Gaye Chand Legeche"—"One Moon is in Contact with Another"*), Lalon is talking about the 'unborn' child—the 'foetus'. He says it is inside a room which has no doors…a living human is confined there but it does not speak…who does feed it…who does pray for it? *(References 8, 9 & 10)*

Now, read a Taoist version of an 'unborn' child's feeling:

> *"Oh! I'm the only one who is quiet and silent, like a baby who is not yet a child. Oh! I'm fastened and tied, and I've no place to return." (Reference 11)* Lao Tzu, the ancient Chinese philosopher was the founder of the Taoist concepts.

This holy foetus has the mind of a fool yet it possesses the highest wisdom. It is quite different from a 'born' child, as it strictly follows and honours the mother-nurse. Here the 'unborn' baby is the follower of Taoism and the mother-nurse is the Tao philosophy itself. The inner meaning here is that the 'unborn' child has no name—and, above all, no 'Ego'. The moment the baby is taken out of the mother's womb and it becomes a 'born' child, and given a name - its 'Ego' starts developing as its tool for survival and growth. And, ego-centricity, while acts as a protective shield, is the cause for all human sufferings, pains, frustrations. This is the Taoist perception.

Lalon, in his song, points his finger towards the 'Power of Egoless-ness'. He indirectly suggests that one should be like an 'unborn' child—who has no 'Ego'—totally respectful towards his (no gender bias) benefactors and care-givers—particularly the 'Gurus'. Taking cue from the Taoist philosophy, he should respect all 'wombs'—in other words, all women, as those are the 'mysterious females' who have given births to all under heaven. They are like the gates to Earth and Heaven. ("Tao is the womb which generates Heaven and Earth, which is the source of life". The most interesting twin concept is that Tao is the 'mysterious womb' as well as the 'mother-nurse' of all beings.). Now, Lalon Sai says in his song: "*Ma ke chule more chele*" (English translation: "*The son dies if he touches the mother*". "*Chele*" means the owner of the male genital. If he touches the womb-owner (who is regarded as the '*Mother*'—

in Bengali, '*Ma*') with his male genital and releases his 'bij' (that is, semen), the experience that he faces is no less than death. Was Lalon familiar with the 'Oedipus Complex' concept of Dr Sigmund Freud where the young boy unconsciously wishes to have sex with his mother and disdains his father for having sex and being satisfied before him *(References 12 & 13)*.

In Taoism, we've been introduced to the 'Mysterious Female' to whom the origin of all under heaven has been attributed. There are 'Non-mysterious females' too, about whom Lalon sings in his song: "*Choy masher ek kanya chilo*". This '*kanya*' or daughter is a non-mysterious female who has 6 (six) vices: Kama (desire/lust), Krodha (anger/aggression), Lobha (greed), Mada (ego/arrogance), Moha (delusion) and Matsarya (jealousy/envy). '*Noy mashe tar garbha holo*'—which means that when the 9 (nine) doors of the body which all male and female children have (2 eyes, 2 ears, 2 nostrils, 1 mouth, 1 genital passage, 1 anus) developed, she developed those six enemies. When 2 (two) more outlets (one for the semen and one for the menstrual/vaginal fluid respectively for the growing boy and the girl) were added, they got ready to produce three children—semen, menstrual fluid and vaginal discharge. Lalon now asks: "*Konta korbe fakiri?*"—out of these three kids, which one will take up the life of a 'fakir'?

Lalon wanted to highlight that common people (who do not follow authentic Baul philosophy) are killing live cells at every act of sexual engagement when the purpose is not reproduction—just for moments of pleasure—for earning the brain's reward molecule 'Dopamine'. This common man, in his one lifetime, how many such deaths has he caused. By understanding the importance of semen preservation ('beej dharan'), one can enhance his level of consciousness and move into the zone of higher vibrations. *(References 14 & 15)*

A man gets exhausted after every act of ejaculation. It tantamounts to precious biological energy loss and energy deficiency. An infant is not attracted towards the opposite sex. Taoists, therefore, recommend one to embody the fullness of innocence like a ruddy infant.

Regarding the ruddy infant, a Taoist verse says:

> *"Wasps, spiders, scorpions, and snakes will not sting or bite him;*
> *Rapacious birds and fierce beasts will stay away.*
> *His bones are weak, and his sinews soft, yet his grip is tight.*
> *He knows not the joining of male and female, yet his penis is aroused.*
> *His essence has reached a peak."*

Lalon wants every individual like this ruddy infant.

That is why he sings:

> *"Chander gaye chand legeche.*
> *Amra bhebe korbo ki?"*

In Baul culture there are 4 (four) 'chands' or 'moons'—semen, urine, stool, and menstrual fluid. "*Chander gaye chand legeche*" means a male is engaged in 'coitus' with a menstruated female. Even if it happens in front of my eyes, I should not be bothered—I should let it pass because my attitude, my mind-set I've managed to groom like a 'ruddy infant'. What a beautiful way of expression!!

In this most difficultly worded Lalon song, I've attempted to discover a Taoist link!!

Lalon's Bio-Poetics

Fakir Lalon Shah's talent for 'Bio-poetics' was really amazing. 'Bio-poetics' is a term I've coined just now to describe poetry, verses, lyrics based on biology. Lalon's verses dealing with the 'Deha Tattva' (Doctrine of the Body) all belong to the domain of 'Bio-poetics'.

Here is an outstanding example. The first line of the song is: "*Ek phoole char rang dhoreche*" (English: "*One flower displays four colours*"). Here, Lalon is talking about the menstrual fluid which changes colour during the period according to the presence, quality, quantity and density of different biological components. Lalon continues: "*Se phool e bhavnagare ki shova koreche...karon barir madhye se phool, bhese beray ekul okul, swet baran ek bhramar bykul...se phooler modhur ashe ghurteche.*" (In English: "*What a beautiful sight it is in the city of thoughts!*

That flower is in the midst of the causative fluid...floating from one side to another...one fair-looking anxious bee... is wandering in the hope of tasting the honey that resides inside the flower."

Lalon beautifully describes how a sperm is most anxiously and impatiently moving from one side to another in the fluid to penetrate into the flower to taste its honey.

In the language of biology, it is like this. The 'menstrual cycle' is the monthly series of changes a woman's body goes through for the possibility of pregnancy. Each month, one of the woman's two ovaries release an 'egg'. This process is called 'ovulation'. At the same time, hormonal changes prepare the uterus for pregnancy. The land is now ready for the seed to be sown. The land-owner is the woman—the would-be mother. The fertility of the land varies from one woman to another and it may vary in the same woman from one time to another. But the fertile land will not be properly utilised if the seed is not sown. The owner of the seed (the 'sperm'—the 'bij' or 'bastu' in Baul language) is a man. If he does not place the seed on the fertile land of the woman, pregnancy will never take place. Therefore, if ovulation takes place and the 'egg' is not fertilised by the 'sperm', the lining of the uterus sheds through the vagina. This is called the 'menstrual period' or 'period' in common parlance. During the 'period', the abandoned, unutilised uterine lining comes out as 'menstrual flow', which might occur once in every 21 to 35 days and last for minimum 2 and maximum 7 days. Menstrual cycles tend to be shorter and more regular as you age. Throughout a monthly menstrual cycle, the body makes different amounts of chemicals called 'hormones' to prepare for pregnancy. These hormones are: Estrogen, Progesterone, FSH and LH. The variation in the level of each of these hormones decides the phase which a woman undergoes.

These phases are: (1) 'Menstrual Phase' (that is, the 'period' lasting from 3 to 5 days); (2) 'Follicular Phase'(an 'egg' is released from one of the ovaries by a matured egg follicle); (3) 'Ovulatory Phase' (ovulation takes place during day 13 to 17, mid-cycle); and (4) 'Luteal Phase' (post-ovulation, where the fate of the 'corpus luteum' is decided—if fertilisation occurs, pregnancy starts—if fertilisation does not occur, the 'menstrual cycle' is repeated). Every phase is influenced by the female hormones described above. A normal 'menstrual cycle' lasts between 24 and 38 days.

On the very first day of the 'period', you observe bright red blood ('Lal' in Bengali). The texture, appearance and amount of discharge change as the hormones fluctuate during the 'period'. If a 'white discharge' occurs before the 'period', then it is most likely coming from the cervix and uterus. These are a combination of cervical mucus and secretion. A woman who is not on contraceptive pills and who is in her reproductive years, may expect to have very few days without some form of vaginal discharge. There are 4 (four) distinctly different types of 'vaginal discharge' *(See Reference 18).*

Lalon, in his song, mentions the 4 (four) colours of the flower as: Red ('Lal' in Bengali), Rose-coloured ('Jarod' in Arabic), Jasmine-coloured ('Sia' in Arabic), and Snow/Milk-white ('Safed' in Arabic). These cover the blood-red menstrual fluid and the white vaginal discharges.

Lalon's poetry continues: "*The flower is creeper-like without any root and it has leaves without any stem—most peculiar it is—you have to visualise it in your imagination as you can't see it physically.*"

Then he continues to say: "*Je phool e Nabi-r janmo hoy...se phool to samanya phool noy...Lalon koy jar mool nai deshe*" (In English: "*The flower that has given birth to the Prophet Muhammad, it is not an ordinary flower...Lalon says its root is not to be seen in the country.*" He wants to highlight the tremendous power of the egg fertilised by the sperm—which has been responsible for the birth of the Prophet!!

A parting thought for this piece! 'Red', I understand, is the colour of Lord Shiva; so is 'White'. And 'Shiva' is 'Purusha'. Does that mean that the red menstrual blood and the white vaginal discharge which are unique to a woman are embodiments of Lord Shiva waiting for the real 'lingam' to snugly fit into the crevice, for the purpose of sowing the 'seed' in the 'land' that is ready?

Lalon's Guru Principle

Each religion has its own Gurus who are sold totally to the religion's special and specific beliefs and rituals. Such Gurus are specialists. Some rare species of Gurus are universal, they are generalists. Lalon was one of those rare breeds. He had composed quite a few songs to convey his ideas about such Gurus. I am quoting only two of those here (English translation and refurbishment mine).

Song No. 1

"You've not realised what kind of a substance is a True Guru,
He is the one who can make you cross the turbulent river of this materialistic world!!
Without him, you'll be utterly helpless.

Who will tell you:
What is the purpose of your life?
Why were you brought to this planet?
What kind of illusions have made you forget such basics?

Your days have been spent totally uselessly,
Dark time had kept you embraced.
Somebody unrefined and of low taste had invaded your spiritual palace of colours.

Wind is blowing in your room—wind of change!!
You may spend some time now in devotion under the tutelage of a True Guru!!
Siraj Sai says—listen stupid Lalon,
If you lose this opportunity, you'll be lost for ever!! (Reference 19)

Song No. 2

The Guru is ready for service at the doorstep of the disciple,
Irrespective of his community and caste:
whether he is Hindu or Muslim,
whether he is of a high or low caste!!

A person belonging to the lowest caste may be mad in devotion.
Saint Kabir was just a fisherman by caste—
Who was disconnected from the world but connected with the cosmos!
Ramdas, the cobbler was a fountain of devotion,
His spirit of service would ring the heavenly bells!

One moon lights the whole world,
One sperm fertilises an egg to create a new life!
These are two of the universal truths!!

Lalon says, only such things are real, the rest is all false
Whatever are the hearsays and social beliefs!! (Reference 20)

Lalon on 'Love'

The anthropologist-researcher Helen Fisher, PhD from the Rutgers University, who has specialised in 'Love'-related studies, writes in the 'Prologue' of her book *Anatomy of Love (Reference 21)*:

> *"I was recently travelling in the highlands of New Guinea in the back of a pick-up truck, talking with a man who had three wives. I asked him how many wives he would like to have. There was a pause as he rubbed his chin. I wondered: Would he say—five? Ten? Twenty-five wives? He leaned towards me and whispered: none."*

Most of the Bauls are against having married wives. They have 'sadhan-sanginis' as we've already discussed—most essential and critical partners for their 'Jugal Sadhana' (joint ritual). They have their own perceptions and opinions about 'lust' (in Bengali: 'kam') and 'love' (in Bengali: 'prem').

There are many Baul songs on 'lust' and 'love', but those composed by Fakir Lalon Shah are particularly allegorical and I like them the best. I'm sharing below three such songs which I've translated in English myself, and while translating, I've dressed them up a little (not much) to convey the inner meaning.

Dying While Living in the Practice of Love:

> *"In the practice and performance of 'Love', can you die while living?*
>
> *I mean, can you defeat all the 'Six Enemies of the Mind' (the 'Sadaripus') and be like a dead man while loving someone?*
>
> *Totally unlike the normal 'Love' in which a young boy and a young girl indulge?*
>
> *It is hard to shake off lust from the body by one who is 'driven' by it.*
>
> *However, it is possible to become lust-free by worshipping devotedly at Kamrup Kamakhya, we hear!*
>
> *But it is too difficult for one to steal the secret strategy.*
>
> *Just like the blooming lotus attracts the golden rays of the sun,*
>
> *The female attracts the male with the help of her physical pheromone in the same way for mating!*
>
> *Both are instinctively aware of the power of the sex hormones,*
>
> *Lalon Fakir is just a watcher and a listener from a distance!*
>
> *In the practice and performance of 'Love' can you die while living? (Reference 22)*

[In the Baul philosophy, 'dying while living' (in Bengali: 'Jyante mara') is a commonly used phrase which means you are living like a dead man without lust, anger, greed, infatuation, ego, and envy. This condition represents a 'Pure Mind'.]

Search for a 'True Lover':

> *"Those who are brimming with 'True Love' in their soul, where have they hidden their erotic lust?*
>
> *Oh, my dear friend, please answer my question and make me free from my mental pain!!*

Lust arises first and, in its wake, semen gets activated; but you've to hold it—restrain it from getting auto-released.

The person with 'True Love' in his heart is unperturbed by the libido
He is aware of the conduct and behaviour of the 'pitridhan'—the wealth inherited from the father—the potent 'seed' of life!!
The 'True Lover' does not ejaculate as he very well knows
That you move towards the life's end if you lose the 'seed' again and again—you lose your power of 'creation' of art and culture!
So, promise to give up the use of empty words, show through your action that 'You Can'.

One who fails to obey what is embedded in the mind has forgotten what he had promised—his resolution!
Fakir Lalon just ponders and says: 'If you call him, he doesn't respond. He, surely can't be a 'True Lover'!! (Reference 23)

[This song describes the natural philosophy of male-female love and how the Bauls and Fakirs are not in favour of following it. They go for the reverse route (in Bengali—'Ulta rasta').]

Root Cause of Love:
(not the whole verse, only some relevant excerpts)

"Whom should I ask what is 'Deep True Love'?
In which love, the 'Guru' represents the boat of life that you're sailing in?
In which love, the 'Devotee', the 'Disciple' is the boatman rowing the boat?

Without knowing the root cause of love, it is useless to have a love-bound relationship,
Siraj Sai says to Lalon." (Reference 24)

[This song is about the importance of the root cause of love.]

Mystic Lalon: The Mysterious Songwriter

More than a decade and a half ago, I had a chance-viewing of an amazing film of deep educational value at The Tata Steel Management Centre. The name of the film was 'The Eye of the Beholder'. The moral was: how we perceive the same situation from different perspectives according to the nature of the consciousness that each of us have. This aligns very well with physician Dr Paul MacLean's (MD) 'Triune Brain Theory' which is a reasonably good yet controversial one. I like it because there is no abstract philosophy attached to it. *(References 25 & 26)*

According to Dr MacLean, the human brain is like a house which has three floors. The ground floor at the base is the 'Reptilian Complex' brain structure that we have inherited from our reptilian past. This 'hindbrain' is present in all kinds of reptiles, birds and such other creatures who lay eggs. These creatures lack in emotions—they are 'Survival and Replication'-oriented. The 1st floor of our brain is what MacLean called the 'Paleo-mammalian Complex' (known as the 'midbrain' in common parlance). This portion has the 'emotional centre'—all mammals who bear babies in their womb, deliver them and nurture them for grooming up are active in this portion of the brain. The uppermost floor is the 'Neo-mammalian Complex' or 'Neo-cortex' (known as the 'forebrain')—present in all higher mammals and is thickest in its layers in the human brain. It contains the social brain and the brain's executive control centre that can logically analyse things for decision-making and problem-solving.

This is modern neuro-science! The ancient Hindu scripture of Taittiriya Upanishad had proposed another beautiful model of the human personality—my most favourite 'Pancha Kosha'. Our 'Soul' is enveloped by 5 (five) sheaths. The outermost is the visible 'Gross Body' ('Sthula Sharira')—the 'Annamaya Kosha' that represents everything materialistic beginning with those that meet our basic needs—food, clothes and shelter. From the 2nd sheath onwards all the sheaths are invisible constituting the 'Subtle Body' ('Sukshma Sharira'). The 2nd sheath is the 'Pranaymaya Kosha' representing the life force—the breath energy. The 3rd one is the 'Monomaya Kosha' representing the people relationships—the emotional energy. The 4th one is the 'Vijnanamaya Kosha'—representing everything related to 'Knowledge and Wisdom'—the intellectual energy. The 5th and the final one is the 'Anandamaya Kosha' which, if you can reach there with full devotion and dedication to anything, you can earn 'Bliss'—the pure, unadulterated cosmic energy. The 'Jivatma' which is a part of the 'Paramatma' is nested within these five sheaths *(References 27 & 28).*

One of the most popular songs of Lalon is: '*Barir kache arshi nagar*' (in Bengali) '*Close to my house is the City of Mirrors*' (in English) *(Reference 29).*

Carol Salomon was a very prominent researcher on Baul songs and philosophy. The scholar who was on the teaching faculty at the University of Washington, Seattle, USA met with a car accident died young leaving her husband and only child. She has translated many Baul songs in English and her best collection is 'The City of Mirrors' *(Reference 30).*

She has translated '*Barir kache arshi nagar*' almost literally assuming that the songwriter is talking about his '*sangini*'—female devotional partner. Salomon's translation goes like this:

> *"I have not seen her even once…my neighbour; Who lives in a city of mirrors near my house.*
>
> *Her village is surrounded by deep boundless water…I long to see her but how can I reach her village?*
>
> *What can I say about my neighbour? She has no hands, no feet, no shoulders, no head.*
>
> *Sometimes she floats high up in the sky, sometimes—in the water!*
>
> *She and Lalon are in the same place…Yet five thousand miles apart!!"*

Very sweet indeed! But where is the philosophy impregnated into the verse through which Lalon wanted to convey something very very deep based on the "Soul Theory"?

Now, read how I've interpreted the same song! Different beholders have different perceptions or impressions of the same incident!! How true it is!!

By 'House' Lalon is referring to his 'body'. My perception of the 'City of Mirrors' is the 'whole body' where there are different organs and systems functioning seamlessly to make us survive and replicate. There are also different layers of the mind—the 'Conscious', the 'Subconscious' and the 'Unconscious'. These are like mirrors where one can see the reflections of his 'Soul' which changes its form and shape with changes in its consciousness. 'Consciousness' changes as per the activation of the 'Hindbrain', 'Midbrain' and the 'Forebrain' in response to different stimuli—external as well as internal.

By 'Neighbour', Lalon means the 'Soul' which is hidden under 5 (five) sheaths according to the 'Pancha Kosha' model. Again, Lalon's 'One room full of neighbours' represent the changing 'Consciousness' at different times—from 'Pre-human' to 'Human' and from 'Human' to 'Post-human'.

Lalon says he has never met his neighbour even once. How can he, unless he can cross all the five sheaths of the 'Pancha Kosha' and reach the 'Jivatma'. This barrier, in Lalon's song, is the deep stretch of water in the village and he cannot see the banks, neither has he got a boat to cross the turbulent vast expanse of water. He is getting pulled by the 'Dietary Sheath' ('Annamaya Kosha'), the 'Breath Sheath' ('Pranamaya Kosha'), the 'Emotional Sheath' ('Monomaya Kosha'), the 'Intellectual Sheath' ('Vijnanamaya Kosha') and the 'Blissful Sheath' ('Anandamaya Kosha').

When Lalon says that his neighbour has no hands, no legs, no shoulder, and no head—how can it be a 'human being' (Carol Salomon perhaps did not think deeply when she interpreted the neighbour as the singer's female companion). I firmly believe that Lalon had the 'Soul Theory' in mind, particularly when he says that for a while it floats on space, at other times it floats in water. Lalon is hungry for the 'Soul's touch as that would have given him an opportunity to unite with the cosmic energy of which the Soul is a part and that experience would have taken away all his pains, brought an end to all his trials and tribulations of the mortal life. Until, he PURIFIES himself, it will remain a distant dream!! What a philosophy!!

References

[1] *Margaret Mead*—Wikipedia.

[2] Daniel Z., Lieberman M.D. and Michael E. Long, *The Molecule of More: How a Single Chemical in Your Brain Drives Love, Sex and Creativity—and will Determine the Fate of the Human Race*, Dallas: BenBella Books, 2018.

[3] Paul J. Zak, *The Moral Molecule: The Source of Love and Prosperity*, New York: Plume (Penguin Group), 2013.

[4] Richard Dawkins, *The Selfish Gene*, Oxford: Oxford University Press, 30th University Edition, 2006.

[5] Paul N. Joseph, Rakesh K. Sharma… Laura K. Sirot, "Men Ejaculate Larger Volumes of Semen, More Motile Sperm and More Quickly when Exposed to Images of Novel Women", *Evolutionary Psychological Science*, Vol. 1, 2015, pp. 195-200.

[6] Saul McLeod, "Freud's Id, Ego and Superego", *Simply Psychology*, updated 2021.

[7] *Konosuke Matsushita*—Wikipedia.

[8] "Chander Gaye Chand Legeche—Gaaner Artha" Wasif Ahmed 26, Bandh Bhangar Awaj.

[9] "Chander Gaye Chand Legeche—Gaaner Mool Artha", nobojug.blog

[10] "Chander Gaye Chand Legeche—Kotha R Sur" Qmin.

[11] Eugeni Tortchinov, "The Doctrine of the 'Mysterious Female' in Taoism: A Trans-personalist View".
In: T.R. Soidla and S.I. Shapiro (ed.) *Everything is According to the Way: Voices of Russian Trans-personalism*, Brisbane, Australia: Bolda-Lok Publishing and Educational Enterprises, 1997.

[12] "Oedipus Complex: Definition and History", *Encyclopaedia Britannica*.

[13] Kendra Cherry, "What is the Oedipus Complex?" *verywellmind*, 20th May, 2022.

[14] Pamela Dussault Runtagh, "The Benefits of Being in a Higher Vibration", *HUFFPOST*, 30th July 2012.

[15] Sarah Regan, "The Law of Vibration, Explained: How to Use This Universal Law to Your Advantage", *mbg*, 17th June 2021.

[16] "Your menstrual cycle" OASH Office on Women's Health.

[17] "Menstrual cycle: What's normal, what's not", *Healthy Lifestyle: Women's Health*, Mayo Clinic.

[18] Deika King, "Menstrual Cycle: 4 Types of Vaginal Discharge" Holistic Breast Specialist and Naturopathic Doctor.

[19] Sanat Kr. Mitra, *Lalon Fakir: Kabi o Kabya* (in Bengali), Kolkata: Pustak Bipani, Bengali year 1367, p. 121, Song No. 1.

[20] Sanat Kr. Mitra, *Lalon Fakir: Kabi o Kabya* (in Bengali), Kolkata: Pustak Bipani, Bengali year 1367, p. 143, Song No. 61.

[21] Helen Fisher, *Anatomy of Love*, New York: W.W. Norton, 2016 (revised edition).

[22] Shaktinath Jha, *Fakir Lalon Sai: Desh, Kal ebong Shilpa*, Kolkata: Sangbad, 1995, p. 48. Song No. 155.

[23] – Do – p. 22, Song No. 56.

[24] – Do – p. 23, Song No. 61/62.

[25] *Triune Brain*—Wikipedia.

[26] "Triune Brain"—*Science Direct*.

[27] Dr Biswajit Satpathy, "Pancha Kosha Theory of Personality", *The International Journal of Indian Psychology*, Vol. 6, Issue 2, April-June 2018, pp. 34-39.

[28] *Pancha Kosha*—vikaspedia.

[29] "Barir kache arshi nagar", Bengali Lyrics, *gdn8.com*/2020/07

[30] Carol Saloman (Texts, Translation and Commentary), Edited by: Keith E. Cantu and Saymon Zakaria, *City of Mirrors*, New York: Oxford University Press, 2017.

CHAPTER 5

A Golden Gift: Birth as a 'Human'

"The creation of the human beings, who are of one species only and who stock their eatables in the belly, is the ninth in the rotation. In the human race, the mode of passion is very prominent."

—Srimad-Bhagavatam 3.10.26

"...the human beings are more passionate than the animals and thus there is a high level of irregularity when it comes to sex life... The animals have due time for sexual intercourse but the human beings have no regular time for such activities.

A human being is given more freedom and facility to do certain things and not to do certain things too. Because of the pleasure in sexual intercourse or sexual attraction, he thinks that whatever endeavour he is doing is ultimately meant for enhancing that. The fine 'rasas' that are possible in the human form are not possible in the animal form. The entire purpose of Vedic culture was to give the human being the fine samples of all the possible 'rasas'." *(Reference 1)*

The human body is a marvel of engineering and technology. It is a most complicated chemical plant. In Baul culture and practices, there is a lot of importance attached to a biological product that the male body produces at the onset of puberty. In a healthy body, this product is auto-generated. In Baul language, it is described as 'Bastu' or 'Bij'—which is nothing but the male 'semen'.

Bauls believe that it is 'Pitri Dhon' (in Bengali)—a Golden Gift that is potent with the power to 'pro-create'. The young adolescent now has the capability to become a 'father' (that is why, the product is assigned the name 'Pitri Dhon'—the wealth that can make you a 'father'). Therefore, this biological resource is needed to be preserved and nurtured to be converted into biological capital. It must not be 'lost' by its owner being a victim of 'lust' (in Bengali, 'kam'). 'Lust' or 'kam' is its enemy—a most difficult one to be won over as it is one of our basic creaturely instincts.

Lalon writes: *"Age kapat maro kam-er ghare; manush jhalak debe roop nihari"* (In English: *"Before anything else, shut the door of the room where your lust resides; if you can keep it captive, under your total control, your body will radiate a glow—you'll shine"*.

Your 'lust' is related to the 'Muladhar Chakra' in your body which is connected with the sex glands—'gonads'. For a male, the 'gonads' are the 'testes' where the 'semen' is created.

The 'semen' contains 'sperms' which are living things. And, since each 'sperm' is living it has a 'soul' of its own. When the 'sperms' are retained by their 'Dad'—the male owner, they remain in heavenly happiness. Collectively, the 'sperms' constitute a storehouse of power, of productive energy. The moment the semen is ejected inside the female vagina, the sperms face a new world full of turbulence and turmoil as the female 'egg' does not allow any odd male sperm to come in its proximity and get attached. The 'egg' is very selective.

The 'sperms' that were happy inside the male testes soon start suffering from unknown, unfamiliar stress—especially if the physical relationship is one of 'lust' (for earning the reward molecule 'Dopamine') and not of 'love' (bathed in the bonding-trust-compassion molecule 'Oxytocin'). Under such circumstances, if the 'sperm' gets connected with the 'egg' and fertilisation takes place leading to pregnancy, the 'zygote' (bundle of flesh and blood) formed is already under stress. Eventually, the baby is born normal physically, but with a built-in stress. All normal babies carry some amount of 'stress' when born because intercourses hardly take place when both the partners are brimming with the love molecule 'Oxytocin'. If the baby is subjected to further stress, post-birth, due to neglect (mother having too many older kids who need more attention; mother widowed after childbirth; inter-parental conflict; mother-in-law-daughter-in-law conflict; working-professionally engaged-career-oriented mother; mother in stress because of absentee father, etc.), the stress multiplies in the growing child leading to subtle problems which the paediatricians cannot smell and diagnose easily. These are typical cases where the conception occurred due to lustful sex.

- **Lalon continues to write:** In Bengali: *"Haoa dhoro, agni sthir koro; marar agete moro; more jeno banchte paro; dekhe shaman jak fire"* (in English: *"Control your breath—hold it and take the reins of the fire inside you; feign death—by holding your breath, before the real end comes; you will live long if you die in that fashion; let the God of Death return from your door hopelessly."*). In the Baul rituals, there is a lot of emphasis on breath control techniques (to be trained in which, of course, you need a 'sadguru') some of which have to be taken advantage of to control ejaculation of semen.
- **Lalon goes on:** In Bengali: *"Bare bare kori mana; leela r deshe ar jeo na; tejer ghare karo tejiana; sadho urdho chand dhore."* In English: *"I warn you again and again; not to go to the land of dirty games; stay with your power and go on strengthening it; instead of releasing your semen downwards with the help of gravity, let it move upward by controlling your breath."* Authentic Baul sadhaks learn breathing techniques from their experienced Gurus and go for physicals with menstruated females and instead of ejaculating inside the vagina allow the semen to move upward along with the menstrual fluid to reach a place where the three rivers meet ("Triveni Sangam"—meeting place of the 'Ida', 'Pingala' and 'Susumna' nadis near the 'Ajna' chakra located deep inside your brain, in between your two eyes). It is a Tantric technique, I presume.
- **Lalon's last stanza is:** In Bengali: *"Jano na re mon, parahin darpan; Kemone hoy roop darshan; Siraj Sai er bachan shon re Lalon; theke hushiare."* In English: *"My dear 'Mind' since you are a mirror without any mercurial layer at the back,* ('para' in Bengali and 'mercury' in English means 'semen' in Baul language)—the sentence means: *"since you have been losing your powerful semen due to frequent ejaculation to earn your pleasure molecule 'Dopamine', you do not have full in-depth knowledge; you do not know how one can witness the real beauty if you do not waste, instead retain your semen and build up 'semen capital'; Siraj Sain (who was Lalon's Guru) says to*

Lalon—listen to me—pay attention to what I say—take care not to indulge in something that is unintelligent and damaging for you". What Lalon wants to say is that by going for such strategically planned and executed physical relationship using some special breathing technique, you will earn your 'Dopamine' without the cost of losing your semen which has the potential for assigning the 'father' role to you. On top of it, if you can develop a loving relationship with your partner through touching and feeling each other's body with affection and compassion, you can earn your 'Oxytocin' too.

Oxytocin Hunt

In Indian mythology, 'Kama Deva' is the god of erotic love and pleasure (in other words, 'lust'—in Bengali, 'kam'). 'Rati', gorgeous and sensual, with thin hips and luscious breasts, is the Hindu goddess of desire, passion, and 'lust'. She is a faithful consort to 'Kama Deva' and the two are often worshipped together as 'Kama-Rati'. *(Reference 2)* You will bump onto 'Kama-Rati' quite often in Baul songs. 'Madan', an equally highly-sexed Puranic male is the brother of 'Kama Deva'. At times, mentioned in Baul songs, he is also regarded as the god of physical love or infatuation. There is a story where it is mentioned that how 'Lord Shiva' had taken the help of his 'Third Eye' to turn 'Kama Deva' into ashes as the latter tried to de-focus the former's mind, with lustful thoughts, while he was engaged in deep meditation. *(Reference 3)*

The very fact that in Indian mythology, there is a god of erotic love and pleasure (aka 'lust') and there is also his consort 'Rati'—the goddess of desire—does that mean that 'lustful sex' had a prominent place in the ancient Indian society—that was the background of Indian mythology? As a matter of fact, in the human society of all ages, there has been the existence of 'pre-human' (people governed by primitive, animalish instincts), 'human' (people in whom the basic instincts do exist but many a times, those are suppressed or repressed due to social norms), and 'post-human' (people who have conquered the basic instincts and exist at a very high level of consciousness with very high frequency vibrations).

'Pre-human' sex is all lustful sex as it is most vital for all non-humans and 'pre-human' humans to produce offspring who can take charge of their own safety and security against all odds in their own typical societies. 'Human' man is essentially a social animal—love plays the most vital role to fulfil his social bonding and relationship-building objectives. 'Post-humans' exist beyond the social plane, even when leading a family life; they are detached.

One distinct gain of 'lustful sex' (typical of a high level of the male sex hormone 'Testosterone') is that it helps the body to release a lot of 'Endorphins'—body's endogenous stress-relieving molecules. *(Reference 4)* So, 'lust' helps people to withstand a lot of 'stress' and to take risks. And, one possible loss of 'lustful sex' is creation of children who are 'attention-hungry' right from their infancy. Experienced child-watchers can make out with or without much effort which is a 'child of lust' and which is not. A 'child of love' is already high in the love molecule 'Oxytocin' so she becomes more of a 'care-giver' than a 'care-seeker'. *(Reference 5)* Hypothalamus makes 'Oxytocin', but your posterior Pituitary Gland stores and releases it into your bloodstream. 'Endorphins' are also created in the hypothalamus and pituitary gland. So, there is a 'see-saw' relationship between 'Oxytocin' and 'Endorphin'. This, one must remember.

Be it between two lovers (same-sex or opposite-sex), or between a husband and a wife, or a Baul 'sadhak' and his 'sadhan sangini'—what different kinds of relations exist, can be expressed in terms of the 'Rasas' prevailing between them. 'Rasa' is the emotional essence, invisible vibrations, the essential feeling that exists between the two. *(Reference 6)*

There are five 'Rasas' that have been identified. Nevertheless, these do not include the lowest of the 'Rasas' which is common in all creatures including in the king of them—the human. This is 'kam' ('lust' in English) that does not spare the five working organs (that is, 'karmendriya') and five organs of intellect and wisdom (that is 'jnaendriya')—which all vibrate at the same frequency to get the pent-up force released; their typical activities all get suppressed under high 'libido'.

Leaving aside this 'Kama' or lustful relationship where the 'Rasa' is absolutely basic and creaturely, we can have the following five types: *(Reference 7)*

- **Santa Rasa:** Keeping cool, remaining totally under control; appreciating each other's good qualities and achievements. Doing everything silently—without any reaction or response whatsoever. There is no free exchange or reciprocation of 'love' in full terms.
- **Dasya Rasa:** In addition to the awe and reverence of the 'Santa Rasa', there is a perceptible service-oriented attitude. There are formality and restriction of complete exchange of 'love'.
- **Sakhya Rasa:** The awe and reverence still persisting, the spirit of service has been replaced by a playful attitude that is typical of what exists between two friends. They eat food together; share each other's food. It is a beautiful state of expression of love; however, there is unavailability of freedom of full expression intimately.
- **Vatsalya Rasa:** Protective and nurturing relationship.
- **Madhurya Rasa:** All the boundaries that were there in the earlier four 'Rasas' are crossed here, leading to complete surrender—'atma nivedanam' with full trust ('Oxytocin'). The flood gates of 'Prema Rasa' are fully open in this 'Rasa' state, and the hearts of both the partners are full of 'love'.

This 'Rasa Theory' is equally applicable in the case of relationship-building between two persons—even two friends, between the 'Guru' and the 'shishya' or between two 'shisyas' of the same 'Guru'.

Fakir Lalon Shah clearly emphasizes in one of his most popular songs, how important is the 'Oxytocin Hunt' activity for one who wants to be a real 'Human Being' ('Sonar Manush' or 'Golden Man' in Lalon's own poetic language):

"Manush bhojle sonar manush hobi,
Manush chara khyepa re tui mool harabi"

(In English: *"You will fulfil your 'human' role only when you get positively connected to other humans; Without any well-bonded human relationship, you will lose your 'root'."*)

Lalon continues beautifully:

> *"Ei manushe manushe gantha, gache jemon alak lata,*
>
> *Jene shune murao matha, jate twarabi."*

(In English: *"Just like a creeper grows along the trunk of a tree, humans are meant to be closely connected with each other. Knowingly, if you get positively connected with other humans, you'll be regarded as a 'human'."*) *(Reference 8)*

Dying While Living

In the East, originating from the Vedic literature, we have the mystic concept of 'Dying while Living'—which means being alive but totally cut off from the external as well as internal environments. That means, you are disconnected from your outside as well as inside—not allowing any stimulus to affect you to dissuade you from focussed pursuit. In that realm, there is no distraction; instead, there is enduring calmness and peace. It is a kind of 'liberation' from the earthly bondage—'mukti' from the 'parthib' 'moha' and 'maya'. *(Reference 9)*

There are 4 (four) types of liberation mentioned in the Hindu scriptures: (i) 'saalokiya'—this is a state where one stays in the intense happiness of god's world; (ii) 'sameepiya'—this is where one is in close contact with god; (iii) 'saroopiya'—where one attains likeness with the god in characteristics; and, (iv) 'saayujiya', where one savours the bliss of identity with the supreme being. All of these take you away from the materialistic world of emotional entanglement and brings you close to divinity. In my opinion, it is equally applicable in a Guru-Shisya relationship where for the Shishya, the Guru is placed on the pedestal and regarded as the god. *(Reference 10)*

The last one applies to where one feels oneness with god. Such enlightened people may not renounce family or possessions, live inside a mountain cave or a seaside bamboo cottage, put on no special attire to be identified with a particular sect, but they emit a special aura that impacts their surroundings. They are 'nitya mukta'—the 'eternally liberated' ones, who perform a divinely ordained task that benefits the entire mankind—not just his family, folks and friends. (Fakir Lalon Shah is the best example for us). *(Reference 11)*

They are inwardly free from all desires but outwardly most energetic and active. They are detached yet most unconditionally attached to their tasks. They are witness to what goes around them but maintain poise in all situations, being pro-active. They are egoless as they are fully aware that ego can deter progress and act as an insurmountable barrier. Here, of course, by 'ego', I mean your sense of 'Self', as a separate identity leading to pride and vanity—not your feeling of consciousness that you 'exist'.

'Dying while Living' means overpowering your 'Selfish Ego' by conquering your body's 'sensory needs' for pleasure, your hunger for the 'reward molecule' 'Dopamine', by erasing your sense of discrimination between good and bad, clean and unclean, fragrant and pungent, tasteful and toxic (which the Baul 'sadhaks' strive for by following the 'chari chandra' ritual—consuming semen, urine, stool and menstrual blood). Such a step lessens the load on your brain's 'Error Detection Circuit' ('EDC') which is responsible for your power of discrimination—thus saving your brain's precious energy. *(Reference 12)*

The 'Dying while Living' that I've in mind is possible when you cut yourself off from all 'Maya' and 'Moha' of 'sangsar' (a householder's life) by de-activating your five 'chakras'—starting with the 'Muladhar' at the root of your 'spine' up to the 'Visuddha' around your 'throat'—by allowing them to work just for keeping your body in the best possible condition without any attachment with anyone or anything. You'll reside mostly at your 'Ajna' and 'Sahasrar' chakra levels which help you to be in touch with the higher vibrations of the cosmic consciousness. *(Reference 13)*

I presume Fakir Lalon Shah had tried to suggest this 'Dying while Living' state in his popular song *"Aat Kuthuri Noy Daroja"*. The first line in English would be: *"Eight rooms and nine doors"*. The eight rooms stand for eight spacious body parts/organs: the skull that contains the brain tissue – 1; lungs – 2; heart – 1; stomach – 1; kidneys – 2; colon – 1; Total = 8. The nine doors mean: Eyes – 2; Ears – 2; Nostrils – 2; Mouth – 1; Genitals – 1; Anus – 1; Total = 9.

Lalon goes on: *"Kono khane noy tala; ghar khana hoy teen tola."* (In English: *"Not a single one is locked. And, the house has three floors"*). Lalon means each one of these is open—nothing is under lock and key. And he is also talking about the 3-storeyed brain. (Professor Paul MacLean's 'Triune Brain' where the Gr. Floor is the Hind-brain, the 1st Floor, the Mid-brain and the top floor, the 'Fore Brain'). *(Reference 14)*

Lalon says:

> *"Gharer opor talay court cachari"*
> (In English: *"The 1st floor has the court room"*)
> *"Majher talay roy bypari"*
> (In English: *"On the middle floor,*
> *buying-and-selling transactions take place"*)
> *"Abar nicher talay karmachari dhyan kore premer mala"*
> (In English: *"Again, on the ground floor,*
> *the employees are meditating by counting beads"*)

My interpretation is: The ground floor is meant for 'routine' ritualistic activities like chanting, meditating with beads, and so on. On the first floor, all input-output (stimulus-response) transactions go on. And, the top floor is meant for judgemental decisions as the forebrain houses the executive control centre.

Lalon continues

> *"Noy darojay no jon dwari beray sada ghure"*
> (In English: *"The nine doors are well guarded by nine security guards"*)
> *"Choy dakate katbe kakhan ghore amay chore"*
> (In English: *"They are keeping vigil on when six robbers will come to steal by breaking in."*)

My interpretation is: All my nine outlets of the body are most alert and sensitive not to be influenced and carried away by the six vices that stand in the way of our spiritual progress and upliftment.

Lalon continues to say:

> *"Gharer monikothay diye chabi, moner sukhe nidra jabi"*
> (In English: *"Get located in the uppermost rooms of your house, lock yourself in; and, go to sleep to your heart's content"*)
>
> *"Jabe choy dakater bhoy bhabona, sukhe robi mon kala"*
> (In English: *"You'll be free from the tension of the six robbers,*
> *Oh! My 'Mon Kala' you will remain restful and in peace!"*)

My interpretation: The highest two chakras—the 'Ajna' and the 'Sahasrar' are meant for higher thoughts related to 'Intellectual Energy' and 'Cosmic Energy'. So, if you get yourself totally engaged and locked up at that level, you will be totally free from negative thoughts and enjoy happiness and bliss.

'Crime' *vs.* 'Sin'

Many of us, many a times, have committed and continue to commit 'SINs'. I classify our misdeeds into two broad categories: 'CRIME' and 'SIN'. A 'crime' is legally and, therefore, socially unacceptable. For example, 'murder' is a 'crime'. It is perceived on the 'gross' plane of our mind. It is an entirely man-made perception and, in the pre-historic, primitive society where there was no man-made law, the word 'CRIME' was not known.

The perception of 'SIN' is on a very 'subtle' plane. My favourite example is how we behave with the trillions of microbes that have made the outside and inside of our body their habitats. As a matter of fact, we are only 10 per cent human, 90 per cent microbial. How? The number of 'genes'—the 'genome', that we have inherited from our family tree on both sides constitute only 10 per cent of our total gene pool that I call 'metagenome', the bulk—that is the balance 90 per cent is made up of the 'microbiome'—the genes of the 'microbes' which are invisible to our eyes—they are so microscopic. *(Reference 15)*

I am concerned here more with our 'gut' microbes—which, in terms of the most subtle Vedic Sciences, are of three types (entirely my own conjecture which incidentally and, most interestingly, tally with the latest biological research studies): 'Sattvic' ('S') (of ascetic temperament—neither very active nor harmful); 'Rajasic' ('R') (most active—loves to work on fibrous dietary inputs like roughages and fibrous fruits and vegetables); and 'Tamasic' ('T') (most inactive and lazy—interested in fine grains, refined and processed dietary inputs like flour, plain rice, sugar, fruit juice, processed cheese, processed packaged fish and meat items like salami, sausages and so on). Those of us who feed mostly on the last types of food are feeding the 'T' microbes which do not produce much beneficial enzymes and chemicals which help us in the digestive process. Since the hard-working 'R' type of microbes are deprived of their fibrous inputs (which our primitive, pre-historic ancestors were habituated to for a couple of million years before the discovery of fire and the advent of agriculture), we become prone to constipation, diarrhoea, irritable bowels syndrome and such gut disorders which are so common in modern times. Are we not 'SINNERS' as we are depriving the 'R' microbes that populate our large intestine of the kind of diet they have been accustomed to for executing their functional tasks? This is the FIRST example of my perception of 'SIN' which cannot be appreciated on a 'gross' mental plane. Sorry, I missed out one important point. We tend to kill our gut microbes by taking, off and on, antibiotic medicine which are deadly killers for them. We are thus not only committing a 'SIN', we are 'KILLERs' as well.

My SECOND example of 'SIN' is taken from the poultry and meat shops. When you buy chicken, do you have the faintiest idea whether when the bird was killed for its meat, it suffered from 'stress' or not? In the first place, it had been under 'stress' in the poultry farm having been caged and fed on antibiotic-laden food. Thereafter it has traumatic stress at the time of being killed releasing stress hormones into its blood from the adrenal glands. So, when we are relishing our poultry chicken preparation at home or in a hotel, it already has some stress hormone left in it even after cooking, which raises the level of our 'stress' (many of us carry some in-built 'stress' due to our life's struggles). Same is the case with the lamb, or the goat meat or the beef or the pork that you are eating. I know that there are some special procedures that the butchers follow while killing the animal in the slaughter house so that the blood of the dead animal is drained out before making pieces. The eggs that we are eating, are they not laid by stressed poultry birds? In my opinion, fish is the best bet; and, it should not be killed by a sledge hammer or something heavy—it should be made to die its natural death by putting it out of water. *(References 16-18)*

My THIRD example of 'SIN' is so common in marital sex-related activities. How many times a lustful partner forces the other one to indulge in sex? If the outcome of such sex is pregnancy, is an abnormal or subnormal child—even a 'premie' is it due to the baby's past life's sin? I don't suppose so, the aggressive sexual partner is the 'sinner'. *(References 19-20)*

I was amazed to find how such 'subtle' phenomena were crystal clear to Fakir Lalon Shah who never went to any formal school, spent his whole life in a remote village of Bengal. He was a pure vegetarian and had recommended vegetarianism to his followers. He was not against marriage; but he was totally against producing any offspring. *(Reference 21)*

Lalon, I presume, talks about such 'SINs' when he sings:

"Ar ki re ei papi r bhagye
Dayal chand er daya hobe
Amar din ei hale jabe
Bahia paper tarani"

(In English: *"I am a SINNER. I've been committing SINs. Will the kind-hearted Almighty ever pardon me? The rest of my life will be spent rowing this SINful boat."*)

Hasten Rebirth!!

Fakir Lalon Shah begins one of his popular songs, with the words: *"Emon manab janam ar ki hobe"* (In English: *"Shall I be lucky to be born as a human again?"* He shows a feeling of HASTE in the next line:

"Mon ja karo twaray karo ei bhabe" (In English: *"Whatever you do in this world, do it in HASTE, do it hurriedly, do it fast"*.).

He continues in the next stanza: *"Ananta roop shristi korlen sai, suni manaber uttor kichui nai, dev-devata gan kare aradhan janmo nite manabe, mon ja karo twaray karo ei bhabe."* (In English: *"The God Almighty created an eternal form, it is beyond the comprehension of common man, even the gods and goddesses pray to be born as humans who have so much available for pleasure; hey, my mind, whatever you do in this world, do it in HASTE!!"*.

The average age of cells in adult human body would be between 7 to 10 years. As we age, our body cells are replaced regularly until a time when the rate of this replacement becomes slow almost to the point of a halt. What we, humans, are today is just because of the process of 'evolution' of the entire biology in all respects—body-brain-wise. However, for us, the physical evolution has come almost to a dead end. The process of 'evolution' is now taking place in 'consciousness' only in respect of the three 'gunas'—from the 'Tamasic' level, moving through the 'Rajasic'—towards the highest 'Sattvic' plane. For any individual, this evolution is being executed through the process of 'reincarnation' or 'rebirth'.

The 'soul' or 'spirit' begins a new life after biological death—in a body that may be human, animal, or spiritual depending upon the moral quality of the previous life's actions. According to Hinduism, even 'Devas' ('Gods') may also die and be born again, although here the term 'reincarnation' may not be strictly applicable. Lord Vishnu is known for his 10 incarnations—'Dashavataras'.

One is reborn through 'desire' (in Bengali: 'kam'). A person 'desires' to be born because he or she wants to enjoy a body which can never bring deep, lasting happiness or 'bliss' (that is, 'ananda'). With every birth, the individual has fresh bodily experience of 'pleasure satisfaction'.

After many births, every person becomes dissatisfied with the same physical experience again and again (external stimulus > desire > action planning > action > pleasure satisfaction response)—represented by the release of the pleasure-related neurochemical 'Dopamine' ('D').

(Reference 24) Being disillusioned, he begins to seek higher forms of happiness through spiritual experience.

In Baul culture, to prevent this physical boredom and stalemate, leading to deep-rooted frustration, due to physical intimacy with the same partner, some Bauls go for multiple 'sadhan sanginis' and, a few others for promiscuous (that is, 'parakiya') relationships, so that time taken for reaching the stage for the longing of the 'post-physical', 'spiritual' satisfaction, is shortened and a few of the normal future REBIRTHs are skipped. *(Reference 25)*

The Baul sings what Lalon had composed:

> *"Kato bhagyer phole na jani; Mon re—peyecho ei bhab tarani; Beye jao twaray tori; Sudharay jeno bhara na dobe; Mon ja karo twaray karo ei bhabe."*
>
> (In English: *"I do not know how much fortunate you've been; Oh! my mind—to get this thought boat; Please go on rowing it fast; Lest you get drowned with the showering of short-term pleasure; Hey—Mind, whatever you want to do in this world, HASTEN—do it fast, do it quickly."*) *(Reference 26)*

The Battle of the Egos

> *"The two most important days in your life are the day you are born and the day you find out why."*
>
> —***Mark Twain*** *(1835-1910), American writer and humourist*

Sex is determined at conception by the combination of X and Y sex chromosomes a baby receives from the mother's 'egg' and the father's 'sperm'. All 'eggs' have one X chromosome each, while 'sperms' contain either an X or a Y chromosome. Embryos with XY chromosomes develop male sex organs, while those with XX chromosomes develop female sex organs. That means father's 'sperm' determines a baby's sex. That is the 'Yogic' or 'Tantric' concept of 'Purusha' or 'Shiva' which I will describe as 'Male Ego' or 'M-E'. *(Reference 27)*

Up to until about week 7 to week 8 of pregnancy, both sexes have what's known as a 'genital ridge'—that is, an identical preliminary set of genitalia that will eventually differentiate to become either male or female sex organs. Incidentally, according to 'Tantras', a wandering SOUL also enters the freshly formed 'Pineal Gland' ('PG') of the foetus's brain around the same time. Therefore, is the foetus's sex also determined by the nature/gender of the 'Incoming Soul'—this question bothers me.

Anyway, it means that our sex organs come from the same foundation: The 'testes' in men are equivalent to the 'labia' and 'ovaries' in women, and the male 'penis' is the equivalent of the female 'clitoris'. The female genitalia together represent the 'Prakriti' or 'Shakti' of 'Yogic' and 'Tantric' Sciences, which I will describe as the 'Female Ego' or 'F-E'.

'Shiva' symbolises 'consciousness', while 'Shakti' symbolises 'power' and 'energy'—that is 'Mother Nature'. The Hindu God Lord Shiva is generally portrayed holding a trident which represents the trinity of 'Ishwara', 'Purusha' and 'Prakriti'. If I use the analogy of electric current, then the electrical energy is 'Ishwara', the 'lamp' it illuminates is the 'Purusha' and the 'object' or the 'environment' that gets illuminated is 'Prakriti'.

'Shiva' resides at the top of the head in the 'Sahasrar' chakra' whereas the residence of 'Shakti' is in the 'Muladhara' at the base of the spine. Since 'Shakti' or 'Prakriti' is feminine and motherly—it desires union with 'Shiva' or 'Purusha'. So, the 'Female Ego' (F-E) tries to control the 'Male Ego' (M-E) by influencing its 'consciousness'—bringing it down from the 'spiritual' to the 'physical' plane. That is the reason why an ordinary man often has sexual thoughts while engaged in meditation.

Unless the 'F-E' develops a spirit of total surrender and an attitude of 'service', the union between 'Shiva' or 'Purusha' and 'Shakti' or 'Prakriti' does not lead to a result that is pure and divine. *(Reference 28)*

This idea is beautifully expressed in one Lalon song (the idea is entirely my own—your perception may be totally different) which goes as: *(Reference 29)*

(In Bengali: *"Amare ki rakhben Guru Charanadasi?"*) (In English: *"Oh, My Guru! Will you keep me as your care-giver maid?*). Kindly note here how the 'F-E' is addressing the 'M-E' as 'Guru' which represents the spirit of surrender and how she is prepared to serve him in all respects.

The next line is: (In Bengali: *"Itar pana karjya amar ghote ahar nishi"*) (In English: *"I do indulge in lowly thoughts and activities every day and night"*). She is admitting how surreptitiously she tries to allure 'M-E' with lowly thoughts and acts.

The next part is amazing:

> (In Bengali: *"Jathara jantrana peye, Eshechilam karar diye, Se sakal giyachi bhule bhabete ami"*)
>
> (In English: *"I was delivered after severe labour pain with an undertaking that I will not indulge in anything lowly and sinful; but having been overwhelmed with worldly desires, my birth resolution has disappeared from my mind."*). How beautiful it is as the SOUL is saying that I had promised while entering the womb not to indulge in any negative behaviour once I am exposed to the light of Mother Earth—but the abundance of items and activities of 'pleasure' has made me forget my promise. I am so weak in character.

Lalon continues:

> (In Bengali: *"Chinlam na se Guru ki dhon; Korlam na tar seba sadhan; Ghurte bujhi holo re mona abar churashi"*) (In English: *"I've failed to realise how precious a real Guru is; I never took care of him with a spirit of total surrender and service; Wandering here and there aimlessly I have advanced in age."*)

The last stanza is full of assurance:

> (In Bengali: *"Guru rup jar bandha hriday; Shaman bole tar kisher bhoy; Lalon bole mon tui amay korili doshi"*) (In English: *"One whose mind has the framed photo of his Guru; Why should he be fearful even at the advanced age when death comes; Lalon says—Hey, my mind! You are making me feel guilty."*). A real, authentic Guru teaches the 'shishya'—how to learn from mistakes and failures and how to face death with the hope that the next life will be virtuous—so oh my

mind, do not suffer from a sense of guilt—plan and prepare for your next birth full of good work and deed for the entire mankind.

The 'Camphor and Black Pepper'

The great Italian polymath Leonardo da Vinci had prepared some drawings depicting the human anatomy and physiology, a few of which dealt with the male genitals. He would have regarded it as a most fascinating biological tool. The European thought at that time was that there was a direct connection from the brain through the spinal cord to the male genitals, perhaps so that an essential component of the male seed (that is 'semen'—'bij' or 'bastu' in the language of the Bauls), presumably originating in the brain, could be transmitted during intercourse.

These ideas were not only common in the West, they were also widely held in East Asia. The ancient Chinese sex manuals frequently referred to the origin of 'semen' and, in many cases, referred specifically to the nervous system as the route by which the transmission of the relevant characteristics of 'semen' was achieved. The idea was also important to the Taoists because they also believed that it was beneficial to a man to preserve his 'semen' and return it to the brain.

The social, religious and medical interpretations were very different, however, and that question deserves a deeper study than we have done so far.

Italian scholars seemed to had emphasized that Leonardo's interest for the seat of the 'virtu generativa' was due to the fact that he believed this to be one of "soul's faculties". To quote Leonardo, from his private notes:

> *"Different foods produce different bloods. And, different bloods make different kinds of 'sperm'; and different kinds of 'sperm' make children of different constitutions.*
>
> *If 'coitus' is made with LOVE and mutual desire, then the child will be of great intellect, witty, lively, and lovable." (References 30 & 31)*

According to the Vedic philosophy, the cosmos ('Brahmanda' in Sanskrit) and the human body ('Dehabhanda' in Sanskrit) are composed of three levels of dimensions. These are united by the union of three 'bodies' ('kayas' in Sanskrit) which results in 'liberation' or 'moksha'. The three bodies are: the 'gross' or 'physical' ('sthula sharira'), 'subtle' ('sukshma sharira') and the 'super subtle' or 'causal' ('karana sharira'). The 'sukshma sharira' is the one which contains all vital functions and helps the physical (gross) body to remain alive. It is believed to exist after an individual dies and operates as a medium for reincarnation. *(Reference 32)* The 'karana sharira' is thought to be the portal to entering higher consciousness when the 'gross' and the 'subtle' body consciousnesses are lost. At the same time, 'karana sharira' is the cause of the existence of these two. It connects both the individual and the cosmic consciousness together, and is believed to store information from past lives. *(Reference 33)* 'Nirmanakaya', 'Sambhogakaya' and 'Dharmakaya' are the Buddhist equivalents of the Vedic concept.

In Ayurveda, it is believed that the 'subtle body' ('sukhsma sharira') of each human has 21 'chakras' of which 7 are most important which serve as the conduits of 'prana' or 'life force/energy'. *(Reference 34)* The first 'chakra' ('Muladhar') or the starting point of the human spine, has an energy charge which can transform and awaken the human brain when moved from lower torso to the head. In its lowest 'crude' form, it is the reproductive energy; and, in its 'refined' form, it is the spiritual 'kundalini' activation. A complete version unites the three 'bodies' dissolving the 'super subtle' body into the 'subtle' body, transforming it from 'yin' to the golden 'yang'. In Chinese philosophy, the 'yin' and 'yang' are opposite forces that are interconnected. *(Reference 35)*

So, the first 'chakra' is the dormant EMBRYO of enlightenment—which may be described as the 'GOLDEN EMBRYO'.

We are uniting 'lunar energy' ('Ida nadi') and 'solar energy ('Pingala nadi') currents within the central channel (the 'Sushumna nadi) of the body. The 'caduceus' (an ancient Greek or Roman herald's wand—typically with two serpents twined around it) is carried by the messenger god Hermes or Mercury—in Greek mythology. The 'caduceus' is the 'Sushumna' and the two serpents are the 'Ida' and 'Pingala', and it represents the triple channel 'Kundalini' activation in alchemical art depiction. *(Reference 36)*

Reproductive energy which is stored in and around the lowest 'chakra' (the 'Muladhar') where the associated glands are the testes and ovaries, gets refined into 'chi' or 'vital energy' which is further refined into 'shen' or 'spirit' ('Kundalini'/'Golden Embryo' in the complete form). The 'spirit' is returned to 'void' and then to 'Tao' (post-conjunction).

Celibacy creates a surplus of reproductive energy. It is a method of energy cultivation based on 'jing', 'chi' and 'shen' or 'nadi', 'prana' and 'bindu'—respectively in the Chinese and Indian systems.

Cross-legged sitting alone can block the 'prana' from travelling up the spine to the head. But Jainism and Taoism often emphasize standing meditation as a more effective method of taking the energy 'chi'/'prana' from the lower torso to the head than just sitting. *(Reference 37)* The singing and dancing styles of the Sufis and the Bauls of Bengal in the standing posture help the performers to get advantage of the upward movement of the 'prana'.

The 'akhara' concept of the Bauls is based on the 'satsang' principle. It is very useful, why you know? The human body is like 'camphor'. When it is in touch with the external public environment where the air may be impure, awakening carnal desire—which is comparable to bad wind that will make the 'camphor' evaporate. But if you mix black pepper with the 'camphor', it ought to remain intact. Lalon, in one of his songs, compares the mind with black pepper. Your body should be restrained by mental force and wisdom. This is just one example of Lalon's "Atma Tattva" ("Doctrine of the Self").

To illustrate this 'camphor' concept of a weak human mind, I quote one line from a most touching Lalon song *"Ekta bod hawa lege khanchay—khanchar ara porlo dhoshe, pakhi ar darabe ki se, oy bhabona bhabchi bose, chamak jara boiche gay…"* In English: *A bad wind has blown to the cage - the stand reside the cage has fallen .... where would the bird stand now - I'm thinking about it and having tingling sensations in my body.*

References

[1] Madhu Pandit Dasa, "Vedic Life: A Sample of Five Primary Rasas", *Srila Prabhupada's ISKCON*, Bangalore, 19th May 2015.

[2] *Kama Deva*—Wikipedia.

[3] Mansee Jain, "The Death and Rebirth of Kama, The God of Love", *Did You Know?* 8th February 2021.

[4] *Endorphins*—Wikipedia.

[5] *Oxytocin*—Wikipedia.

[6] *Rasa (aesthetics)*—Wikipedia.

[7] Madhu Pandit Dasa, "Vedic Life: A Sample of Five Primary Rasas", *Srila Prabhupada's ISKCON*-Bangalore, 19th May, 2015.

[8] "Manush Bhojle Sonar Manush Hobi", *Ponno Lyrics*, mStock.

[9] Dr Satish K. Kapoor, "Dying while living: Experiencing death is withdrawing one's consciousness from mundane to higher aspects of being." *The Tribune*, 29th December 2022.]

[10] T. Singh, "Four Kinds of Liberation", *Gurbano.org*, Reflections on Gurbani.

[11] *"Nitya Mukta means"*—Vaniquotes

[12] M V Kireev *et al.*, "The Brain's Error-Detecting Mechanism—a PET Study", *Neuroscience and Behavioral Psychology*, Vol. 43, 2013, pp. 613-616.

[13] Celina Wang, "The Meaning of the 7 Chakras and How to Unblock Them", *Buddha and Karma*, 12th February 2022.

[14] *Triune Brain*—Wikipedia.

[15] Alanna Collen, *10% Human: How Your Body's Microbes Hold the Key to Health and Happiness*, London: Bryan K. Williams, 2015.

[16] Apolo A. Carrasco-Garcia *et al.* "Effect of stress during slaughter on carcass characteristics and meat quality in tropical beef cattle", *Asian-Australian Journal of Animal Sciences,* Vol. 33, No. 10, October 2020, pp 1656-1665. Published online Jan 13, 2020.

[17] Giancarlo Bozzo *et al.,* "Analysis of Stress Indicators for Evaluation of Animal Welfare and Meat Quality in Traditional and Jewish Slaughtering", *Animals*, 2018, Vol. 8, No. 4, p. 43.

[18] *Animal Slaughter*—Wikipedia.

[19] "No lust, only veg, pure thoughts: AYUSH ministry's bizarre advice to pregnant women", *The NEWS Minute*, 14th June, 2017.

[20] "Lust vs. Normal Sexual Desire", *Focus on the Family*.

[21] In Bengali: "Fakir Lalon Shah", *Bhaba Ghure Katha*.

[22] "Reincarnation: religious belief"—*Britannica*.

[23] A.K.M. Nagaraj, R.B. Nanjigowda and S.M. Purushattama, "The mystery of reincarnation", *Indian Journal of Psychiatry*, 2015, Vol. 57. No. 4, p. 439.

[24] Daniel Z. Lieberman and Michael E. Long, *The Molecule of More: How A Single Chemical in Your Brain Drives Love, Sex & Creativity*, Dallas, Texas, USA: BenBella Books, Inc., 2018.

[25] Joseph Morales, "A Sufi View of Spiritual Rebirth: Bawa Muhaiyaddeen".

[26] "Emon Manab Janam Aar Ki Hobe"—Lalon Geeti Lyrics (Search on 'Rockol'. "rockol.com/uk/lyrics-2023.

[27] Colleen de Bellefonds, "When Your Baby's Sex is Determined", *what to expect*, 9th July 2021.

[28] "Shiva and Shakti: Consciousness and Energy", *Yoga Principles; Chakras. net.*

[29] "Amare ki rakhben Guru charanadashi" *Ponno Lyrics.*

[30] Leonardo da Vinci, Private Notes.

[31] Denis Noble, Dario Di Francesco, and Diago Zancani, "Leonardo da Vinci and the origin of semen", *Notes and Records of The Royal Society of London*, 20th December 2014, Vol. 68, No. 4, pp. 391-402.

[32] *Sukshma Sharira*—Yogapedia.

[33] *Karana Sharira*—Yogapedia.

[34] Vinita Rashinkar "Sri Chakra and the Human Body", *Vinita Rashinkar Blog*, 14th April 2020.

[35] *Yin and Yang*—Wikipedia.

[36] *Caduceus*—Wikipedia.

[37] Barclay Powers, "Integral Immortality: The Kundalini/Golden Embryo: Theory of Everything" *Integrated World Exploring Theories of Everything.*

CHAPTER 6

Iron into Gold

Turning Wrought Iron into Glittering Gold

Keep your right hand on your chest—touch your heart and make a cross-check as to whether you have ever asked yourself questions such as:

- Why have you been born?
- Are you pursuing the real purpose of your life for which you have been brought to this beautiful planet?

Once we are born, we get so much engrossed in the fulfilment of our physical, material and emotional desires that such probing, soul-searching, questions disappear behind our selfish, ego-centric mental screen. In fact, to get a proper answer to these questions, one may need the blessing of an authentic Guru. And, who is an authentic Guru? An authentic Guru is a pious person who can 'Turn Wrought Iron into Glittering Gold'.

It is not that Fakir Lalon Shah and his ardent followers were/are the only creators of most soul-touching Baul songs from which we derive such very special insights. I've learnt it from a Baul song composed by a relatively unknown Baul Kala Shah, sung by Baul Gaurab Tarafdar.

However, in this piece, I'm taking up for discussion a smart, short and sweet Baul verse composed by Late Radharaman Dutta, which carries the same message in a slightly different style.

Radharaman Dutta (1833-1915) was born Radharaman Dutta Purakayastha in the Sylhet region of undivided Bengal. He was a Bengali litterateur, sadhak poet, Vaishnava Baul and father of the 'Dhamail' style of folk singing and dancing. To folk art lovers, he is known simply as Radharaman. *(Reference 1)*

The song that I've in mind begins as:

(In Bengali: *"Mon pakhi boli tore...Bolo bolo Krishna Krishna o Hare Hare"*)

(In English: *"Oh! My mind bird! Let me tell you that you must not fail to sing—Krishna Krishna O Hare Hare!"*)

The song exposes the truth now:

(In Bengali: *"Mon Re! Luv korite ailam ami ei bhaber bazar e-Luv moole sab harailam loha kinlam sonar dore!"*)

(In English: *"Oh My Mind! I came to this world market to make some profit, to gain something for my upliftment...But instead I lost everything...I purchased iron at the price of pure gold...am I not stupid?"*).

The songwriter wants to say that he was born in his present life to gain something for his development and spiritual progress. But he was so stupid that he engaged himself in pursuits, all with a selfish motive; so, all his transactions did lead to a loss. He could never figure out before acting that if you're selfish in anything, you'll be paid back in the same coin.

The next line goes as:

(In Bengali: *"Mon Re! Hasta pade bandhan chilo Janani jathare... Bandhan mochan ke korilo—ke anilo e sangsar e?"*)

(In English: *"I was all tied up in my hands and legs inside my mother's womb...Who did cut the ropes, freed me up, and brought me to this householder's life?"*)

(In Bengali: *"Mon Re! Bhai Re! Radharaman bole janam gelo hele, Churasi lakhkha joni bhraman kore janam munishya kule"*)

(In English: *"Oh My Mind! Oh My Brother! Radharaman says that this birth has been totally futile, despite the fact that after having passed through eighty four lakh vaginal passages I'm lucky to be born in the human form."*)

The essence is: We are so stupid that despite the fact that to be born a 'Human', one has to be born so many innumerable times in inferior 'Pre-human' forms, we don't lead our life virtuously enough so as to bear golden fruits. If you don't avail of the opportunity for soul upliftment and spiritual progress in the present life, with full heart and spirit, you may not get this chance again.

Scatter-Brained!!

Prehistoric men (whom I call 'pre-human') were 'scatter-brained'. They did not think seriously about things—they moved from one thing to another, they were totally unfocused unless the task or activity was related to their 'survival' or 'replication'—fulfilment of the mundane purposes for which they were brought to this planet—for consolidation of the human species.

Leaving aside those 'core' purposes, most of the time, they could not decide what to do; they could not set their priorities. Even for fulfilment of those 'core' purposes, they had to struggle so much, had to cope with so many odds and so many uncertainties—typical of an unorganised, unsettled existence in the wild. Today, even after many millennia of 'human' existence, many of us who are settled in the true sense of the term having assured food, clothes, shelter, physical and economic security, have unsettled minds—brains vibrating at a higher rate (25 to 32 Hz) than what is desirable and ought to be (14 to 25 Hz) under circumstances where there are no justified reasons for the occurrence of any stress.

The reason is simple yet most subtle. We have evolved from the 'pre-human' to the 'human' stage only superficially. All our 6 'Negative Propensities/Enemies of the Mind' (in Sanskrit/Bengali: 'Shada Ripu') which were necessary for the 'pre-human' life—for 'survival' and 'replication', have not left us—they still exist as our companions most of the time. Our core is still 'pre-human'. *(Reference 2)* When one of these negative propensities (desire, irritability, greed, ego, attachment, partiality) do not get gratified, the brain loses its homeostatic balance and starts vibrating at a higher rate than what makes us happy; the outcome—we become 'scatter-brained'.

There is, of course, a solution. Is it 'meditation'? No. The solution is to identify your 'True Passion' and pursue it to allow your brain to move smartly into the 'FLOW Brain State' ('FBS'). *(Reference 3)* where you will lose the sense of time, place, space, and all your 6 enemies of the mind. (Read '*Reference 4*' on how to discover your 'True Passion').

The idea of the 'Scatter-brained Brain State' ('SBS') has been expressed beautifully in a Baul song (In Bengali: *"Tomar ghore basat kore koy jona?"*) (*Reference 5*) (In English: *"How many people reside in your house?"* composed by Zahid Ahmed. The song talks about someone who has multiple interests—but he is not serious at all in or about any of those—a typical case of 'SBS'. I'll be sharing the English version of the song with you.

"Oh My Mind! You do not know who all reside inside you—you do not know how many are such residents."

"Oh My Mind! One of them is engaged in painting pictures; another one keeps seated and applying paints to himself; And, then again, who spoils the painting?"

"Oh, My Mind! You do not know how many reside inside your mind"

"Oh, My Mind! One of them plucks the string of the 'Ektara'; Another one taps on the percussion!"

"Oh, No! Who starts singing out of tune—please check"

"Oh, My Mind! How many people reside inside you?"

"One has lost his balance after having consumed the 'Rasa' of the music—just see how he loses control of the reins of his horse!"

"Just check who takes the reins from him"

"Who all live inside your mind? Who all and how many of them?"

What a messy mind! Born 'human' with a 'pre-human' core! "Am I one such specimen?" I ask myself. I request you to ask yourself also.

Focus is Power

I don't know much about Zahid Ahmed, lyricist and composer of the Bengali Baul song *'Tomar ghore basat kore koy jona?'* (In English: *"How many persons live in your house?"*) which I had used to highlight the 'Scatter-brained Brain State' ('SBS'). I find the same message has been conveyed, in a different style, in the verse of a song by the Late Bengali mystic, composer and songwriter Bhaba Pagla: (In Bengali: *"Amar Nitai Chander bazare...Gour Chander darbare...Ekmon jar sei jete pare...O, Bhai! Sei jete pare"*) (In English: *"Oh! Brother! Only he who is totally 'focussed' can go to the gatherings of Nitai Chand...the courtroom of Gour Chand...nobody else!"*) The 'key' idea is to have a 'Focussed Mind' ('FM') which gears up your brain for high quality output at a high speed.

Every human brain has a typical circuit which is called the 'Default Mode Network' ('DMN'). It gets switched on automatically when the brain is idle, not engaged in any task. Like a few other brain circuits, DMN used to be very helpful in the case of primitive, pre-historic ancestors of ours. 'DMN' disengages 'focus' on the 'present'—brings the 'past' into 'focus'. So, our ancestors used to plan for their 'future' taking cues from the 'past' experiences of 'successes' and 'failures'. It was a very handy 'brain tool' for the management of their daily life and resources to fulfil the twin objectives of 'survival' and 'replication', as social life as well as the environment in which our ancestors lived—in those days, were totally disorganised. Today, most of us are much better organised as our brain remains in the 'Task Mode Network' ('TMN') or 'Task Positive Network' ('TPN')—we are engaged in some meaningful task or another, for living and working. For example, we know what provisions we have in stock and when should we place order for the next lot of supplies—which items, at what cost and in what quantities. But even then, periodically, when our brain is not 'TMN'/'TPN'-engaged, the 'DMN' automatically gets switched on and the brain becomes preoccupied with thoughts of negative experiences of the past and apprehensions for the future. Besides, the idle brain gets disturbed by the 'Six Enemies of the Mind'—the 'SadRipus': Kama (Desire), Krodha (Anger), Lobha (Greed), Mada (Ego), Moha (Attachment), and Matsarya (Envy).

Even if you leave the idea of filling your mind with thoughts of godmen like Bhagawan Mahapradhu Sri Chaitanya (Bhaba Pagla's 'Gour Chand') and his protégé Shri Shri Nityananda, for anything to be achieved you have to set a CLEAR GOAL—not in abstract but in concrete terms. This is why, to my mind, the proponents of Hinduism had conceived the idea of Gods and Goddesses who can be concretely visualised as being 'sakar' (having a body) and 'saguna' (having certain qualities). To set a CLEAR GOAL and to pursue that GOAL, you need a 'Focused Mind' ('FM'). The music-maker Bhaba Pagla has brought the analogy of a goldsmith who knows his metal: (In Bengali: *"Jemon swarnakare sona chine, abar nyay se tare parakh kore"*) (In English: *"Just the way a goldsmith knows what is gold and what is not, and he conducts all the typical tests for validation"*).

Bhaba says: (In Bengali: *"Abar dui mon hole porbi fande khyepa re...abar dui mon hole porbi fande...ore parbi na pare jete"*) (In English: *"Again, if you have two minds—unfocussed, you will be caught up in a trap...you will not be able to cross the river of life and go to the other shore!"*). I'd take the lesson from the mystic that we must keep our brain's 'DMN' under control and ensure to keep the 'TMN'/'TPN' on to manage ourselves and our lives purposefully.

Two Bundles of Flesh

In the Yogic and Tantric concepts, the place of the 'Purusha' or the 'Male' consciousness is at the top of the head—the 'Brahma Randhra'—the 'Sahasrara' or the 'Crown' chakra, whereas the place of 'Prakriti' or the 'Female' consciousness is at the tail end of the spine—at the 'Muladhara' or the 'Root' chakra—between the anus and the genitals. The 'Muladhara' represents the 'Prithvi' or the 'Earth' element of the 'Pancha Bhootas'—the five basic elements. So, the 'Prakriti' at the 'Muladhara' attracts the 'Purusha' at the 'Sahasrara' by the force of gravity. If the 'Purusha' moves downwards by this attraction, in Tantric terms, this is an 'Anulom' activity (or 'kriya') *(Reference 10)* This is nothing but the sexual drive or 'libido' which is one of the basic instincts that had formed the core of Sigmund Freud's 'psychoanalysis' and 'psychotherapy'. *(References 11 & 12)*

The genital of a male ('poong-linga'), which is a bundle of flesh, that becomes taut and erect when excited—gets attracted by another bundle of flesh—the female genital ('stri-linga') which gets inflated into a three-inch long crevice under excitement. Thus the Baul poet

Ashim Sarkar writes: (In Bengali: *"Duti mangso pindo londo bhondo korilo ei sonar desh...tin inchi nadi te pore sare tin hat nouka sesh"*) (In English: *"The boat having a length of equivalent to three hands and a half gets totally lost in a river which is only three inches long... Two bundles of flesh are playing havoc in this land of gold"*).

Whoever is our creator, call him 'God' or by any name, had designed all our organs and activities to fulfil certain specific purposes. The sexual act and the organs for its performance had originally been designed for 'creation'—'procreation' in this specific case. And, in the prehistoric society, pre-humans would follow it generally as there was no fixed bonded relationship for sexual activities. Sex had to be performed at random as the mortality rate for the newly born was also very high. As 'pre-humans' became civilised 'human' partnerships became more organised offering licensed sexual acts, another utility of sex emerged and, that is, 'Sex for Pleasure'. 'Sex for Procreation' took a back seat.

And, if sex for pleasure would lead to chance pregnancy and eventually childbirth, how many of those children would be considered worthy of the expectations of their parents as their birth had not been planned. We have two types of sense organs—'jnanendriyas' (knowledge organs)—eyes, ears and nose—and 'karmendriyas' (working organs)—hands, legs, genitals and mouth (including lips). During impulsive, lustful sex ('kam rati') all the energy ('prana') carried by the blood and other secretions move to the 'working organs' keeping the 'knowledge organs' alive but not active. The partners involved lose control over their logic, intelligence and rationality. They earn their reward molecule 'Dopamine' ('D') but not the love and trust molecule 'Oxytocin' which would be released during love-filled sex ('prem rati'). The former is 'pre-human' sex and not 'human' sex. We have not really fully evolved to be regarded as 'humans' as, in sexual activity, we are still 'pre-humans'.

So, the poet says: *"The two bundles of flesh have massacred this land of gold"*. Really, if our kids would have all been products of love-filled sex ('prem rati'), can you imagine what would have happened? This land would have been inhabited by 'Human Capital' and not just 'Human

Resource'. What a beautiful idea! Hats off to Baul poet Ashim Sarkar!! *(Reference 13)*

It's never too late! We all can take a lesson from this song. Use you brain—your intelligence, judgement and rationality to go for planned sex—as all Baul philosophers led by Fakir Lalon Shah had been advocating! Use sex for planned creation and not merely for pleasure!

Female *vs.* Male

Haore Gossain is a relatively unknown (to me at least) Baul poet who has composed a wonderful song regarding female biology. *(Reference 14)* From the surname 'Gossain', we can guess that he belonged to the 'Shaiva or Vaishnava' religious group and not the 'Sahajiya' Baul background.

The song begins: (In Bengali: *"Mashe mashe joar ashe tribenir sanghati... Meye Ganga Jamuna Saraswati"*) (In English: *"Every month, in every female, tide comes at the meeting point of three rivers... Ganga Jamuna Saraswati"*). The poet is talking about the menstrual cycle in females. Every post-puberty female is subjected to the 'menstrual cycle' which has four phases: menstruation (1-5 days); the follicular phase (before release of the egg, 6-14 days); ovulation (day 14); and, the luteal phase (after egg release, days 15-28). *(Reference 15)*

Which or what are the rivers Ganga, Jamuna and Saraswati? The poet has compared the three main subtle energy channels or 'nadis'—Ida, Pingala and Sushumna to the three rivers—Ganga, Jamuna and Saraswati. 'Prana' (or the 'life force'/'biological energy') flows through the 'nadis' in our body, according to 'Subtle Biology'.

Ida (feminine energy) is on the left side of the body, catering to the right side of the brain. Pingala (masculine energy) is on the right side of the body making right-handed people more active on the right side, catering to the left side of the brain. These two 'nadis' start from the tailbone (the Root chakra or 'muladhara') and terminate at the 'Third Eye' or 'Ajna Chakra'. Sushumna is at the centre, starting at the tailbone ('Muladhara') and ending at the Crown Chakra or 'Sahasrara'. 'Ida' is lunar energy—its colour is silvery white. 'Pingala' is solar energy—its colour is golden yellow. 'Sushumna' is a mixture, fiery-red in colour. *(Reference 16)*

During menstruation, when there is a high tide of menstrual blood flow, the female provides an opportunity to the male partner for 'bastu' or 'bij' 'dharan' (that is, retention or withholding of 'semen'). The song goes like this. (In Bengali: *"Abar sei nadite snan korile...abar sei nadite snan korile hoy Gourango mati...Meye Ganga Jamuna Saraswati"*) (In English: *"Taking a bath in that full-blown river gives an opportunity to develop a Gourango-like mind-set"*). By 'Gourango mati' the poet means the mind-set of a controlled person who knows how not to waste his semen. One essential feature of 'Baul Sadhana' is to go for sexual intercourse during the female partner's menstruation period (and not during 'ovulation') and enjoying 'orgasm' and, at the same time, withholding 'ejaculation' for retention of the 'bastu' or 'bij' (Bengali for 'semen') which is 'pitridhan'—a property that the son inherits from the father, biologically, which contains the power to 'create' another human being. We are created by sexual energy and we own sexual energy to create other humans. This concept as well as the technique are borrowed from Taoism. *(References 17-20)* The technique avoids too much pressure on the prostate gland and the testicles which may be caused if one practises 'coitus reservatus' (that is, just not allowing the semen to be released).

Two of the three girls are full of love for Lord Shiva who is the embodiment of 'Purusha' or male consciousness and creative power. The song says: (In Bengali: *"Meyer goon ke bolte pare—kinchit jane Maheswware...Ekjon shire, ekjon book-e dhore Pashupati"*) (In English: *"Who can talk about the good qualities of the girls...Lord Maheswar may be familiar to a certain extent—as one girl has him on the head, another one holds him on the chest"*). The third girl is very clever, she knows how to enjoy the whole world sitting secretly at home—without any physical contact she enjoys masculine love using her power of 'visualisation'. The song says: (In Bengali: *"Rasik meye gopan thake ghore bose jagat dekhe, sati hoye dharma rakhe loye upopati go...sakkhshi tahar Gopir meye gokul-e bosoti...Meye Ganga Jamuna Saraswati"*) (In English: *"The intelligent girl keeps it secret—watches the world sitting at home, keeps her reputation by being a non-promiscuous 'sati' taking an imaginary husband...her witness is the Gopi's daughter who lives in 'Gokul'"*).

The songwriter's wish is expressed in the last and final stanza. It goes like this. (In Bengali: *"Ebar more nari hobo prem sagar-e santar dibo, mahat sange jene nebo premer reeti-neeti, Gossain Haure bole rakhbo na ar bongse dite bati...Meye Ganga Jamuna Saraswati".*) (In English: *"When I die this time I will be reborn as a female to swim in the ocean of love...shall get to know about the rules and regulations of love from wise company...shall abdicate the responsibility of carrying my lineage."*)

If you're born male, you've the prime responsibility of continuing the lineage by passing your 'sperms' (your 'pitridhon', inherited from your father) to create a male child. You are free from that responsibility if you're born a female. As, in that case, your responsibility is limited to the extent of providing a fertile land for your male partner to sow the seed of his lineage. This is indeed most interesting as this fact puts the 'Purusha'—the male, on a much higher pedestal than 'Prakriti'—the female. In the case of flowers and fruit-bearing trees also the land or the soil matters but what matters much more is the quality of the seed that is planted on the soil. The Austrian clergyman Johann Gregor Mendel's (1822-1884) work on pea plants led to the discovery of the fundamental laws of inheritance. *(Reference 21)*

The Menstruating Goddess

Lalon's popular song (In Bengali: *"Samay gele sadhan hobe na"*) (In English: *"Once the proper time has passed, you won't manage to get your job done"*) *(Reference 22)* just reminded me that once the date and time scheduled for the 'Ambubachi' mela and puja *(Reference 23)* have passed, you cannot get the blessings of the menstruating goddess much though you may worship her with a lot of fanfare.

Who is this menstruating goddess? Is there any such deity? I suddenly remembered that I had read long ago that ancient Egyptians used to worship a male God 'Khonsu' who was the God of the Moon. 'Khonsu' means 'traveller'—it comes from how the moon moves or travels across the sky like a 'wanderer'. During the New Kingdom of Egypt, 'Khonsu' was worshipped not only as the moon god but also as a god of 'love' and 'fertility'. 'Fertility' is related to the 'Menstrual Cycle'—which has the four phases including the 'ovulation' phase which is when the female sex organ is most fertile—ready to accept and nurture the 'seed' from the male. *(Reference 24)*

Greek philosopher Aristotle had claimed in the 4th century BCE: "The menses tend to occur naturally during the waning moon. [...] For this time of the month is colder and more humid because of the wasting and disappearance of the Moon." Age-old parallels between the menstrual cycle and the phases of the moon have likely also led to some females referring to their 'periods' as "moon cycles" to this day. One full revolution of the Moon around the Earth takes 27 days, 7 hours, and 43 minutes. One menstrual cycle can be in the range of 25-30 days, with the median duration of 28 days. A 1986 study conducted in the Dept. of Gynaecology at the Canton Traditional Chinese Medical College did seem to find a link between menstrual and lunar cycles. The researchers deduced that the 'ovulation' periods tended to coincide with the full moon. *(Reference 25)*

The Lalon song which has prompted me to write this piece also has a mention of the lunar cycles in a stanza: (In Bengali: *"Amabasya o Purnima hoy...Mahajon se diner uday"*) (In English: *"Moonless and full moon nights come and go leading to the appearance of daylight"*).

In the beginning of this piece, I'd mentioned a Hindu festival by the name of 'Ambubachi'. Why did it suddenly occur to me? It occurred to me because during the three days of 'Ambubachi' puja in the month of June every year, the 'Kamakhya' temple in the outskirts of Guwahati, the capital of the State of Assam, remains closed as the Goddess 'Kamakhya' (whose other name is 'Kameswari') menstruates inside.

The Goddess 'Kamakhya' is present not in the idol ('murti') form. It is in the form of the 'Yoni'—the genitals of Goddess Sati. According to the Hindu Purana, Lord Shiva got married to Devi Sati against the wishes of Sati's father—King Daksha. Once the King was having a big puja—a Maha Yagna where his son-in-law Lord Shiva was not invited.

Totally outraged, Sati Devi committed suicide and Lord Shiva, the 'God of Destruction' took up her lifeless body on his shoulders and started dancing the 'tandava' dance. He just could not be stopped. Ultimately Lord Vishnu had to intervene. He put his 'Sudarshan Chakra'—the sharp-edged wheel into motion which cut Sati's dead body into 108 pieces which got scattered and fell all over the place. The Devi's sex organs fell near Guwahati in Assam and that is how it became a pilgrimage and a centre for Tantra and Aghori sadhana. The stone-carved sex organ is placed in a pool of water where water is coming up from the earth below like a spring.

During the 3 days of 'Ambubachi' this pool of water becomes red with the flow of the menstrual blood from the Goddess's vagina and if you leave a piece of white cloth with the priests to be placed near the spring, after the 3 days of the puja when the temple doors are open, you will get back the cloth which has become bloody red losing its white colour. The spring water also becomes red and flows to the River Brahmaputra nearby. If you preserve the blood-red cloth in your custody, it is believed that it will give you protection from all health-related problems. *(References 26-28)*

In the Tantric aspect of Hinduism, menstruation is not considered an inauspicious event in the life of post-puberty females. The menstruating Kamakhya goddess is worshipped as the goddess of fertility. Menstruation is regarded as the symbol of fertility and menstruated women are regarded as goddesses—potential mothers. This belief is also nurtured in 'Baul Sadhana'. And the best opportunity to avoid conception and, at the same time, enjoy orgasm is when the female partner has her monthly 'period'. So, if the male partner has missed the date, then for him that twin opportunity is lost.

I've gone through the whole Lalon song and that is my interpretation. Others might interpret it differently. My interpretation is biological.

References

[1] *Radharaman Dutta*—Wikipedia.

[2] *Arishadvargas*—Wikipedia.

[3] Mihaly Csikszentmihalyi, *FLOW: The Psychology of Optimal Experience*, New York: Harper Perennial Modern Classic, 2008.

[4] Siddhartha Ganguli, *Smart Leading & Parenting of Teenage Kids in the Digital Era: A Neuro-managed Way*, New Delhi: Allied Publishers Pvt. Ltd., 2021.

[5] Anirban Sur "Tomar Ghore Basat Kore"—*Bengali Lyrics*.

[6] *Bhaba Pagla*: Wikipedia.

[7] "Amar Nitai Chander Darbare"—lyrics in Bengali—*Subhanjan Basu Blog*.

[8] *Arishadvargas*—Wikipedia.

[9] Nadia: "Samudra theke jal nile ki Samudra sesh hoy"—*Anandabazar Online (anandabazar.com)*

[10] "Anulom Vilom—Alternate Nostril Breathing", *Arhanta Yoga Ashrams*.

[11] *Psychoanalysis*—Wikipedia.

[12] Jennifer Kunst PhD, "The Difference between Psychoanalysis and Psychotherapy", *Psychology Today*, 14th June 2017.

[13] "Tin inchi nadite pore sare tin haat nouka sesh"—lyrics and explanation in 'Nari'.

[14] "Meye Ganga Jamuna Saraswati"—Bengali lyrics, *Folksonglyrical*.

[15] *Phases of Menstrual Cycle*—Menstrupedia.

[16] "Ida, Pingala, Sushumna—Three Main Nadis in Yoga"—*prana sutra*.

[17] Miroslav Zec, "The Secrets of Taoist Sexology", *Volonte*, 25th May 2019.

[18] Marisa Fanelli, "Losing Jing: The Taoist Perspective", 13th May 2011.

[19] Arpita Halder, "Experience bliss: Spiritual sex through Taoist sexology", *Deccan Chronicle*, 8th May 2019.

[20] "Are there any Side Effects of Not Releasing Your Sperms (Ejaculating)?" *healthline*.

[21] *Gregor Mendel*—Wikipedia.

[22] Ambubachi Mela—Wikipedia.

[23] "Somoy gele sadhon hobe na"—lyrics by Lalon Fakir, *'Bangla Song Lyrics'*.

[24] "Egyptian God Khonsu—Facts, Mythology Depictions and Symbols", *Study.com*

[25] Maria Cohut, PhD, "Menstrual cycles and lunar cycles: Is there a link?" *Medical News Today*, 12th February 2021.

[26] Bhairavi Sharma, "Kamakhya Devi Temple: Story and History", *Mystical Bee*.

[27] "Know about the miraculous temple where the Devotees get wet cloth stained with blood in the prasad", *myjyotish*, 4th June 2021.

[28] "This Indian Temple Celebrates its Menstruating Goddess Breaking the Stigma around Periods", *Curly tales.*

CHAPTER 7

Baul, Vayu and Prana

Gross Body ('Sthula Sharira') is the one made of flesh-bone-and-blood which we can see, touch, and feel. 'Subtle Body' ('Sukshma Sharira') is the one that makes the 'Gross Body' live and work. I was a little confused about the 'Causal Body' ('Karana Sharira') until I started going deep into the 'Deha Tattva' ('Doctrine of the Body') of the Bauls of Bengal. The body that is responsible for making the 'Gross Body' for its life's journey would be the 'Causal Body' and that consists of the two elements having the potential to create a human being: the sperms contained in the semen of the male—the 'sukranu' in the 'birja' and the ova released during the menstrual cycle of the female—the 'dimbanu' contained in the 'raja'. That is why, the Baul says: (In Bengali: *"Je bastu jibaner karon... Tai Baul kore sadhon"*) (In English: *"The matter that is responsible for life... The Baul does his 'sadhana' for that"*).

The Baul's 'sadhana' is with the body—both inside and outside. For maintaining health and well-being, for keeping all diseases away, he follows 'Chari Chandra Bhed'. He consumes the wastes eliminated by the body which do contain some useful nutrients unutilised by the body during the 'processing' function. The 'Chari Chandra' or the 'Four Moons' are: semen (containing sperms), menstrual blood (containing plasma and sex hormones), urine (containing minerals) and stool (containing bacterial biomass and undigested carb, fibre, protein and fat). According to the Baul theory: (In Bengali: *"Jibon i tirtha dharma path...Ei katha Baul er mat"*) (In English: *"Life is the path and journey for pilgrimage... This is the opinion of the Bauls"*).

For creating a new human, whatever ingredients are necessary—are available within the male and female bodies, only the life-force (that is, 'prana') to run the body created, has to come from outside—from the environment. Thus, the sloka says: (In Sanskrit: *"Sukra dhatu bhabet pita...Raja dhatu bhabet mata...Shunya dhatu bhabet prana.*") (In English: *"The sperm-bearing material comes from the father...the ovum-bearing material comes from the mother...But the life-force comes from the space*"). It makes real sense now how the 'Pancha Bhuta' are responsible for making and running the living and working human machine. Earth (the Prithvi), Water (the Apa), Fire (the Agni), Air (the Vayu) and the Space/Ether (the Sunya/Akasa).

There is a school of thought that the name 'Baul' has originated because they deal with 'Vayu'—that there is a lot of thrust on techniques of 'breathing'—emphasis on the 'Pranamaya Kosha' (which deals with the 'Breath Energy' or 'B-E') of the Upanishadic 'Pancha Kosha' model of human personality. It does make some sense because of the following reasons: (i) the activities of the Bauls are largely oral which relates to transactions of the 'Breath Energy' ('B-E')—whether they sing songs singly or in pairs or in groups or the Baul Gurus preach and teach their disciples—there is no writing involved. The Baul songwriters like Fakir Lalon Shah, his followers Panju Shah or Duddu Shah, and others like Kangal Harinath, Gagan Harkara, Bhaba Pagla, and Hason Raja—all used to create songs just like that, from nothing but air, 'ex-nihilo', like magic—without scripting anything; (ii) practising pranayama (that is, 'Breath Energy Management') is a must for all Bauls as taught by their Gurus; and, (iii) their withholding ejaculation in order to preserve the semen and its contents—the sperms (that is, 'bij' or 'pitridhon' in Bengali) is possible with the help of some special breathing technique which again has to be learnt under the Guru's direct supervision. Like the most effective training in Indian Classical Music—both vocal and instrumental is obtained by living with the Gurukul, training in Baul Sadhana is totally Guru-badi. You cannot become a real Sadhak Baul by attending classes in a school or college or by participating in a seminar or even by spending a few weekends with a Baul Guru in a retreat.

The Guru explains to them how 'Vayu' is the 'Prana' and the entire journey through life is nothing but a 'Domer Khela' or 'Breathing Game'. The more you can save the 'Breath Energy' ('B-E') by effective 'Management of Prana', the healthier you will be and the longer will be your life. Having a balanced nutritious diet (that is the 'Dietary Energy'/'D-E' related to the outermost sheath 'Annamaya Kosha') is not enough for such purposes. That caters only to your 'Gross Body' or 'Sthula Sharira'. Proper care-giving to your 'Subtle Body' or 'Sukshma Sharira' starts with 'Management of Prana' or 'Breath Energy Management'.

The Breathing Game ('Domer Khela')

We are breathing in Oxygen and breathing out Carbon Dioxide, about 22,000 times a day. It goes on in a cyclical fashion all the time and stops automatically when life comes to an end. The average adult, when resting, inhales and exhales 7 to 8 litres of air per minute—totalling about 11,000 litres per day. *(Reference 7)*

In Yogic Sciences, this 'life force' that keeps us alive is called 'Prana' and the breath energy—the 'Pranic Energy'. 'Prana' moves through the 'Subtle Body' (that is, the 'Sukhsma Sharira') and the conduits through which it moves are called 'nadis'. There are 72,000 main 'nadis' in an adult human body.

'Prana' takes the form of 'Vayu' (that is, 'Air') and, most interestingly, there are 5 (five) types of 'Vayu' that are needed for the proper functioning of our body. 'Vayu' is the most unstable element amongst the 'Pancha Bhuta'. There can be 'zero-wind' situation at one extreme and 'ghastly-stormy wind' at the other.

The first type of 'Vayu' is the 'Prana Vayu' ('PV') which is the air that moves inside the body from the outside environment, through the nostrils which are the receptor organs meant for the purpose. Use of the mouth for the input-output of air is not desirable at all unless you have a blocked nose or are gasping for breath when a larger quantity of air is needed than what is required under normal circumstances. Once it is 'in' through the nostrils, the 'PV' moves automatically inward and upward. The 'PV' is a vibrating or oscillating wind energy and its vibrations or oscillations get affected by your emotions. Thus, you can control your emotions by controlling your 'PV' vibrations. That is the basic purpose of the Yogic practice of 'Pranayama', which involves controlling your breath in different styles and lengths. *(Reference 8)*

'PV' is the fundamental energy in the body and it directs and feeds into the four other 'Vayus'. It nourishes the brain and the sensory organs—eyes, ears, nose and tongue and governs the reception of all things—food, air, senses and thoughts. 'PV' relates to water within the 'Subtle Body' ('Sukshma Sharira') and allows us to absorb sensations, feelings and thoughts within the mind. When you speak too much or sing too much, in other words, you're in an oral or vocal profession, then 'PV' gets affected and, therefore, it has to be taken care of properly.

'PV''s place is also in the chest, heart and lungs and, apart from the breathing activity, it is also involved in swallowing (re: eating and drinking) and, of course, in speaking and singing. The 'Udana Vayu' ('UV') covers from the neck to the head through its vertical movements. The 'Samana Vayu' ('SV') which has got nothing to do with the external environment, is involved in the absorption of food, and located in the diaphragm and the abdominal region below it. Its movement is in the horizontal plane from the left to the right of the body and vice versa. It performs the 'balancer' role.

The 'Apana Vayu' ('AV') which is a downward-moving energy covers the region from the pelvis to the feet and is involved in all elimination or release-oriented movements such as: urination, defecation, ejaculation, menstruation and childbirth. It operates through biological tubes, pipes, tunnels and crevices. In its activities, it gets the support of the force of gravity.

The last one—'Vyana Vayu' ('VV') circulates throughout the body including the limbs in the form of churning circles. *(References 9 & 10)*

'Yoga' divides the mechanism of breath into 3 (three) parts: 'puraka' (inhalation), 'rechaka' (exhalation) and 'kumbhaka' (retention). 'Yoga' also prescribes a ratio between the three. Generally, the time taken for 'puraka', 'kumbhaka' and 'rechaka' would be 1 : 4 : 2, in the case of 'Conscious Breathing'. During 'Puraka', you're taking in 'PV' which takes a little longer time, during 'Kumbhaka', to get distributed as 'UV', 'SV' and 'VV' then it takes double the time of inhalation to get it exhaled. During breathing, one should feel that the purest elements in the universe are being inhaled, while negative stuff in the body and the mind are being exhaled. *(Reference 11)* The 18th century Hatha Yoga Pradipika states that the highest breath control (which it defines as inhaling to a count of 8, holding to a count of 19, and exhaling to a count of 9, confers liberation and 'Samadhi'. The 'kumbhaka' or breath retention forces the retained breath into the central 'Sushumna' nadi (allowing 'kundalini' to rise and cause liberation). Death is impossible when the breath is held in the body. *(Reference 12)* The name 'Kumbhaka' is from Sanskrit 'Kumbha'—a 'pot', comparing the torso to a vessel full of air.

I suppose, during the initial training for 'Baul Sadhana', the interns are made to practice different kinds of 'Kumbhaka' (retention or holding of breath): (i) Antara Kumbhaka—breath retention after inhalation (lungs full); (ii) Bahir Kumbhaka—breath retention after exhalation (lungs empty); (iii) Sahaja Kumbhaka—when breath retention becomes natural at the stage of withdrawal of the senses—'Pratyahara'—the fifth of the eight limbs of 'Yoga'; (iv) Kevala Kumbhaka—when inhalation and exhalation are suspended at will—parallel with the state of 'Samadhi' or union with the divine, the last of the eight limbs of 'Yoga'. *(Reference 13)* 'Kumbhaka' types (iii) & (iv) are meant for advanced 'pranayama' practitioners.

"Anulom-Vilom' is a specific type of 'pranayama' that involves holding one nostril closed while inhaling, then holding the other nostril closed while exhaling. The process is then reversed and repeated. *(Reference 14)*

Vayu Flow Reversal

One of the first steps in doing 'Baul Sadhana' is self-purification through breath control. Traditional Bauls describe it as 'Vayu Dharma'. According to them, 'Baul' is equal to 'Vaul' which, again, is equal to 'Vayu Tula'—which means to lift up the vital air. *(Reference 15)* I do not know whether, by this, they mean reversal of the air flow which is an essential ritual in 'Baul Sadhana'.

Reversing the flow of the downward-moving 'Apana Vayu' is not that simple as, to achieve that goal, one has to work against the gravity. First of all, it will require a perfect gut health to be ensured so that there is no sign of constipation, diarrhoea, 'Irritable Bowels Syndrome' ('IBS'), or any other gut-related problems, which obviously tend to affect the normal flow and other properties of the 'Apana Vayu'. Assuming that the person has a perfect gut health, he has to be trained to make conscious contraction of the muscles around the anal region so that it allows the Apana Vayu to move upward against the force of gravity. The movement of the body waste like urine, faeces and menstrual blood and potent stuff like semen, and vaginal discharge containing ova also get affected if the gut health is not in order. Besides, frequent blow-out of fart and gas is also a sign of ineffective 'Vayu Management' inside the body.

Now, let me move a little deeper into the 'Science of the Vayus'. The nose feels congested with nasal fluid after prolonged sexual stimulation. Medically it has the name: 'Honeymoon Rhinitis'. *(Reference 16)*

Biologically, your nose is lined up with the same kind of erectile tissue as your genitals and those tissues become swollen when you get excited. German physician Richard Kayser had observed way back in 1895, periodic cycles of congestion and decongestion that alternated between the right and the left nostril which was later termed 'Nasal Cycle' ('NC'). *(Reference 17)* As a matter of fact, the existence of 'NC' had been known on 'Yogic Sciences' from the time of the great sage Patanjali who lived between the 2nd & 4th centuries CE. Authentic Yogis have been making use of this biological phenomenon to change the body's temperature, temperature of the 'Vayu' ('Air') and one's mental state.

Scientific observations on the 'NC' phenomenon are as follows:

1. At any given moment, you are both breathing in and out through one dominant nostril. Then, some time later, you switch to the other automatically. The interval between the two is usually 2 to 2.5 hours; and, it continues in a rhythmical fashion.

2. This rhythm changes over time for most people.
3. It seems to be controlled by our brain's 'Central Nervous System' ('CNS') which consists of the brain tissue and the spinal cord.
4. 'Swelling' of the nostril is related to the activation of the 'Sympathetic Nervous System' ('SNS') that triggers the 'fight-or-flight' response; and, 'Shrinking' of the nostril corresponds to the 'Parasympathetic Nervous System' ('PSNS') triggering the 'rest-relax-and-digest' response.

At any given moment, you have 'SNS' dominance on one side of the body (breath mostly through the nostril on that side) and 'PSNS' dominance on the other. Then, after some time, the order reverses. So, basically, 'NS' is an indicator of the switch that happens between the 'SNS' and 'PSNS' from one side to the other.

When the 'SNS' is dominant on the right side of your body, you have (i) increase in body temperature; (ii) reduction in prolactin secretion (prolactin stimulates breast development and milk production in women—has no known normal function in men, although men with well developed breasts are observed to have some feminine propensities); (iii) increase in male sex hormone 'Testosterone'; (iv) increase in the neurotransmitter 'Endorphin' which is our internally generated stress-reliever and pain-killer.

When the 'SNS' is dominant on the right side, all these bio-markers indicate a reduction in value and intensity. *(Reference 18)*

Yogis and Tantrics use a different language. According to them, the energy balance in our biology is affected by the flow of energy along the 'Ida' nadi (lunar), 'Pingala' nadi (solar) and the 'Sushumna' nadi. Pingala is solar and warm like sunshine—it has masculine quality and terminates at the right nostril INCREASING YOUR SEXUAL DRIVE & LIBIDO.

Your sexual drive and libido can be inhibited by breathing in through the left nostril which is where the 'Ida' nadi ends—and breathing out through the right nostril. This practice is called 'Chandrabheda' in Yogic Sciences.

'Right Nostril Breathing' ('RNB') involves alternate cycle of inhalation and exhalation through the right nostril while the left nostril is occluded and 'Left Nostril Breathing' ('LNB') involves alternate cycle of inhalation and exhalation through the left nostril while the right nostril is occluded. *(References 19 & 20)*

Nadi Dominance

At any given time, one of the two nadis, 'Ida' and 'Pingala', is predominantly active and much of airflow happens through one of the nadis. This, 'One At A Time' ('OAAT') or bilateral way of functioning of some of our organs and body parts is due to Nature's remarkable 'conservatism'—its beautiful way of saving the most precious biological energy. (*Reference 21*. Read my notes on 'The System of Proportions'.)

There is a reversal of role between these two nadis after a regular period of interval, This, as I have mentioned, is the 'Nasal Cycle' ('NC'). This cycle is important because the change in breathing cycle ensures that the nostrils don't get dry and sufficient moisture levels are maintained.

'Ida' and 'Pingala' have energies of opposite nature. 'Ida' energy flow is cool like the cool lunar energy of 'moonshine' whereas that of 'Pingala' is warm like that of 'sunshine'. Based on this basic difference, 'Ida' and 'Pingala' would be dominantly active while doing any daily task.

Yogic Sciences are based on 'Subtle Biology' and if one of the two nostrils remain predominantly active for a much longer time than normal, then that would be an indication of some body-brain-mind-soul issue which can manifest on the surface—on the 'Gross Biology' front much later. One example is: continuous hoarseness of voice may be indicative of some brewing throat disorder.

An overactive 'Ida' nadi means that the left nostril is being used dominantly for a longer period of time. It would mean a more than optimal level of coolness in the body. This results in under-performance of the thyroid gland, known as 'hypothyroidism' leading to lowering of the metabolic activity, ineffective digestion, too much energy wasted in getting your dietary inputs digested—making you feel weak. Naturally, you always remain sluggish or lethargic. There is an increase in gas and flatulence in the body. Downward flow of the 'Apana Vayu' gets affected making you constipated and susceptible to diabetes. The quality and productivity of your performance drops. You become an energy-costly person. Moreover, the creative, intuitive, visualising faculties of your 'Right Brain' get affected making you passive and depressed in temperament. Despite being on a healthy diet, you feel the burden of fatigue. The root cause is most ineffective 'Vayu Management'.

When the 'Pingala' nadi (connected to the 'Left Brain' which is responsible for goal-oriented movement, language-based effective communication, planned reproduction, and logical thinking) is overactive, energy flow through the right nostril is predominant. There is excessive heat in the body which can even take the form of fever. There is proneness to hyperthyroidism, excessive food intake and frequent craving for eating something. This can also result in acidity and peptic ulcer, dryness of skin, throat and excessive sexual energy (I will talk about it in the next piece). Inflammation issues such as bronchitis and arthritis can also arise. There could be imbalance in body fluids. This can have effect on kidney and liver functioning. There is excessive load on the logical, left side of the brain, which may increase the mental stress level and blood pressure.

Authentic Baul and Fakir sadhak interns are taught by their Gurus 'Vayu Management' techniques which have been passed down the line in Guru-Shishya Parampara, to take self-remedial actions. The 'Chandra Bhedi' pranayama is used in case of an overactive 'Pingala' whereas 'Surya Bhedi' pranayama for overactive 'Ida'. The Guru may also guide the shishya in the right practice of 'Anulom-Vilom'.

Sexual Transmutation

In Ayurveda, one drop of semen is said to be made from 40 drops of blood. Similarly, Tibetan medicine says that it takes one cup of the vital essence of blood to produce one drop of the vital essence of semen. Western medicine says that semen has over 200 different proteins, vitamins, minerals, and amino acids. It's a treasure chest of nutrients that the body and mind own to perform at their best. By this measure, semen is even more precious than blood.

In 2011, Alexander Rhodes, a young programmer in USA came across a study on the website 'Reddit' which revealed that men who refrained from wasting their semen for 7 days experienced a 45.7 percent spike in their male sex hormone 'Testosterone' ('T') levels on the 7th day. Rhodes decided to abstain from all sexual activity for a period and started noticing considerable changes in his life. He founded the 'NoFap' community to encourage others to do the same. Today the 'NoFap' has more than 600,000 members with 5 percent of the members being women. *(Reference 23)*

"A river may be dammed, and its water controlled for a time, but eventually it will force an outlet. The same is true of the emotion of sex. If it is not TRANSMUTED into some creative effort, it will find a less positive, less productive outlet." (*Reference 24*; Napoleon Hill, In: '*Think and Grow Rich*')

In the case of men, when semen is retained, it is absorbed back into the body to nourish the higher energy centres ('chakras'), nervous system, and the brain.

One of the three most critical enemies of the mind is: 'strong desire' or 'lust' (in Bengali: 'kam') which is concentrated mostly in the pelvic region—in the 'Muladhara' and 'Swadhisthana' chakras. When the sexual energy located there is arrested by special breathing technique and semen is retained, the energy bundle tends to stimulate the abdominal region where the 'Manipura' chakra is located. 'Manipura' is associated with another most critical enemy of the mind—'greed' (in Bengali: 'lobh'). You become greedy for food—'lust' becomes converted into 'greed'. If you cannot transcend this level, you eventually get taken over by chronic ailments like diabetes, fatty liver, peptic ulcer or 'Irritable Bowels Syndrome'. If you can settle with the 'Manipura' amicably, your energy travels to the 'Anahata' or 'Heart' chakra and there is every possibility that you fall a victim of 'infatuation' (In Bengali: 'Moha') which is the third critical enemy of your mind. So that the disciple does not get infatuated by his female partner, the traditional Bauls adopt the twin strategy of: first offering his girl to the Guru and shares her with him; and, secondly, by having more than one sadhan-sangini.

Once the 'Heart Chakra' hurdle is over, the powerful energy reaches the 'Visuddha' or the 'Throat Chakra'. Voice is the main organ used by a Baul as he sings one song after another while going for his 'Madhukari' (begging trip). He needs concentrated accumulation of energy in his vocal apparatus so that his songs touch the hearts of the rural householders and they come out voluntarily with generous alms. Lalon, Guddu Shah, Panju Shah, Kangal Harinath, Gagan Harkara, Hasan Raja, Bhaba Pagla were all songwriters, composers and singers like Bob Dylan, Pete Seger and our Kabir Sumon in modern Bengal. All of them needed an equal amount of creative energy ('Sexual Energy' gets transmuted into 'Creative Energy') at the level of their 'Ajna Chakra' which is the centre of imagination, intelligence and intellect.

The energy now multiplies as its vibrations are very high. The lowest vibrations are at the 'Muladhara' level—the higher you rise along the chakra route, the higher become the energy vibrations. The high energy now stimulates the 'Sahasrar' chakra—the 'Crown' and this is when the opportunity for liberation arises—you CAN PREVENT THE POSSIBILITY OF REBIRTH. The 'Birth-and-Death' cycle stops in the case of an authentic sadhak, provided, of course, he conquers the other three enemies of the mind—'Anger', 'Ego' and 'Envy'—(respectively, 'Krodh', 'Mod' and 'Matsarjya'—in Bengali), which raise their silly heads when you feel ownership of the moving energy (you are not the owner, it is a part of the cosmic energy) develop a competitive and combative attitude. The rising sexual energy is what is known as the serpentine 'Kundalini' in Yogic and Tantric Sciences. Making the 'Kundalini' power enter the Crown Chakra and make you feel one with the cosmos is the ultimate aim of authentic Baulgiri and Fakiri. This is my perception and I'm indeed open for challenge.

References

[1] Sudhir Chakrabarti, *Baul Fakir Katha* (book in Bengali), Kolkata: Ananda Publishers, 8th Impression, January 2022.

[2] Sebastian Bruno, "The 5 Vayus Explained", Video Presentation (You Tube).

[3] Geetha M. Kanthasamy, "The Five Pranas that fuel functional systems of body", Video Presentation (You Tube)

[4] Olgakabel, "Five currents of prana and how they organize your physiology (5 Vayus)", *Sequence Wiz.*

[5] "What is Prana? Understanding flow of 5 Vayus", *FITSRI.*

[6] "Domer Gari Dibe Faki"—Lyrics by Obujh Musahid Jibon, *Apon Gallery HD.*

[7] "How Many Breaths you take per Day and Why it Matters", *ADVENT Blog.*

[8] "What is Pranayama?"—Medically Reviewed by Dan Brennan, MD on 22nd April, 2021.

[9] Olga Kabel, "Five currents of prana and how they organise your physiology (5 Vayus)", Sequence Wiz, 3rd September 2014. Video Presentation (You Tube).

[10] Geetha M. Kanthasamy, "The Five Pranas that fuel functional systems of body: Prana—Apana—Samana—Vyana—Udana)". Video Presentation (You Tube).

[11] Satish K.K., "Controlling the vital force within", *The Tribune*, 31st March 2020.

[12] "In yogic ways Rechak, Purak and Kumbhak are the path to vigour and good health", *Vastutantraastro*, 23rd April 2020.

[13] "Puraka, Kumbhaka, Rechaka + Shunyaka" *prana-sutra.com*, 29th July, 2022.

[14] Ann Pietrangelo, "How to Practice Anulom-Vilom Breathing", *healthline*, 25th March 2022.

[15] Babu Kishan Aka Krishnendu Das Baul, "Baul History 101", *Speaking Tree in.* 11th May 2011.

[16] *Honeymoon rhinitis*—Wikipedia.

[17] *Nasal cycle*—Wikipedia.

[18] R. Kahana-Zweig and M. Geva-Sagiv, [....] and Noam Sobel, "Measuring and Characterizing the Human Nasal Cycle", *PLOS ONE.*

[19] Rinku Garg and Varun Malhotra, [.....] and Ritu Agarwal, "Effect of Left, Right and Alternate Nostril Breathing on Verbal and Spatial Memory", *Journal of Clinical and Diagnostic Research (JCDR)*, July 2016, Vol. 10, No. 2, pp. 1-3.

[20] Olga Kabil, "Yogis ahead of science: One nostril breathing determines how you feel", *Sequence* Wiz; sequencewiz.org/201.

[21] Siddhartha Ganguli, *Human Engineering for Better Management*, Kolkata: Kwality Book Co., 1978.

[22] Aashish Nanda, "What goes wrong when Ida and Pingala do not perform properly?" *moksha mantra life gupshup.*

[23] Anoop Abraham, "Sexual Transmutation (NoFap): How to Transmute Sexual Energy", *The SoulJam.*

[24] Napoleon Hill, *THINK and GROW RICH*, Mumbai: First Jaico Impression, 2016.

CHAPTER 8

Study of Man
(Manush Tattva)

In the Baul-Fakir culture, 'MAN' is the central character. Bauls & Fakirs worship MAN, they believe that to find GOD, you need not go to a temple, mosque, church, or gurdwara, you will find godly qualities in humans. Before 'Man' or 'Humans', there were 'Pre-historic Men' or 'Pre-humans' (In Bengali: 'Bon Manush'). I had proposed in my 'Manush Tattva', the existence of a 'Post-human' stage beyond the 'Humans'. Most interestingly, Bauls & Fakirs follow the concepts of 'Sahaj Manush' ('Simple Man' who is not artificial) and 'Moner Manush' (who is 'Egoless'—egocentric people cannot share love with others, their 'self-love' element is so strong). These two concepts somehow fit in quite snugly with my 'Post-human' paradigm.

While reading Utpal Fakir's Bengali book 'Jibon Nadir Kule Kule'—released in the 2023 Kolkata Book Fair, I was amazed to come across an unusually long song by Late Sanatan Das Baul's Guru Nitai Khyepa which starts as: (In Bengali: *"Ache manush ei manushete…Je pare manush dekhite chinite"*) (In English: *"Man is there in every human … Who can read and understand people"*). *(Reference 1)* It reminded me of the classical research project on 'Reading and Judging People' that I'd spearheaded at the University College of Medicine (Goenka Hospital), University of Calcutta, during the period 1972-78 which had led to my favourite 'FAT' formula. *(Reference 2)* Since I find my research was lab-based collecting elaborate physical, physiological, medical and psychological data on 3,000 adult, able-bodied, able-brained healthy test subjects from the University's student population, I am sharing the essential outcome with my readers here so that they can get some practical tips about reading and judging people. I classified my test subjects into three broad groups: (i) Fat (F); (ii) Athletic (A); and (iii) Thin (T). I am sharing my FAT formula below:

1. *F (Fat):* Fatty tissue predominant in the body. Landmark to be studied is the wrist joint. In Fat people, the bony prominence in the wrist joint is not visible—the joint is covered under a layer of fatty tissue. There is a prominence of 'round' shapes in the body (face is round, body is apple-or-pear-shaped, round nails). Generally short to medium in stature.

   Such people are strong in the 'Kapha' dosha of Ayurveda—physically lazy and lethargic in nature (although may be very creatively productive emotionally-mentally); averse to physical-manual work which requires physical energy expenditure. Likes desk-based work, work-from-home. Avoids physical exercise. Fond of good food and entertainment like going to movies and theatres or concerts where you have to be seated to watch—not art exhibitions or fairs where physical movement would be necessary to do full justice to your visit.

   Highly people and social oriented; extraverted; very friendly and sociable; polite and sweet in talking. Very sharp and intelligent to the point of being shrewd, tactful and diplomatic—not straightforward at all, which would be a strength in human relations. Could be emotionally and sentimentally driven, while taking decisions, solving problems and in relationships.

2. *A (Athletic):* Bones, muscles and joints are predominant in the body; those body parts are gainfully utilised also; not hesitant to take moderate physical risks. Medium in stature. Bony prominence in the well-developed wrist joint visible. There is a predominance of square to rectangular shapes in the body—to be noted in the face and nails. Powerful eyes—full of self-esteem and confidence.

   Such people are strong in the 'Pitta' dosha of Ayurveda—highly energetic and active by nature—physically as well as behaviourally. They like sports, games, physical movement, physical exercise (gym-based or with exercising tools, gadgets and accessories at home). Highly disciplined and controlled in everything. A noticeable strength is effective planning and time management.

Brainpower is logical and analytical—takes a rational and scientific approach in anything, which tends them to be a little slow in certain critical decision-making/problem-solving situations. Far from being impulsive—emotional and sentimental. Extraverted but controlled; strong in oral and written communication. But their honesty, integrity and straight-forwardness make them unpopular at times with both 'F' and 'T' type people.

3. *T (Thin):* Thin and lean in constitution. There is predominance of oval and inverted triangular shapes (watch the face and the nails). Long extremities—both upper (hands) and lower (legs)—long fingers and toes, thin lips, sharp pointed nose. Medium to tall in height. Eyes full of expression and insightful.

   Introverted by nature, such people are strong in the 'Vata' dosha of Ayurveda—highly imaginative but unsteady and fickle-minded. Inclined to live in their own imaginary world. Thinking tends to be abstract and philosophical. Poetic by nature. Weak in practical intelligence and goal-orientation. Being confused in a materialistic environment, tends to move towards religious faiths. However, not all of them, advance spiritually because lack of dedicated focus. Physically not lazy but not too energetic and active—moderate in scale. Well-matched with people having high vibrations.

Practical Application: Nobody is a pure F, pure A or pure T. Everybody has all the three components, representing 'Kapha', 'Pitta' and 'Vata' of the Ayurvedic 'Tridosha' in different proportions. *(References 3-5)* A typical Baul-Fakiri temperament would have a TAF constitution—predominantly thin, lean, tallish, longish with an oval or inverted triangular face with prominent bony landmarks on face. A person of such description would not be materialistically inclined unless there is a large proportion of 'F'—fatty tissue, present in the body. Nevertheless, mind you, with any change in the body profile there will also be a change in the temperament which would be perceptible.

You have to be very careful in studying people using the FAT formula. It requires long practice to master the skill.

The Man of My Heart (In Bengali: 'Moner Manush')

My very first exposure to *'Moner Manush'* (In English: *"The Man of My Heart"*) was through the Baul poet Gagan Harkara's famous song: (In Bengali: *"Ami kothay pabo tare...Amar moner manush je re...?"*); (In English: *"Where shall I find... The man of my heart?"*). Gagan Chandra Dam (1845-1910), whose pseudonym was 'Gagan Harkara' was a postal courier in the Silaidaha post office which was located close to the ancestral estate of poet Rabindranath Tagore. In addition to his job as a govt. peon, he was a most talented poet, songwriter, composer and singer. Tagore's song (In Bengali: *"Amar sonar Bangla...ami tomay bhalobashi..."*) (In English: *"Oh! My Golden Bengal...I love thee"*) was composed in the shadow of Gagan's above song and, after the liberation of East Pakistan, it became the national anthem of the newly founded Bangladesh. *(References 6-8)*

The Bauls & Fakirs of all times have been thinking, talking and dreaming of 'Moner Manush' and, as far as I could understand reading the work of lead researchers and interacting with enlightened people who are close to Baul sadhaks, their perception of 'Moner Manush' is a person who is full of unconditional love for everyone irrespective of race, religion, caste, creed, gender, age, status and occupation. The idea is no doubt great, but I'd be educated if someone can explain how to attain that 'Moner Manush' ('Man of the Heart') state so that you're EGOLESS. 'Ego' is an armour that a child develops as it grows from infancy to protect itself from onslaught from others and ensure its survival. Even the Yogi meditating in a Himalayan cave, totally bare-bodied in the bone-chilling and freezing weather, has an 'Ego' which makes him to remain isolated from others to prevent wastage of energy in useless social interactions. You become a 'Moner Manush' ('Man of the Heart') for all others when you surrender yourself to their desires and plans just like good shishyas surrender to authentic Gurus and become absolutely empty vessels.

In modern times, every human phenomenon or concept is being expressed in terms of BIOLOGY. Even abstract mainstream philosophy is being modernised by 'Neuro-philosophy'; thanks to the Canadian-American philosopher Professor Patricia Churchland of the University of California, San Diego, USA. *(Reference 9)* I've been trying to link 'Music' with 'Biology' through my brainchild 'Bio-musicology'.

In terms of 'Biology', the 'Moner Manush' mental state can be obtained if one has a handsome level of the chemical 'Oxytocin' ('O') in his blood. 'O' is a neuro-transmitter released from our brain's 'Pituitary Glands' which are located near the 'Ajna Chakra' (known as the 'Third Eye') in Yogic Sciences. Only a few years ago, the existence of 'O' was known only to gynaecologists and obstetricians as it would get released in the vaginal passage of a pregnant lady during labour pain to facilitate vaginal delivery. 'O' will also be released inside the brain of the would-be mother who is most anxiously waiting for the baby's arrival. On delivery, 'O' will be released inside the brain of the infant also as it starts on breast-feeding to develop a trustful bonding between the mother and the child. The mother can never think of doing any harm to her child; and this feeling is reciprocated by the child.

Only a decade and a half ago, Dr Paul Zak took 'O' out of the dark slippery ally of the woman's vaginal region and, through his classical research, gave it a much higher status of the love-compassion-empathy-trust-bonded relationship-building molecule, as he founded the new science of 'Neuro-economics'. *(References 10 & 11)* Zak has clinically established that compassionate, empathetic, trustworthy people have a high level of 'O' in their blood. So, we can find out who can qualify to be 'Moner Manush' ('The Man of the Heart') by testing the level of 'O' in their blood at different times, whether it maintains a steady state.

You can increase the 'O' level in your blood by taking 'O' inputs through nasal sprays. *(Reference 12 & 13)*

In my research on 'Bio-musicology' I suddenly bumped on to a case which led to a brainwave regarding 'O' generation without nasal sprays, using melodious music. I came across a very reputed vocal musician who shared with me his blissful experience with a particular Raga. He enjoys singing many classical Ragas but over the last few months he is finding a very close bonded relationship with one particular Raga with which he must start his Riyaaz every morning without fail. He has observed that he gets so much carried away by this Raga that his 'Stupid Ego' disappears and he develops a very warm feeling with everyone he meets in course of the day. Pursuit of the same habit every day has helped him to conquer his Ego in human relationships. This is the gift of the 'O' release in his brain. I'm in the midst of following up with the case.

Meanwhile, let me tell you if you are a Baul or Fakir singer or you are a music lover—you listen to Baul songs. Identify a few (not more than 3 or 4) Baul songs which gives you that 'egoless' feeling. Sing or listen to those regularly early in the morning to increase the 'O' level in your blood so that you move towards the 'Moner Manush' ('The Man of My Heart') model.

Lalon researcher Sanat Kr. Mitra says: "Unless your mind is like an used white cloth…unless your culture, your tradition is like an unclothed, uncovered child, how can you become a 'Baul'?" Is Mitra talking about the 'Moner Manush' ('Man of the Heart')? *(Reference 14)*

Soul Search for theGolden Man (In Bengali: 'Sonar Manush')

Before I could get a breathing break after sharing my last piece on 'Moner Manush' ('The Man of My Heart'), I got two nudges from two of my young followers—one from the Nadia District of West Bengal, India and the other from the Chittagong District of Bangladesh indirectly drawing my attention to Lalon's famous song: *"Manush bhojle SONAR MANUSH hobi"*. The verb 'bhoja' in Bengali means 'bhajan kara' (In English: *"To sing in praise…to eulogise"*). So, according to Lalon: *'if you sing in praise of MAN, you will evolve into a GOLDEN MAN'. (Reference 15)*

Let me share with you what would be my interpretation. Each individual is born with enough resourcefulness (equivalent to the 'Raw Gold' extracted from the gold mine in the Kolar Goldfields, Karnataka, India or the Goldfields in Central Zambia, Africa) in his (no gender bias) body and brain, but those are full of 'impurities' which need to be removed to obtain 'Pure Gold' and for refining the 'Raw Gold' for removing the impurities the best possible strategy is to mix with various types of people without any discrimination. And, while mixing with all types of people closely, ignoring their race, religion, community, caste, creed, gender, age, family background, and socio-economic status, they would need to follow the 4A strategy which I have developed through a few years of field research (in order to sift out the 'most liked' people from those who are 'not so much liked' and 'disliked'—this was conducted in differently-sized organisations in different parts of India):

1. A: Attention (establishing and sustaining positive eye contact and paying uninterrupted attention to the other person when she/he speaks). [Opposite Stand: Lack of Attention]
2. A: Acceptance (accepting the person as a friend by forgiving and forgetting her/his past misdeeds and the conflicts that you two might have had). [Opposite Stand: Rejection]
3. A: Affiliation: (including her/him into your close affinity circle providing her/him with the feeling that you CARE.) [Opposite Stand: Exclusion]
4. A: Appreciation (acknowledging even simple favours by saying 'Thank You' and expressing 'Gratitude' for larger favours) [Opposite Stand: Keeping mumb]

Does this strategy release any happiness chemical inside the brain of the 'Recipient'? Yes, it does release the 'feel good' reward chemical 'Dopamine'. By making others happy you emerge as a 'Sonar Manush' (the 'Golden Man').

In another of his sugar-sweet songs, Fakir Lalon Shah says: *(Reference 16)*

(In Bengali: *"Dekh dekhi mon, dekhte jar oi basana hriday, lonthone ruper bati jalche re sadai"*); (In English: *"Oh, my mind—you can clearly see, if you have the desire in your heart; the flame of your beauty is burning in the lantern all the time!"*).

By 'lantern', the songwriter means your 'body'. By 'ruper bati', he means your 'Jivatma'—your 'Personal Soul'—your 'True Self' which represents your 'swarup'—your 'personality', your 'attitude', your 'mind set'.

The poet continues: (In Bengali: *"Dekh na re mon dekhte jar basana hriday!"*) (In English: *"Oh my mind! If you have a desire to find out what it is like, why don't you have a look?"*)

Lalon goes on: (In Bengali: *"Ratir gire faska mara, sudhu kathar bybsa kara, tar ki hobe rup nihari, miche gol badhay"*). (In English: *"Physical union is forsaken, the only transactions are through the exchange of words, what is the use of looking at its nature, you may be confused unnecessarily."*

In the next stanza, we have: (In Bengali: *"Jedin bati nibhe jabe, bhaber sahar andhar hobe, sukh-pakhi tor palaiibe, chere sukhalay"*) (In English: *"When the lamp will go off, the city of emotions will plunge into darkness, the bird of happiness will fly away, leaving the abode of contentment."*)

In the concluding stanza, Lalon says: (In Bengali: *"Siraj Sai bole re Lalon, Swarup e tui de re nayan, tabe hobe rup darashan, poris na dhanday"*.) (In English: *"Siraj Sai says Oh, Lalon, please look at the real appearance – only then you'll be able to know the truth, don't get lost in the maze"*).

The last stanza is potent with yoga philosophy. 'Yoga' can be defined in many ways. To my mind, the simplest definition is: merger of the 'Jivatma' with the 'Paramatma'. 'Jivatma' is the 'Self' within your 'Soul'. It is not pure. It is contaminated with the 'Sada Ripu'—the 'Six Enemies of Your Soul'. 'Paramatma' is the 'Universal Self'—the 'Cosmic Consciousness' which is pure. Unless you purify yourself by transcending above your 'Ripus', much though you may try, you can never reach the level of the pure 'Universal Self'. So, you must take a good look at your 'Swarup'—your 'True Self'—what and where are the impurities and chalk out a plan for remedial actions and implement that plan, you should never aspire to reach the level of 'Paramatma'. And, this is your opportunity for self-appraisal as once death comes, you would have missed your chance in this life. This is what happens to us every time we are born. We must make it a point, at least in the present birth, to make a beginning to the self-cleansing process.

For your clear understanding, I am explaining below in most realistic/practical terms the "Six Enemies of Your Soul", each of which makes your body and brain vibrate at a low frequency: *(Reference 17)*

1. ***Kama (Desire):*** Drive for anything which is 'temporary' and 'transient' helping you to earn the reward molecule 'Dopamine'—lust for sex included. Sex for lasting happiness (that is 'procreation') is OK but not sex for pleasure (that is, for earning 'Dopamine')
2. ***Krodha (Anger):*** Even slight irritability due to frustration, disagreement etc. releases the aggressive chemical 'Adrenaline' or 'Epinephrine' from your Adrenal glands which switches on your 'Sympathetic Nervous System' and puts you in the 'fight mode'. This is not good for your physical as well as mental health.
3. ***Lobha (Greed):*** Adequate inputs for your minimum needs satisfaction are good enough; seeking more is not good for you as it makes you a 'Dopamine'-hungry person. Addiction to a neuro-chemical is as bad as addiction for nicotine, alcohol or narcotics.
4. ***Mada (Sense of 'I'—Ego):*** A balanced 'Ego' that provides you with self-esteem and confidence is good enough—a bloated ego is a sign of inferiority complex.
5. ***Moha (Attachment):*** Your goal should be: 'Attachment with Detachment'. You should be happy with something when you get it but not unhappy when you don't get it. You shouldn't MISS anything—which makes you feel like a LOSER and your Adrenal Glands start secreting 'Cortisol'—the stress hormone.
6. ***Matsarya (Envy):*** You become the source of your own unhappiness by comparing yourself with others. Do you ever try to find out what you have which the person that you envy does not have? If you do, then you have a mature mind—fit to be regarded as 'human'. It is the 'pre-human' mind that compares itself with others.

'Moner Manush' (The Man of My Heart) Revisited

The elusive 'Moner Manush' ('The Man of My Heart') has been the target of a certain segment of the artistic human society everywhere.

Even the 2016 Nobel Laureate poet-songwriter-singer Bob Dylan, the unparalleled Beatles, the energetic Sir Mick Jagger lead vocalist and founder member of the rock band Rolling Stones have not been exceptions, not to speak of our own Fakir Lalon Shah and a few other creative geniuses who have contributed to the world of music, poetry, drama, and performing arts.

All of them did apprehend that this 'Man of the Heart' was within one's own 'Self'. And, they realised that it is that part of the 'Self' which you can TRUST, which gives you CONFIDENCE to take up a challenge, which tells you 'YOU CAN DO'. But, in order for that part of your 'Self' to come out of its hard protective shell, it needed a trigger, and that trigger had to be acquired from outside—it was nothing but a 'Phyto-cannabinoid' like 'Cannabis'—which is known by many names like marijuana, pot, grass, hemp, and 'ganja' (in Bengali/Hindi). *(Reference 18)* 'Cannabinoids' are a group of compounds found in the plant 'Cannabis', also known as 'marijuana'. *(Reference 19)* Similar to 'opioids', 'cannabinoids', produce their effects by interacting with specific receptors, located within different parts of the 'Central Nervous System' ('CNS'). 'Opioids' are substances that act on opioid-receptors to produce morphine-like effects—medically used for pain relief, including anaesthesia.

'Cannabis' belongs to the group of 'Narcotic Drugs' which are banned in most places. Although not legal, Cannabis has been cultivated in Afghanistan for centuries and in 2010, the United Nations reported that Afghanistan was the world's top Cannabis producer. Cannabis is put under the group of 'Drugs' because it has medicinal value, but the use in the artistic circle that I'm talking about is for pleasure, motivation and recreation only. In order to get a kick of confidence, the drug-user becomes dependent on it as it is highly addictive like nicotine and alcohol. There are nasty withdrawal symptoms also.

The habituated ganja-smoking people do not know that there are 'cannabinoids' inside our brains also which are known as 'Endo-cannabinoids'. 'Anandamide', a fatty acid neurotransmitter, was the first endocannabinoid to be discovered. It binds on the same cannabinoid receptors that the phyto-cannabinoid 'cannabis' ('ganja') acts in. *(Reference 20)* The brain chemical gets its tongue-twisting name from 'ananda', the Sanskrit word for 'happiness, joy, contentment and delight'. After the discovery of 'Anandamide' (also known as the 'Bliss Molecule'), scientists began searching for cannabinoid receptors and found that the human body is brimming with them. They are in the lungs, liver, kidneys, white blood cells, reproductive organs, and in the gastro-intestinal and urinary tracts. The effects of 'Anandamide' are thus much more widespread than 'ganja'. Suboptimal levels of 'Anandamide' can drain you of happiness, make you feel insecure and diffident, increase fear and anxiety, and rob you of the ability to cope with stress—the circumstances which make a habituated 'cannabis' ('ganja')-smoker to go for a 'pot'. So, if your 'Anandamide' level in the body and brain is OK, then you do not need any phyto-cannabinoid to make up the deficiency.

Here comes the importance of 'Neuro-management' ('NM')—the new and novel multi-disciplinary domain that I'm trying to develop for the last 6-7 years. You have to discover your TRUE PASSION (one and only one) by using my 3D (Dream-Drive-Domain) approach which I've discussed in detail in my book published by Allied Publishers in 2021. *(Reference 21)* Once you have discovered your 'True Passion' and pursue it whole hog by utilising all your personal resources, you will remain in the 'FLOW Brain State' ('FBS') which will help you to access the 'Bliss Molecule' sources in your brain and different parts of your body. *(Reference 22)*

I am grateful to Late Professor Raphael Mechoulam of the Medicinal Chemistry Dept. at the Hebrew University of Jerusalem who is considered the father of medical cannabis research. He discovered the 'Endocannabinoid System' ('ECS') in the 1980s and collaborated with his students and post-docs to identify and isolate the vital endogenous cannabinoids of the ECS including the 'Anandamide'. *(Reference 23)* 'Anandamide' was first described (and named in 1992) by Prof. Mechoulam And his lab members W.A. Devanne and Lumir Hanus. I've learnt a lot from their work and also from the work of other medical cannabis researchers in Europe and USA with whom I've been in regular touch. 'Anandamide' plays a role in hunger, sleep, pain modulation, working memory, identification of novelty and interpretation of environment. In the pre-historic days, when health and medical sciences were totally unknown, 'Anandamide' was Mother Nature's gift for safe and secure survival and growth. *(References 24 and 25)*

'Endocannabinoids' are released from the brain cells or 'neurons' wherever they are present in the head brain (between the ears in the cranium), the heart brain, and the gut brain. Levels are especially high in certain brain regions, including the 'striatum' (in the subcortical Basal Ganglia of the Forebrain) and the 'brain stem' (lower part of the brain connected to the spinal cord) that regulates most of the body's automatic functions that are essential for life, including breathing and heartbeats. *(Reference 26)*

The Bauls & Fakirs have the practice of smoking hemp (the unreal 'Moner Manush') because, they possibly haven't got the faintest idea as to how to awaken the real 'Moner Manush' ('Man of the Heart')—the 'Bliss Molecule'—'Anandamide', which is present not only in the brain but spread all over the body in different organs and biological systems to facilitate overall well-being and homeostasis. I emphasize, that most Baul rituals and practices ought to be reviewed in modern times from scientific angles.

'Moner Manush' ('The Man of My Heart') Review

As a Baul or Fakir, whether you are going on 'Madhukari' seeking alms or performing, all dressed up with accompanists, on stage—charging a fee, you are not 'selfless'; you have a SELFISH MOTIVE. Naturally, therefore, there is an element of ANXIETY in your heart as you are driven by a desire—a desire to collect alms, a desire to earn money for your subsistence. 'Desire' is 'Kam'—one of the 6 Ripus/Enemies of the Mind. You are not a court musician like Miyan Tansen in Mughal Badshah Akbar's time or like Late Ustad Baba Alauddin Khan in the court of the Raja of Maihar in Satna, Madhya Pradesh where all your and your dependents' needs are met by your employer or sponsor.

Where does that ANXIETY take place in your brain? ANXIETY fills your brain's 'Default Mode Network' ('DMN')—a special circuit, which gets engaged when the brain is idle—it is not focused on any meaningful task. Negative neuro-chemical 'Cortisol' is released and your brain cells have negative vibes. This is where the ganja/bhang-smoking Hindu God Lord Shiva emerges as the 'Role Model' for Bauls, Fakirs, Darbeshs, Sadhus, Yogis, Tantrics and Aghori Babas.

Lord Shiva is considered as one of the supreme forms of gods who can save nearly everything from falling apart. Being regarded as a 'destroyer', symbolises his massive power. He is one of the three in 'Trimurti'.

Lord Shiva is a complex person—an ascetic as well as a family man, beautiful but terrifying, an ace dancer but can be absolutely still. Worshipped by gods as well as by demons and evil spirits, lives in green forest but meditates in burial grounds and or burning cadavers. Some people are biased when they picturise Lord Shiva as smoking pot ('Cannabis'). They do not know that 'Cannabis' is one of the most sacred plants like the 'tulsi' or the 'bel' and it is documented in the Vedas that it relieves ANXIETY.

Actually, as the Hindu mythology says, during the 'Samudra Manthan'—cleaning of the ocean, a lethal poison named 'Halahal' was released which was so poisonous that it would have ended the entire creation. To avoid that happen, Lord Shiva consumed the whole poison on his own to save the Earth and became known as 'Neelkantha'. To clear his system of the poison, gods offered him 'bhang'/'ganja' (Cannabis).

For members of the artist community, 'poison' is the pre-performance ANXIETY and to clear their minds of this poison, they have made Lord Shiva their 'Role Model', and go for smoking the pot. In order to throw away the chilim (the ganja-smoking pipe) and be free from any such substance-dependence, you have to choose one of two following strategies:

Strategy 1: Find out your 'True Passion' and develop your 'Unique Buying Proposition' ('UBP'). 'UBP' is a 'Neuro-management' ('NM') concept that I've developed. Develop yourself, UNIQUELY, in 'Skill', 'Intelligence' or 'Talent' or in two or all the three—to counter competition. In 1962, I had spent three nights and two full days with the sitar maestro Late Pt. Ravi Shankar in my host Late Prodyot Sen's house in Finsbury Park, London and I was amazed to find how laboriously Ravi was trying to develop his UBP. I did not find him smoking cigarettes, not to speak of 'Cannabis', nor did I find him having even a glass of port or beer (he was a teetotaller like me) and we were on vegetarian diet.

Strategy 2: If you are into music—whether classical, modern, folk or Baul—vocal or instrumental, discover your domain. Then do a SWOT Analysis of your 'Music'—which is a 'product' and 'You'—the 'Musician' as the 'Service-provider'. In the SWOT formula, 'S' represents 'Strengths' or 'Plus Points', 'W'—'Weaknesses' or 'Minus Points'—of 'Your Music' and 'Yourself' vis-à-vis your 'Competitors'. 'O' stands for 'Opportunities' and 'T' represents 'Threats' which are related to the 'Environment'—the 'Market'.

Hone up your 'Strengths' and reduce your 'Weaknesses' continuously vis-à-vis the Market where you're operating. I don't know Parvathy Baul but for her the entire world is the market. Her music, her way of presentation, her style, her personality is being attuned regularly in relation to the market and the audience. She has been following the SWOT Analysis strategy unknowingly, although she has not composed 36 original Ragas like Pt. Ravi Shankar. Paban Das Baul and Mimlu Sen is a pair for whom also the entire world is the market and they have developed themselves accordingly.

Adoption of either Strategy 1 or Strategy 2 will hopefully help you to throw away your Cannabis pipe and/or the wine glass. I'd a direct witness to this happening in the case of Pt. Ravi Shankar; I'm afraid I cannot comment on either Parvathy or Paban Das-Mimlu on this count.

'Moner Manush' ('The Man of My Heart') Micro-analysis

Normal, healthy newly born kids have 'Anandamide' ('AEA') molecules present in their blood. They also get a supply of 'AEA' from their healthy mothers' milk during breastfeeding, in addition to 'Oxytocin'—which I've identified as the 'Moner Manush' neuro-transmitter which is the 'love-compassion-empathy-relationship-building-bonding' molecule. The whole purpose of this biological initiative is to make the growing child amenable to receive support from its social environment so that it becomes eligible for receiving the 4-A's (Attention, Acceptance, Affiliation and Appreciation) from all humans in its social environment and get the showering of all happiness chemicals in the infant's growing brain (Read *Reference 27*: "Survival of the Socially Fittest"). Herbert Spencer (1820-1903) was an English philosopher who initiated a philosophy called 'Social Darwinism'. He coined the term 'survival of the fittest' 7 (seven) years before Darwin's publication of his theory of natural selection, 'The Origin of Species' in 1859. *(References 28 & 29)*

Kindly note that newly born kids with lower 'Anandamide' ('AEA') in their brains are most likely to become victims of 'Autism Spectrum Disorder' ('ASD') the main symptom of which is 'Social Inactivity' including lack of 'Response' to 'Social Stimuli'. Such has been the finding of a research study on autistic and normal control children at USA's Stanford University Autism and Developmental Disorder Clinic. *(Reference 30)*

One major role of 'Anandamide' ('AEA') in a growing child's brain is to provide 'Cognitive Focus' to facilitate fast learning and memory development. 'Cognitive Focus' helps in planning for any future work assignment. For 'AEA' to play this specific role effectively, the growing infant must not be exposed to too many things which are alien to it—like any language other than its mother tongue. Secondly, it must be exposed to new things—even play things in the morning hours when its mind is fresh after a good night's sleep as 'Anandamide' release in the blood follows the 'Circadian Rhythm'. *(References 31 & 32)*

The moment the infant has become a child of school-going age, starts attending a school and learning multiple subjects even at the initial entry point, the 'Cognitive Focus' is tampered with and the concentration of 'Anandamide' ('AEA') in the child's blood plasma is reduced and the growing child starts suffering from 'academic stress'. I've seen our local slum children of age 7/8 years, studying in 2nd/3rd Standard, smoking 'bidis' and 'ganja' in local parks and blind alleys hiding themselves from elders. They suffer from academic anxiety. The more number of subjects they are exposed to as they go on to higher classes and still higher educational institutions like colleges and universities, they become more attracted towards nicotine and cannabis. In our local Ashutosh College, a reputed institution under the University of Calcutta the College's side and back alleys are full of ganja-smoking teenage boys and girls. This habit is not pursued only by students who have found studying different subjects enjoyable. They have novelty-seeking circuits in their brains, about which I will talk in one of my future articles. Their method of studying is different. They will take up a topic in Science. Let us say, 'Sound' in physics. Go to the library. Consult 3-4 different books by different authors on the same topic 'Sound'. Note down the basics and then go on adding the new bits and pieces learnt from the different books. Do self-brainstorming. If they come up with some new thoughts, add them to the notes already written. Now, they will have that write-up as their text for preparation. This method will release 'Anandamide' ('AEA') molecules in their brain.

The Bauls & Fakirs who are sparingly literate—may be up to the primary level only, but has "Novelty-seeking" circuits in their brains, will have several permanent sadhan-sanginis, would have many songs in stock, and can write verses and compose songs very well, would have good amount of 'Anandamide' ('AEA') in their brain and body, and might not be addicted to or dependent upon cannabis although might have tried it out regularly during their youth when they had embarked upon this freelancing career.

'Novelty Seeking' ('NS') Man

'Novelty Seeking' is in-grained in human nature. In the pre-historic days, both men and women used to seek new sexual partners. This propensity did not stop in the days of Rajas and Maharajas, Sultans & Badshahs who, apart from a few married wives, used to have paramours and mistresses. Even today, many Arab Sheikhs would be following the same practice. For the Bauls of Bengal, the only difference is that the female partners for them are not married wives, they are known as 'sadhan-sanginis'—women who play an indispensable role in the Baul sadhanas like 'Tantric Sex' serving the twin purpose of retention of semen and, at the same time, enjoying orgasm.

'Novelty Seeking' ('NS') is a personality trait associated with exploratory activity in response to novel stimulus. *(Reference 34)* The same food, the same clothes, the same routine—get stale. Therefore, our brain's 'NS' circuits look for some change—something new and novel. Bauls have the same simple food every day; sadhak Bauls put on the same orange or white clothes everyday (designer clothes or robes with cut pieces stiched to make it look colourful is not the classical Baul style); there is no change in their akhras. The only change that they can bring is in their songs, singing styles, accompanying instruments; but such changes are also not allowed in the traditional Baul and Fakir cultures. So, they look for novelty in the physical relationships.

When there is no change, there is no excitement; and, when there is no excitement, there is no release of 'Dopamine' ('D') molecules—brain's 'Reward Circuit' remains unused and dry. No human brain can afford to keep its 'Reward Circuit' remain unused and dry. That is why schizophrenics hear voices, suffer from hallucination, narcotic addicts need hallucinatory drugs; and, godmen like Ramakrishna Paramhansa needed to talk to Goddess Kali (who was imaginary); prophets like Muhammad needed to hear the voice of Allah. Bauls & Fakirs, who do not earn their 'D' molecules from material objects endeavour to get it from varied sexual experiences with different female partners and, for learning the right kind of techniques, they needed knowledgeable and experienced 'Gurus' and 'Murshids'. Late Prof. Sudhir Chakrabarti's award-winning Bengali book's one chapter talks descriptively about the Bauls' sadhan-sanginis—whether they remain happy or unhappy as they are not allowed to conceive; there are strict birth control practices; and, being women, many of them get frustrated when their masters do not allow them to get pregnant and become mothers which they long for. *(Reference 35)*

Let us look at the 'NS' behaviour, as such. Is the trigger for exploratory behaviour a novel stimulus; or, whether there is an innate propensity for seeking novel objects and novel experience? In the case of sadhak Bauls & Fakirs, the new human partner is a novel object and the sex-related transactions with her/him constitute a novel experience. And, as already mentioned, low dopaminergic activity leads to high NS behaviour.

Let us speculate what happens when a Baul's female partner becomes pregnant although the chances are very remote, the 'zero-pregnancy' training is so foolproof. The roving musician is at a cross road. Rather, I would say, there is a chemical tug-of-war inside him. On the one hand, there is the strong male sex hormone 'Testosterone' ('T') which is causing 'Irritable Male Syndrome' ('IMS') in him as only the sexual act will help him to earn his reward molecule 'Dopamine' ('D'). So, he neglects the pregnant devotee and gets physically involved with a new female. [Some sadhak Bauls mate with married women/wives of close disciples also possibly to make their husbands responsible if there is any pregnancy caused by accident during Baul jugal sadhana.]. I wonder if there has been any case when the Baul became overwhelmed by 'Oxytocin' ('O') and/or 'Vasopressin' ('V')—the love-empathy-compassion-bonding molecule to accept the illegitimate fatherhood and allow the pregnant woman to carry the child and deliver at the end of the term. Another alternative would be to make the pregnant female to get married to a loyal devotee. Certain aspects of the Baul/Fakir society are so much under the veil, that from outside we can only speculate—we just cannot say anything for definite. It requires in-depth research.

References

[1] Utpal Faqir, *Jibon Nadir Kule Kule* (in Bengali), Kolkata: Shompa Books, 2023, pp. 105-107.

[2] Siddhartha Ganguli, *Live Happily, Work Happily: A Window to the Science of Happy Living and Working*, New Delhi: Allied Publishers Pvt. Ltd., 2008 (Endorsement by Prof. Darrin McMahon, professor at the Dartmouth College, USA, author of 'Happiness: A History').

[3] Y.S. Raghuram and Manasa, "Tridosha Theory in Ayurveda", *EASY AYURVEDA.*

[4] Marc Halpern, "Tridosha: The Science of Ayurveda and the Three Doshas (Vata, Pitta, Kapha)", 17th September 2010, *California College of Ayurveda.*

[5] Kanchan Joshi, Anil Thapliyal and Varsha Singh, "The Tridosha Theory According to Ayurveda", *International Journal for Modern Trends in Science and Technology*, Vol. 7, No. 8, August 2021, pp. 120-124.

[6] *Gagan Harkara*—Wikipedia.

[7] *Amar Sonar Bangla*—Wikipedia.

[8] *National Anthem*—Banglapedia.

[9] Patricia Churchland, *Neuro-philosophy: Towards a Unified Science of the Mind-Brain*, Cambridge, Mass.: MIT Press, 1989.

[10] *Paul J. Zak*—Wikipedia.

[11] Paul J. Zak, *The Moral Molecule: The Source of Love and Prosperity*, Boston, Mass: Dutton, 2012.

[12] Lindsay Konkel, "What is Oxytocin?", *Everyday Health*, Reviewed on October 20, 2015 (This article talks about 'Oxytocin Nasal Sprays').

[13] *Oxytocin Nasal Spray*—Empower Pharmacy.

[14] Sanat Kr. Mitra, *Lalon Fakir: Kabi o Kabya* (in Bengali), Kolkata: Pustak Bipani, 1960, p. 35.

[15] "Manush Bhojle Sonar Manush Hobi"—*jiosaavn.com/lyrics*

[16] "Lonthone ruper bati"—*Lyrics, ITBD.*

[17] *Arishadvargas*—Wikipedia.

[18] A. Douglas Kinghorn, Heinz Falk, Simon Gibbons, Junichi Kobayashi, Editors, *103 Phytocannabinoids: Unravelling the Complex Chemistry and Pharmacology of Cannabis sativa*, Switzerland: Springer International Publishing, 2017.

[19] Loralie J. Langman, Paul J. Jannetto "Toxicology and the clinical laboratory: Cannabinoid" In: *Contemporary Practice in Clinical Chemistry* (Fourth Edition), 2020, Science Direct.

[20] Deane Alban, "Anandamide: Bliss Molecule for Happiness and Mental Balance", *Be Brain Fit*, 16th January 2023.

[21] Siddhartha Ganguli, *SMART Leading and Parenting of Teenage Kids in the Digital Era: A Neuro-managed Way*, New Delhi: Allied Publishers Pvt. Ltd., 2021.

[22] Mihaly Csikszentmihalyi, *FLOW: The Psychology of Optimal Experience*, New York: Harper Perennial, 2008.

[23] "Medical Cannabis Research: The Man Who Started It All – Raphael Mechoulam", *hempstreet*, 6th September 2021.

[24] "Anandamide"—Wikipedia.

[25] David A. Greenberg, "Endocannabinoids", *Encyclopaedia of the Neurological Sciences*, 2003.

[26] Mamta Rana, "Shiva and the cannabis", *Reader's Blog, The Times of India*, 25th October, 2019.

[27] Cay Leytham-Powell, "Survival of the Socially Fittest", Essay/*Stranger Lands; sapiens.org/biology*

[28] "Herbert Spencer on the Survival of the Fittest", *Works & Days, Kalantzis & Cope*, 2023.

[29] Charles Darwin, Origin of Species, New York: *P.F. Collier & Son*, (Available in Harvard College Library).

[30] Debra S. Karhson, Karolina M. Krasinska, [.......], and Karen J. Parker, "Plasma anandamide concentrations are lower in children with autism spectrum disorder", *Molecular Autism*, 2018, Vol. 9, No. 18; Published online on 12th March, 2018.

[31] L.K. Vaughn, G. Denning, K.L. Stuhr, H. de Wit, M.N. Hill, and C.J. Hillard, "Endocannabinoid signalling: has it got rhythm?" *British Journal of Pharmacology* [Internet], 2010.

[32] C.J. Hillard, "Circulating endocannabinoids: from whence do they come and where are they going?", *Neuropsychopharmacology* [Internet] 2018, Vol. 43, pp. 155-172; Published 17th June 2017.

[33] 'Se ki amar kabar katha'—*All lyrics in one place.*

[34] *"Novelty Seeking"*—Wikipedia.

[35] Sudhir Chakrabarti, *Baul Fakir Katha* (in Bengali), Kolkata: Ananda Publishers, 8th Impression, January 2022.

CHAPTER 9

Essence of Sufism

('Sufi Rasa')

First alternative: you can know and reach God through the scriptures. Second alternative: you can know and reach God by singing or listening to songs eulogising God, like hymns, bhajans or stutis, or by chanting 'mantras' Third alternative: you can know and reach God by hearing from a more knowledgeable and experienced person. Fourth alternative: you can know and reach God through direct personal experience (like meditation, yoga and other techniques). Fifth alternative: you can know and reach God by pursuing, wholeheartedly, a set of work activities that you enjoy most—which together constitute the family of your 'True Passion'. I follow the fifth route, whereas Sufis follow the fourth one. Sufism aims at finding the truth of divine love and knowledge through direct personal experience of God. Sufis are also generally known as the 'poor'—Arabic "faqir", Persian "darvish", and English "fakir" and "dervish". "Little sleep, little talk, little food" were fundamental for preparing for a Sufi style spiritual life. *(Reference 1)*

Sufism is the mystical tradition of Islam, where the central theme is 'Unity with God'. Sufi thoughts might have emerged from the Middle East in the 8th century CE, but adherents are now found around the world. Sufism essentially deals with the purification of the 'Self' by eradication of the 'Sadripu' (The Six Enemies of the Mind') which are the causes of all our miseries. This is the strategy Sufi sadhaks recommend for reducing the difference between 'divinity' and the 'humankind'; in my language, to evolve from the 'pre-human' and 'human' to the 'post-human' stage of consciousness. Like the monastic traditions of Hinduism, Buddhism and Christianity, Sufism has its ascetics—the 'Fakirs' and the 'Dervishes'.

The Sufi philosopher Ibn Arabi applies deep analysis on the issue of 'Oneness with God' through the metaphor of 'MIRROR'. In this metaphor, he compares an object being reflected in countless MIRRORs to the relationship between God and his creatures. God's essence is seen in the existent human being, as God is object and human beings the MIRRORs. God is free from 'Sadripu' (The Six Enemies of the Mind'); so you, as a human being, in order to progress spiritually, must check whether you can find the reflection of God in the MIRROR that you represent and continue self-remediation and self-appraisal/re-appraisal.

In Sufi language, 'Hal' is a state of spiritual consciousness that one is born with, whereas 'Maqam' is one's spiritual station or developmental level which is attained by one's effort to transform oneself. 'Manzil' means destination—a plane of consciousness. There are 7 (seven) 'manzils' along the path of God. 'Fanaa' is the Sufi term for extinction—the state of 'samadhi' with no touch with the outside world. It is the total abstention from sin and expulsion from the heart all love other than the 'Divine Love'—total freedom from 'Sadripu'. 'Baqaa' is equivalent to 'Nirvana' in Buddhism, 'Salvation' in 'Christianity', 'Najat' in Islam, and 'Mukti' or 'Moksh' in Hinduism. 'Haqiqat' is the supreme truth or absolute reality. 'Marifa' means knowledge or recognition—spiritual truth reached through ecstatic experiences (like 'singing' and 'dancing' in a special style that is suitable for releasing 'Anandamide' in the brain and body). 'Ihsan' is 'excellence' when one has surrendered and submitted completely to the will of the Allah. *(Reference 2)*

The greatest mystical poet in the Persian language, Jalal al-Din al-Rumi (1207-73) was moved by the mystical love to compose his lyrical poetry and it is he who inspired the organization of the 'Whirling Dervishes'—who sought ecstasy through an elaborate dancing ritual, accompanied by superb music exposing the participants to an enduring 'Anandamide' experience.

Sufi Practice ('ASC')

In the wakeful 'conscious' state of mind, we are aware of the 'realities' in the environment around us as different kinds of stimuli are entering into our brain through the various receptor sensory organs. The 'Altered State of Consciousness' ('ASC') takes one away from those 'realities' which, in fact, are responsible for stimulating one or more of our 'Sadripus'—the 'Six Enemies of the Mind'. For example, when a young man sees an attractive young woman, he develops a 'desire' ('kam' in Hindi/Bengali) to have physical relationship with her. Similarly, when a musician meets another musician of the same age but more successful in name, fame and prosperity, he is most likely to develop 'envy' ('matsarya' in Hindi/Bengali).

There are 4 (four) different modes of 'consciousness': (1) the fully waking mode; (2) the deep sleep mode; (3) the REM sleep or 'dreaming' mode; and, (4) the integrative mode (many 'ASC's are defined as belonging to this mode). *(Reference 3)*

There are several ways of getting into 'ASC' as follows: (i) physical and physiological (fasting, sex, dancing); (ii) psycho-neurological (music, meditation, hypnosis); (iii) spontaneous (dreaming during sleep, daydreaming, near-death-experience/NDE); pharmacological (psychoactive substances like cannabis/marijuana/ganja, psychedelic drug like psilocybin); pathological (epilepsy, schizophrenia, Alzheimer's, brain damage). *(Reference 4)*

Animals also want to get into 'ASC'. They have sex available to them for this purpose, but their sexual intercourse is not as long lasting as for their human counterparts. They can get drunk by eating rotten fruit like grapes or drinking some fermented drink available in the forest. But there has been a most recent revelation which was totally unknown to us earlier. A recent research conducted by the Dept of Psychology at the University of Warwick in UK (with a linguist faculty member from the University of Birmingham in UK) have found that the great apes go for 'SPINNING' activity to get into 'ASC'. *(Reference 5-8)*

This confirms the earlier observations of the famous British primatologist Jane Goodall who had left her homeland at a very young age in order to attend to her calling to study chimpanzees in their natural habitat in Africa. Goodall would frequently come across spinning chimpanzees while taking bath in the waterfalls.

To quote Dr Adriano Lameira, Associate Professor of Psychology at the University of Warwick who was the lead researcher in the cited 'Spinning Great Apes' project: "Every culture has found a way of evading 'REALITY' through dedicated and special rituals. If all great apes seek dizziness, then our ancestors are also highly likely to have done so."

I am adding to what Lameira has said—chimpanzees being are our closest ancestors sharing 98.5 percent genes with us, I'll be surprised if humans also do not follow some of their ritualistic practices. In fact, Lameira and his co-researchers did find such instances in the western ballet dancing, and in the middle-eastern Sufi devotees whirling dances. *(Reference 9)* They did not know about the spinning dances of some of the Bauls and Fakirs of Bengal.

While cannabis/marijuana/ganja can lead to 'ASC', the 'spinning' and 'whirling' activities of the Sufi Dervishes and the Bauls and Fakirs of Bengal apparently lead to the release of the endocannabinoid 'Annandamide' in their brains and bodies. The 'Anandamide' experience is nothing short of a spiritual ecstasy—when we experience freedom from 'REALITY' provided by the 'Sadripu'—the 'Six Enemies of the Mind'.

What are the other confirmed 'key' benefits of 'spinning/whirling': improvement of cardio-vascular health; improvement of lung health; relief from stress; burning of calories; and, building of lower body strength. *(Reference 10)*

Sufism 'Key' Lessons

Lesson 1: The Mystical Path

According to the Sufis, the mystical path is like a ladder, a staircase, that leads to heaven, on which the Sufi Sadhak slowly and patiently climbs towards higher and higher levels of experience. There is also another way of reaching higher experiences—a totally focused "attraction" (which the Sufis call "jadhba" or "jazba") by which a person can be exalted, in one single spiritual experience, into a state of ecstasy and "perfect union with God". In my vocabulary, this "attraction" is "True Passion" and "perfect union with God" is the "FLOW Brain State" ('FBS') attained by pursuing it whole-heartedly. "True Passion" is equivalent to "God" in this case. *(References 11 & 12)* The "perfect union with God" and the "FLOW Brain State" ('FBS') are both 'Altered States of Consciousness' ('ASC').

When someone becomes mad through longing for Allah, he does not care if people stab or kill him. Those in 'jazba' are unaware of themselves and what is happening around them. This is what does take place in the 'FLOW Brain State' ('FBS'). Some scholars have used the metaphor of a bird and cage to explain the state of consciousness. A man's body is like a cage, and his 'Soul'—a bird in the cage. When the 'Soul' is agitated, it tries to break out of the cage like the captivated bird. This is why some Sufis, during their 'sadhana' do things like rolling on the floor.

Some other scholars say that your passion for Allah is like the water in the pot. The water is boiling and with increased passion, the water starts spilling. Then, you lose control of the rhythm of your movements during the 'Whirling Dance'. This is when 'jazba' happens. Cases of musicians losing control and dying during 'jazba' are not rare. Such deaths are the most elevated kinds of death—to die not out of any disease or sudden organ failure—instead dying with one's true feelings and "iman" (faith).

Dance movements help one to enter 'jazba' because when the body suffers (the bird-cage is made of raw/unseasoned bamboo, and it may break), the 'Soul' would like to be released. The more intensely one moves the body, the freer and happier one's 'Soul' will be. You cannot sing and dance at the same time but you can chant God's name (which is 'dhikr'). So there may be songs sung by singers separately in the session, but the lyrics or the melody do not affect the whirling dancers. However, the 'dhikr' (the name chant or 'japam') should preferably be silent.

Every time you practice 'jazba', you get emotionally engaged into it and, after one or two hours of such engagement, you are generally in a good mood for several days at a stretch, and do not feel disturbed by worldly affairs which evoke the 'Sadripu' (the ' Six Enemies of the Mind').

'Dhikr' is the ritual of remembering God through reciting his names (like the Vaishnava 'Hare Krishna Hare Krishna, Krishna Krishna Hare Hare'). This ritual helps your brain to develop concentration and focus, whereas the 'Whirling/Spinning' body movement may help in Left Brain-Right Brain balancing, subject to confirmation through neuro-imaging studies on such dancers.

Incidentally, the 'Whirling Dance' movements were not the idea of the mystic Sufi poet and philosopher Rumi but of his eldest son Sultan Walad several years after Rumi's passing. *(Reference 13)*

Lesson 2: Rumi: Seven Stages of the 'Ego' (Arabic 'Nafs')

The First Stage: 'Depraved Ego': the 'Soul' is entrapped in worldly pursuits—holding others responsible for one's continuous unhappiness. This happens when one or more of the 'Sadripu' ('Six Enemies of the Mind') is/are active. The Second Stage: 'Accusing Ego': instead of blaming others all the time, blaming one's own self. The Third Stage: 'Inspired Ego': display of patience, perseverance, wisdom and humility; the world will feel new and full of inspiration. The Fourth Stage: 'Serene Ego': generosity, gratitude, feeling of indebtedness, unwavering sense of contentment. The Fifth Stage: 'Pleased Ego': pleased with whatever situation God has placed you in. The Sixth Stage: 'Pleasing Ego': lantern to humanity, radiating energy to everyone who asks for it, teaching and illuminating like a true 'master'; may have healing or influencing power; The Seventh and Final Stage: "Purified Ego': a perfect human being—a secret state which is not discussed much. *(Reference 14)*

Sufi-Baul Interface and Music

Our environment—both outside and inside of us is a mixture of 'GOD' and 'NOT GOD' both. By 'GOD' I mean 'PURE' and by 'NOT GOD' I mean 'IMPURE'. Our aim should be to bring the 'NOT

GOD' to 'zero' and make it 'ABSOLUTE GOD'. Much though we may clean our external physical environment in an attempt to 'purify' it, it will remain clean for some time and, then, would again become unclean within a short time. Let me talk about the backyard of my house. It has a few big trees—mango and jackfruit which bear delicious fruits and wood rose ('champa' in Hindi/Bengali) which bears fragrant flowers. Either I clean it or get it cleaned up by someone to make it spick and span. Within an hour, unfortunately, it loses its clean state with fallen twigs, leaves and flowers. Endeavour to clean the outside could thus be most frustrating, but we have to do it regularly to prevent the breeding of mosquitoes and insects of various kinds. We should rather concentrate on cleaning up our internal environment, the inside of us—the circuits of our brain that constitute our minds.

Unless you are PURE inside, you must not dare to aspire to reach GOD, because GOD represents PURITY. If you're still overpowered by one or more of the 'Sadripu' (the 'Six Enemies of the Mind'), you cannot dream of reaching GOD because of the presence of IMPURITY in you. Thus, going to temples, mosques, churches, monasteries or gurdwaras have no meaning if you're IMPURE, although the religious shrine is as pure as mineral water.

The Sufis adopt a wonderful strategy for 'inner purification' to reach GOD. They use MUSIC, which is both harmonious and beautiful. This process is known as 'Tasawwuf' in Arabic. Listening to poetry or music is a natural spiritual practice for them. This devotional application of 'listening' or 'audition' is called 'Sama' in Arabic. 'Sama', sometimes, involves the movement of the body or dance. There are also special occasions when musical instruments are also used.

Sufis have very strong theoretical and practical ideas about 'Music' and its effects—its role in the metaphysical and cosmological scheme of reality, which are all very fascinating. Music is 'Harmony' and it is strongly connected to mathematics and the Spheres of the Heaven according to the Sufi philosophers who are 'Nature-watchers'. Music is not made of 'matter'—it has no physical form—it deals with and consists of all spiritual substances, namely the SOULs of those who perform it and also those who listen to it. The SOULS are emitting quantum vibrations composed of infinitesimal particles which the human eyes are not capable of seeing. Music thus works on the souls of humans and animals. *(References 15 & 16)*

The celestial spheres are all rotating. Music is harmony and is strongly connected to mathematics and the spheres of the Heavens according to Sufi philosophers, who are driven by a higher level of consciousness than typical orthodox law/rule-bound 'Sariyati' muslims. The harmony and beauty of music reminds of the harmony and music of the celestial spheres and the divine realm. All creations of Mother Nature follow a beautiful opening up process which is full of harmony and unstruck melody. The 'Whirling' dance of the Sufi Dervishes are based on the principle of rotating movements seen in the Universe and in Nature.

"Creation begins with the activity of consciousness, which may be called vibrations, and every vibration starting its original sense is the same, differing only in its tone and rhythm caused by a greater or lesser degree of force behind it.

All actions and movements made in this visible and invisible world are musical. That is, they are made up of vibrations." (Hazrat Inayat Khan, *Reference 17*)

Bauls, the wandering mendicants, originally emerged from Buddhist Sahajiya background, have been converted as Sahajiya Vaishnavas, while Sufism came with the spread of Islam since the 13th century AD through the Fakirs and Darbeshes with similar views as expressed in earlier Sahajiya philosophies. *(References 18 & 19)* The mystic 'Sadhaks' of both the faiths would, fundamentally, attach equal importance to music and dancing to its tune and rhythm for divine enlightenment. *(Reference 20)*

Lalon's Sufi Connection

Engaged in his secret path towards 'self-realisation', the 'Sadhak' 'Fakir' or 'Baul' is associated with a sober and secluded life in the reliable and modest concealment of the village, in contrast with the 'Gayak'

'Fakir' or 'Baul' who is an entertainer. Lalon was a 'Sadhak' 'Fakir'; he never introduced himself as a 'Baul'. He was a 'Soul'-searcher like a Sufi minstrel.

The Sufi philosophy talks about four stages of learning and meditation. The first is 'Shariyat'—which is a set of Islamic religious laws that govern aspects of day-to-day life for Muslims, in addition to religious rituals. The next stage is: 'Tariqut'—the Sufi doctrine or path of spiritual learning. The third one, 'Haqiqat' is a mystical path. And, the last one is: knowledge acquired through experience. *(References 21 & 22)*

The Sufis mostly believe in a strong SOUL as it brings a Sufi follower close to the DIVINE SOUL. The belief is strengthened by the spiritual training given by the perfect spiritual guide—the 'Murshid' (Arabic for 'teacher'). This eventually leads to the nearness to 'Allah'. Whoever recognises and is in close touch with his 'Self' undoubtedly recognises and comes close to 'Allah'.

Most interestingly, like the modern 'Triune' brain theory of Dr. Paul Maclean MD (1913-2007) where he clearly demarcated 3 (three) different levels or storeys in our cranial brain (the brain between our two ears) *(Reference 23)*, the Sufi philosophers had proposed a 2-storeyed SOUL. The lower level 'Soul' is crude—full of desires and vices, lacking in refinement; whereas the higher level 'Soul' is relatively pure and refined. The Sufi mystics, therefore, always endeavour to move to the higher 'Soul' level through a ritualistic self-purification process—just as much Fakir Lalon Shah had preached through his songs and oral teachings. Sufis are allowed to enjoy freedom and ease in marriage for the sake of granting their lower 'Souls' their worldly pleasures.

I'm making an attempt to establish the Lalon-Sufi connection through one of Lalon Shah's immortal songs: "*Khanchar bhitor achin pakhi*" (In English: '*The unknown bird inside the cage*'). Here 'cage' is the 'human body' and 'unknown bird' is the 'unfamiliar SOUL'.

The next line is: "*Kymne ashe jay*" (In English: "*How it comes and goes*"). My interpretation is based on my 'Soul Theory'. When someone dies, the 'Soul' leaves the body and starts wandering in the 'Akasa' (space) looking for a suitable womb in a woman's body which could be its home in its rebirth where it can comfortably and conveniently fulfil its past lives' unfulfilled desires. So, for the woman in whose womb the wandering 'Soul' enters, it is like an 'unknown bird'. When, after the term of pregnancy, the baby is born, its body becomes the 'Soul's cage. If the Soul is still too much attached to its previous birth's family and friends, during sleep sometimes it leaves the body and goes on 'astral travel' to the place and family which it had belonged to in its last birth.

Can the 'Soul' be caught and chained up? That is perhaps the question that bothers Lalon and he sings: "*Tare dhorte parle mono beri ditam pakhir pay*" (In English: "*If I could catch the bird, I would have tied up its delicate legs with a chain and not allow it to fly away from time to time*"). If, in its present birth, the 'Soul' is given enough 'unconditional love' (that is, bathed in the love-compassion-empathy-compassion-trust-bonding molecule 'Oxytocin') particularly by its mother, why should it wish to go out of the cage for its astral travel? Here, on a second thought, I feel that Lalon might also have been wondering if life could be prolonged so that one could have lived with the same 'Soul' for a long time. In fact, many of Lalon's rituals were meant for increasing longevity (like: retention of 'bij' or 'semen').

There are 8 (eight) main organs inside the body: the skull, the lungs, the heart, the stomach, the liver, the small intestine, the large intestine, and the gonads (testes/ovaries). There are 9 (nine) doors: 2 eyes, 2 ears, 2 nostrils, 1 mouth, 1 genital, and 1 anus. These in Lalon's song are: "*Aat kuthuri noy darja anta*" (In English: "*8 rooms and 9 doors which are shut*"). The main room (In Bengali: "*Sadar Kotha*") is the brain—but whatever the brain sees, hears, or feels are just reflections on our mind which is like a mirror (In Lalon's song: "*Ayna Mahal*"). The 'mirror' metaphor is a Sufi concept about which I have already talked to you in an earlier piece. However, all these are nothing but 'illusion' or 'maya', which Lalon wants us to realise. The truth lies in understanding the 'Soul'—in Sufi language, whether it is the 'lower level' or the 'higher level' soul, that 'drives' you. In terms of the 'Triune' brain theory, whether your Soul is operating largely from the 'hind', or the 'mid' or the 'fore'-brain.

If the Soul finds the body (the bird finds the cage) comfortable and convenient to continue living inside it, it is a very healthy and welcome situation, but if the cage (the body) is getting old, diseased and decrepit due to lack of proper care, then one day the cage will collapse all of a sudden and the Soul will have no choice but to leave the dead body; the bird will have no choice but to leave the broken cage which was made of green, unseasoned bamboo and start wandering in 'akasa' until it finds another suitable cage to enter into and make it its home.

I'll conclude with another interpretation. I'll make it very brief. The 'Unknown bird' is our 'pranik energy'—the life force which is the 'breath energy'. 'Breathing in and out' is the 'coming into and flying out of the cage—of the unknown bird'. Fakirs and Bauls are 'air-meditators'; they attach a lot of importance on 'Dam-er Khela'—the 'breathing game' in their sadhana.

How beautifully Lalon had explained a very deep philosophy through a metaphorical song!! *(References 24 and 25)*

References

[1] "Sufism"—*Britannica.*

[2] *Sufi Philosophy*—Wikipedia.

[3] *Altered state of consciousness*—Wikipedia.

[4] A.P. Garcia-Romeu; Charles T. Tart, 2013, *The Wiley-Blackwell Handbook of Transpersonal Psychology* (First ed.), Hoboken, New Jersey: John Wiley and Sons Ltd., pp 123-134.

[5] "Dizzy apes provide clues on human need for mind-altering experiences", *WARWICK News and Events,* Press Release, 14th March 2023.

[6] "Dizzy apes give clues on human drive for mind-altering experiences", *University of Birmingham,* 13th March 2023.

[7] "Gorillas love spinning—and enjoy being dizzy"—YouTube.

[8] Sade Agard, "Spinning apes offer insights into the origin of mood manipulation in humans", *Interesting Engineering,* 13th March 2023.

[9] "Dervish Dancing"—*Britannica.*

[10] "Spinning: What are the Health Benefits?" *Backroads.*

[11] Mu Qian, "Pulled by God: Sound and Altered State of Consciousness in the Halqa-Sohbat Ritual of Uyghur Sufis", *European Journal of*

Musicology, University Bern, Switzerland, Vol. 20, No. 1, 2021, pp. 173-195.

[12] 'The FLOW Zone' by Andrew Lawrence-King, *Altered States of Consciousness (ASC).*

[13] Shahram Shiva, "Rumi's Untold Story", *Rumi Network.*

[14] Elif Shafak, "Rumi: Seven Stages of the Ego" *awakin.org*

[15] "The Spiritualty of Music (According to Sufism)"—Video Talk by Filip Holm.

[16] "What is Sufi Music?" (The Sound of Islamic Mysticism)—Video Talk by "Let's Talk Religion".

[17] Hazrat Inayat Khan, *The Mysticism of Sound and Music*, Shambala, 2022.

[18] Premangshu Chakrabarty and Tushar Mandal, "Baul-Sufi Interface and Cultural Tourism: A Study in Northern Rarh of West Bengal, India, In: *"Practising Cultural Geographies"*, Springer Link, First On-line: 21st May 2022, pp. 467-484.

[19] Erum Hadi and Samrat Khan, "Baul-Fakiri: The Musical Art of Syncretic Living", *CCH Learning Together*. 5th June 2018.

[20] Sumit Paul, "Divine dancers, bauls and Sufis", *The Times of India, TOI Crest*, 7th January 2011.

[21] *Sufi Philosophy*—Wikipedia.

[22] *Influences of Sufism on Lalon Fakir*—Tanvir Mokammel.

[23] *Triune Brain*—Wikipedia.

[24] Md. Joynul Abedin, "Lalon. An Undervalued Philosopher" *daily sun*, 18th October 2019.

CHAPTER 10

The Essence of BaulOlogy
(*'Baul Rasa'*)

In order to understand the 'core', the 'essence' of Baul Philosophy (shall we say 'Baul Rasa'), let me try with the 'Trinity' concept of Hinduism, which is based on our own life on this planet. We are born (we are 'created')! We take all care to 'preserve' ourselves! Lastly, our life comes to an end (our tissues get 'destroyed'). So our life is a process of 'Creation', 'Preservation' and 'Destruction'—in Sanskrit, 'Shristi', 'Sthiti' and 'Laya'. The puranic Hindu sages had attributed these tasks to three different Gods. Thus, 'Lord Brahma' is responsible for 'Creation'; 'Lord Vishnu' for 'Preservation' and 'Lord Maheswara/ Shiva' for 'Destruction'.

[Mind you, the concept I'm in the midst of developing may not tally with what you know and you had in mind. Please remain open-minded. I'm not at all going into any disagreement or argumentation. I'm just presenting my own point of view.]

Those who denied the 'Vedic' thoughts and nurture, are known as 'vratya', according to hard-core Vedic philosophy. These people ('vratya') were the founders of the Baul School. In Bengal, the Baul School was developed by the co-ordination of 'Sufi' and 'Nath' Schools. The Buddhist 'Shunyabad' would also have also penetrated into Baul songs.

In Bengali:

> *"Eke Eke miliye gelo hate kichui roilo na.*
> *Guru tomar pathshala te anko sekha hol na"*

In English:

> (*"One merged in one—nothing remains in hand,*
> *O' Guru, I didn't learn arithmetic in your school."*) *(Reference 1)*

(This refers to Lord Maheswara's act of 'destruction'—'pralay')

In ancient Hindu society, those who have the wisdom ('gyan') of 'Brahma' (the cosmic energy—the universal energy around us) came to be known as 'Brahmins'. If you read about the history of the Bauls of Bengal, orthodox brahmins in the past could not stand the Bauls and their culture. The reason might have been (although I'm not sure—correct me if I'm wrong) because the Bauls did and still believe that whatever is there in the 'Brahmand' (the 'cosmos') exists in the 'Deha Bhanda' (the physical body container). As a biomedical scientist (not wearing my 'Brahmin' hat while I'm writing this) I'd say: the Bauls are right. There are trillions of stars in the galaxies of the 'Cosmos'. The human body has millions of cells (in the brain tissue alone—approx. 8,500 to 10,000 million cells) and trillions of infinitesimally tiny microbes on the surface and inside. The genes of the human cells constitute the 'Genome' and the genes of the microbes constitute the 'microbiome'. Together, they make the 'metagenome' in the 'Deha Bhanda'. Although the Bauls have never been 'Brahmins' (correct me if I'm wrong) but they certainly had no less Brahminical outlook.

Moreover, those Bauls who had composed baul songs, they were no less than Brahmins. Composition of poetry, lyrics stands for 'Creation'—that is Brahminical. Lalon Fakir, the King of the Bauls, alone had composed a few thousand songs. It isn't a matter of joke. He was the godson of Goddess 'Matangi'.

Who is Goddess 'Matangi'—do you have any idea? She certainly existed in the mind of prolific creative minds like that of Lalon's. 'Matangi' is one of the Tantric goddesses and one of the Hindu Divine Mothers. She is considered to be the Tantric form of Goddess Saraswati, the goddess of music and learning. She governs speech, knowledge and the arts.

This is the beauty and versatility of Hinduism. [I do not know whether Devdatta Pattanayak, who is the forerunner of puranic writing in English today will agree with me.] I refer to the 'Triguna' concept now. The three gunas: 'Sattva' (purity and nobility), 'Rajas' (energy, drive and action orientation), and 'Tamas' (inertia, lethargy, vices—'sada ripu') are present in different proportions in every individual—and in every god and goddess. In 'Matangi', the Tamasic propensities are present in greater proportions, followed by the action-centric 'Rajas'—which are typical in some songs of the Bauls of Bengal, dealing with conception, contraception and other rituals of 'Baul Sadhana'.

Basically, our body is made up of 'Pancha Bhoota'—five great elements of perceptible matter: Earth (Prithvi, Soil), Water (Varuna), Fire (Agni), Air (Vayu), and Ether (Akasa). The philosophy of the Baul community is to remain content with proper management of these 'Basics'. From this angle, some scholars say that the Baul School is related to the primitive Indian 'Lokayata' or 'Charvak' philosophy. 'Charvaka', also known as 'Lokayata', is an ancient school of Indian materialism. It holds direct perception, empiricism, and conditional inference as proper sources of knowledge. It accepts only the 'reality of the material world'. In other words, 'Charvakas' are those who are more concerned about the pleasures and happiness of the individual and the specific community to which he belongs—and not those of the society and the greater world.

The 'essence' of 'BaulOlogy' (or 'Baul Rasa') can be summarised with the help of 10 (ten) discoveries that I have made in course of my deep study of the rituals, practices and the philosophy of the Bauls and Fakirs of Bengal.

Discovery 1

The 'Love and Trust Molecule'

(In Bengali: *'Moner Manush'*

In English: *'The Man of My Heart'*)

Bauls represent an ancient culture—typical of the undivided Bengal—now, even after the partition and compulsive split-up, like the Bengali language, it is still a factor that unifies the two Bengals: West Bengal, India & Bangladesh. Although our Indian border guards do not allow the Bangladeshi cattle to graze on our land and eat Indian grass, they listen, with heart-felt interest, touching songs by Bangladeshi Bauls having their 'akharas' ('hermitages' and 'practice centres') in across-the-border villages.

'Baul' is a term derived from the Sanskrit 'Batul' which means 'crazy' (in Bengali 'khyepa' or 'pagol') as members of this sect do not identify themselves with any specific religious group, although you'll find people from Hindu, Muslim, Christian, and Sufi Fakir backgrounds have adopted a 'Baul' lifestyle. Most interestingly, these people do not subscribe to any religion, do not believe in the existence of any God as such, neither do they worship any god or goddess. They firmly believe in the most important role of our BODY (which they call 'Deha-Tattva'—may be translated as the 'Theory or the Doctrine of the Body') according to which the entire universe is there in the human body—it is like a multi-departmental power station or a huge chemical plant. This vibes very well with the concept of 'Human Engineering' *(Reference 5)* which I had pioneered as I embarked on my career to study and investigate into the functions of our body, brain, mind and soul from an engineering angle.

Most of the Bauls express their thoughts and ideas by singing melodious songs, the lyrics of which are written in a language which is neither bright and clear like daylight nor it is too dark and unclear like the night—it is called the 'sandhya bhasha' (the 'twilight language'). The reason is: their philosophy is so very unlike the common religious doctrines that their audience may not make any sense and figure out any meaning as to what they want to say. And, of course, not all singing Bauls do understand the 'Baul Philosophy'. They only sing out the melodies that they have picked up from their 'Gurus'.

The first lesson that I learnt by reading several authentic articles and watching video talks by scholars like Prof Shaktinath Jha, Prof Debaprasad Bandyopadhyay, Dr Atish Dasgupta and others and also by watching several Indian and foreign documentary films on Bauls is that they feel that the ultimate goal in life is to have, in my language: 'Sustained Happiness'.

You may recall that I classify 'Happiness', that we all strive for, into three (3) categories:

- *The first one is:* 'SMART Happiness' where some stimulus that you receive leads to a 'happy' response thereby releasing some happiness chemicals—which are 'neurotransmitters' like:

(i) 'Dopamine' (which is the 'reward molecule' that is released when we anticipate some ensuing or forthcoming happy experience as well as when we get or go through that experience); (ii) 'Serotonin' which is released when we 'feel good' and enjoy a balanced mood; (iii) 'Endorphin' which relieves us from stress and pain and is released when we indulge in games, sports, take some exercise, or perform some manual work; and, (iv) 'Melatonin' which is released from the 'Pineal Gland' ('PG') of our brain to make us restful and put us to sleep.

- *The second one is:* 'SHORT-LIVED' or 'SHORT Happiness' where the happy experience is not just 'temporary' or 'transient' as in the case of 'SMART Happiness' but the trace remains for a longer period and gets stored in the memory being retrievable or 'on call' whenever you wish to remember it and re-feel the happy experience.
- *The third and the final one is:* 'SUSTAINED Happiness' which provides you with a permanent or steady state of happiness which provides you with the power to remain happy even under most unfavourable circumstances. The easiest way to earn 'SUSTAINED Happiness' is by having relationship with someone whom you can trust, you can rely on—you know that the person will never go against you. There is a happiness chemical that is the basis for such well-bonded relationship—which is called 'Oxytocin' ('O'). 'O' used to be known to gynaecologists and obstetricians as 'O' injection is used to begin or improve contractions during labour. 'O' facilitates childbirth and also is used to reduce bleeding after childbirth. Dr Paul Zak, founder of 'Neuroeconomics' brought it out from the labour room and established it as the 'Trust Molecule' as it is produced in the mother when she nurses and breast-feeds the new-born baby. The lifelong strong bond between the mother and the child is based on the neuro-chemical 'O'. The male counterpart of 'O' is 'Vasopressin' ('V') which creates the bonding between the father and the child. Dr Zak researched extensively to find out that 'O' is responsible for 'empathy' that makes us connect to other people; it makes us 'moral'.

On 'morality', what Dr Zak says makes me proud of my alma mater. While working as a research scholar at the University of Glasgow,

Scotland, I used to pass by the stone statue of Sir Adam Smith daily. Smith was the professor of 'Moral Philosophy' at the University and in his treatise called 'The Theory of Moral Sentiments' he had hypothesized that we, humans, are moral creatures not because of a top-down but a bottom-up approach. Being social, we share the emotions of others. So, if I do something that makes you happy, I get the share of that joy. So, most of the time we tend to do such things, and when we do, we have transcended our 'ego'—we become egoless. Seventeen years later, the same great philosopher wrote another book—a little one called 'The Wealth of Nations'—the founding document of 'Economics', which highlighted the selfish facet of humanity which makes us traders—which always makes us expect a 'Return on Investment' ('ROI') of the time, energy and effort that we invest. The language of 'Economics' is based on 'money'—the treasury. In the Baul culture, such a language is forbidden.

The king amongst the wandering minstrels, Late Lalon Fakir's concept of 'Moner Manush' (the 'Man of My Heart') is based on the 'Mutual Trust' principle. A mutually trustful well-bonded long-term relationship gives you 'SUSTAINED Happiness' and a Baul is always on the lookout for such relationships which is 'pure' which is 'without any expectation'—its essence is unconditional love.

Such a person is none else than God because all human relationships have 'self' in it—those are far from selfless and unconditional. Ever since there has been the advent of trading, man has lost his purity. He has become the 'Economic Man'. He is no longer 'Homo Sapiens'. He is an out-and-out 'Homo Economicus'. So, the Baul is constantly looking for a person who will not set the relationship on any 'trading'—any 'give-and-take' condition.

Discovery 2

The Soul Theory

(Song in Bengali: *'Achin Pakhi'*

In English: *'The Unknown Bird'*)

The context here is Fakir Lalon Shah's famous song: (In Bengali: "*Khanchar bhetor achin pakhi*") (In English: "*The unknown bird inside the cage*").

My perception of 'Human Resource' ('HR') is a combination of four constituents—body, brain, mind and soul. 'Body' and 'brain' are tissues—the characteristics of which are stored in 'genes' inherited from the parents and the family ancestors. 'Mind' consists of the neural networks—brain circuits, which are formed as a result of the genes' interactions with the environment. The more exposure an individual has, the wider would be his (no gender bias) 'mind'. That is how two identical twins become different having been nurtured in two different families or social environments.

'Body', 'Brain' and 'Mind' constitute the '*Khancha*' or '*Cage*'. 'Soul' which is a stranger is the '*Achin Pakhi*'—'*The Unknown Bird*'.

'Soul' is invisible and indestructible. A dying person's soul leaves the body wandering in the space looking for an opportunity to get into a womb, to be born into a family environment where it can get its unfulfilled desires fulfilled or complete its incomplete assignments which could not be finished in its earlier mortal lives. Although a controversy exists, we can take it that the soul enters the 'Pineal Gland' ('PG'—which is the only unpaired endocrinal gland in human biology) of the foetus on the 49th day—just 7 weeks after conception. The interaction of the 'Soul' nested inside the womb begins right away through sound waves generated inside as well as outside the womb as the foetus's listening power is the first and earliest sensory power to develop. There are 'unstruck sounds' ('Anahat Naad') produced inside the womb by way of the mother's heart beats, sounds of blood circulation, respiration and peristaltic movements. There are also 'struck sounds' ('Ahat Naad') generated outside the womb from different sources including the speaking voices of the care-givers—primarily of the mother.

Up to 2 years after birth, the baby is asleep most of the time, its brain being in the 'Delta' wave state: 0+ to 4 Hz is the frequency, spending least amount of the costly biological energy as the bulk of the energy is dedicated to the baby's growth and development. At times, the sleeping baby may move its tiny body and soft limbs which would mean that the brain has shifted to the 'Theta' wave state, for which the frequency range is 4 to 7 Hz. During these two brain states, especially 'Delta', the 'Soul' of the baby may leave the physical body and start wandering around to get familiar with the environment. It may also travel to its past life locations if it has strong emotional ties still.

Later in life, in the case of a young adult or even an elderly, during deep sleep when the brain has 'Delta' wave, the Soul may leave the body and go for astral travel. The wandering Soul can see the 'live' body lying below with the life force being supplied by the 'prana'—the biological energy is stored in each cell in the form of 'Adenosine Triphosphate' ('ATP'). 'Prana' is different from the 'Soul' which is related to the 'Cosmic' energy.

Lalon, in his popular song, is talking about an unknown bird inside the cage. Lalon's cage is the human body and his *'Achin Pakhi'* is the unknown soul which has come from outside. Lalon is wondering how and why the bird comes and goes. In reality, the Soul leaves the living body for astral travel. It happens if the Soul is emotionally attached to the contacts and contexts of its past life and becomes restless residing in its present body. It leaves when the soul-owner is asleep with all its outlets shut. These outlets are: 2 eyes, 2 ears, 2 nostrils, 1 mouth, 1 genital, and 1 anus: total 9. Like a mirror, the Soul can see the reflection of the Soul-owner deep asleep down below. It happens when there is Soul-Womb Misfit: the Soul did not find the Womb where it was nested, to be a zone of comfort and convenience. In Lalon's language, the cage is not solid and stable. It is made of unseasoned bamboo. It is too flimsy to break down and collapse with a little force or impact. To sum up what Lalon wants to say in this song is that most people's souls are not happy in their present life's circumstances. In my opinion, the root cause is because they have not been able to discover their TRUE PASSION which represents their Souls' natural vibrations.

DMT (the 'Spirit Molecule') researchers believe that while the soul leaves the body at the time of death as well as when a baby is being delivered normally, DMT gets released from the Pineal Gland and previous lives' memories get erased. If that happens, the dying man sees flashes of white light; what the newly born sees, we can't say. The aborigines of the Amazon Valley drink brewed Ayahuasca leaves to get their past memory erased. *(References 19 & 20)*

Discovery 3

The Cosmic Energy Domain
(Song in Bengali: *'Arshi Nagar';*
In English: *'The City of Mirrors'*)

(*Note:* I have already analysed & interpreted this poem under the Chapter 4 on the 'Aura of Lalon' under the sub-title of 'Mystic Lalon: The Mysterious Songwriter'. Please get to know my additional insightful thoughts in the present piece. Some of Lalon's songs can be most meaningfully explained in different ways, he was such an amazing intellectual!)

The great Lalon Fakir was at the height of his metaphysical creativity when the image of *'Arshi Nagar'* flashed on his mind's screen. Sigmund Freud (1856-1939), the founding father of 'Psycho-therapy'—an essential adjunct to Neuro-psychiatric medical treatment, had developed the concept of a three-level mind—the 'Id' (the creaturely basic instincts), the 'Super Ego' (the societal value system of 'good' & 'evil', 'Do's' & 'Don'ts', 'virtue' and 'sin'—totally man-made) and the 'Ego' (the mediator between the two, the individual's own decision-maker, own guide—as to which path has to be chosen).

Lalon has gone beyond the societal 'Super Ego'. His '*City of Mirrors*' is the cosmic energy domain (where the common man believes God exists). That energy is PURE, uncontaminated—it can catch the reflections of all the activities of the inhabitants of the Planet Earth—both good and bad, both virtuous and sinful, like a mirrored surface.

The goal of the SOUL of every spiritually inclined person is to get merged with that pure cosmic energy at the moment of death, but that wish does not get fulfilled because between the house where Lalon lives and Arshi Nagar—his neighbourhood, there is a huge expanse of water, almost like an ocean, the shores of which one cannot see. This ocean is the domain of all our negative emotions and carnal desires—the six (6) vices: lust, anger, greed, attachment, infatuation and envy that are essential for fulfilment of, what I call, our 'Biological Objectives' ('BI'): 'Survival & Replication'. These six vices reside inside Freud's 'Id' and, in terms of Brain Science, in the 'Creaturely Brain'.

In order to explain what is 'Creaturely Brain', I've to refer to Professor MacLean's 'Triune Brain' ('TB') theory. 'TB' is a three-layered concept. The lowest part of our brain of which the 'Brain Stem' is a portion, is the 'hind brain' inherited from our reptilian and avian past. The 'mid brain' is the 'paleo-mammalian' heritage which all mammals have. The 'forebrain' is the more recent addition and is thus called 'neo-mammalian' or 'neo-cortex' which all higher order mammals have and happens to be the thickest in humans. When some stimulus is disliked by us, we respond immediately using the freeze (fear/anxiety) – fight (anger/aggression) – flight (escape) strategy which certainly is a 'creaturely' action, which is 'soul-destructive' behaviour. According to Lalon, living the usual life of a mortal human does not help us to reach the *'City of Mirrors'* as we do not have any boat to cross the vast expanse of water. He did perhaps lose sight of the presence of the 'Pre-Frontal Cortex' ('PFC') portion of our forebrain which has the 'Executive Control System'—that, if activated, can help us to restrain ourselves from soul-destructive behaviours.

As I've already mentioned in Chapter 4, we do find an analogy of Lalon's model in the 'Pancha Kosha' concept of Taittiriya Upanishad according to which the pure Soul which is a part of the cosmic energy is enveloped by five sheaths—the 'Annamaya Kosha' is the 'materialistic energy' sheath; the 'Pranamaya Kosha' the 'breath energy' sheath; the 'Monomaya Kosha'—the 'emotional energy' sheath; the 'Vijnanamaya Kosha' is the 'intellectual energy' sheath; and, lastly, the 'Anandamaya Kosha' which is the 'bliss energy sheath'. These five layers constitute Lalon's vast expanse of water between his house and *Arshi Nagar*. His *Arshi Nagar* is beyond 'Anandamaya Kosha'—the cosmic energy ocean.

Why Lalon's ultimate goal is beyond the 'Anandamaya Kosha', let me explain to you. You can get access to the 'Anandamaya Kosha' and earn the 'Bliss Molecule' 'Anandamide' (AEA) which is an endocannabinoid (you're already aware that ganja, hemp, cannabis, marijuana are phyto-cannabinoids which one can mobilise from external sources) by pursuing tasks related to your 'True Passion' which helps to get into the 'Flow Brain State' ('FBS').

You can also have access to the 'Anandamaya Kosha' through the devotional route or 'Bhakti Yoga'. Let me give you an example by quoting from 'Sri Sri Krishna Lila Prasanga':

> *"Be it the name of Lord Hari, or his handsomeness or shining qualities, sprightly personality or softness, meditating on or singing 'kirtans' on his various role plays—all smack absolute purity. He is the destroyer of all the ill-wishers of his devotees, and the protector of his ardent followers. He resides in the core of their hearts. As a matter of fact, he cannot stay without his devotees and followers. By residing inside their souls, he slowly and gradually helps them to get rid of all the worldly desires and hankerings. In course of time, they lose their identities and get merged into the spirit of Lord Hari. They get into the relationship with him of unconditional devotion. Their minds & souls start brimming with 'Hari'." (Reference 21)* This is the 'FLOW Brain State' ('FBS') that releases 'Anandamide' ('AEA') in the body & brain.

Lalon's goal is to earn the 'Spirit Molecule' ('Di-MethylTetramine'—'DMT') which helps you to forget your past memories of your birth as a human and makes your 'Soul' ('Jivatma') move upward to be united with the 'Paramatma'—the 'Universal Self'. *(References 22 & 23)*

Discovery 4

The Mystery of Procreation

(Song in Bengali: *"Chander Gaye Chand Legeche"*;

In English: *"One moon is in touch with another"*)

Songwriter Bauls use 'metaphors' in their lyrics and Lalon Fakir was the 'King of Metaphors'. As a matter of fact, in reality, because Bauls have their own language and styles of expression, for common people their songs remain good to listen to but difficult to decipher, hard to understand. The listener remains half-satisfied. The song has only partial impact on listeners, in general. But there is a common belief that the most deeply knowledgeable ones in the Baul community, do not want ordinary people to understand their philosophy—what they want to say. They want their concepts and principles to remain restricted to the members of their own sect, who have dedicated their lives to the practice and promotion of the Baul culture.

Let me expand a little. 'Primary Consciousness' is a common phenomenon. It can be defined as simple awareness that includes perception of the environmental happenings and also of emotions (like anger, fear, pleasure and pain) which are natural responses to stimuli. As such, it is ascribed to animals. It is 'Pre-human' consciousness related to the domains of the Reptilian and Paleo-mammalian (Hind & Mid Brains) portions of the brain.

By contrast, 'Secondary Consciousness', depends on and includes such features as self-reflection, awareness and understanding of one's own thought process, abstract thinking, and volition. The term was coined by Physiology/Medicine Nobel Prize-winning American biologist Gerald Edelman (1929-2014). *(Reference 24)*

The source of this type of consciousness is the 'Neo-mammalian Brain' or 'Neo-cortex'—but, let me tell you, all humans don't have it in equal degree or strength—it is a faculty that only those whose consciousness is between the 'Human' and 'Post-human' levels, they have.

There is also a 'Proto-consciousness' theory which proposes a primordial state of brain organisation that is the building block of consciousness. The propounding scientist is J. Allan Hobson. *(Reference 25)* The role of sleep and dreaming in maintaining emotional stability represents a very tangible and practical example of 'proto-consciousness' as a mental state that supports the proper functioning of normal waking consciousness. According to Hobson, brain activation in sleep allows the development and maintenance of circuits necessary for higher brain functions, including consciousness.

Listeners of Baul songs possess 'Primary Consciousness'. Only an exceptional few may nurture 'Secondary Consciousness'. Same applies to the Baul songwriters and singers also.

To my mind, Fakir Lalon Shah was a very rare exception. He was most active in all the states of consciousness—'primary', 'secondary' and 'proto' to be able to compose such beautiful songs with unparalleled metaphors and unique imagery.

Let us discuss one of his most popular songs '*Chander gaye chand legeche*" from the perspective of Lalon's tri-dimensional consciousness. *(Reference 26)* I have already analysed it once at a different place in Chapter 4 ("The Aura of Lalon"—subtitled "Lalon's Taoist Link"), but here I am bringing it up again in a different context

In the first line of this song: "*Chander gaye chand legeche*", (In English: "*One moon is in touch with another moon*"), Lalon is metaphorically talking about the emergence of erotic emotions at the onset of puberty. "Chand" or "Moon" represents Bharata Muni's erotic "Sringara" Rasa—the emotion that is typical of attraction towards the opposite sex. *(Reference 27)*

Lalon is talking about how a 'sperm' (one emotion-laden planet moon) gets attached to another emotion-laden moon the female 'egg' or 'ovum'—which is the beginning of the creation of a life. Lalon's expression of the emotional state when one steps into post-adolescence youth is really unique.

Lalon then continues: (In Bengali: "*Jhi er pete Ma yer janmo*") (In English: "*The mother is born in the womb of the daughter*". Lalon's '*Jhi*' or '*daughter*' means the 'female body' where the male 'semen' is planted. The 'semen' contains the 'sperm'—carrying the seed of a new life to be fertilised after being fused to an ovum—thus Lalon compares the fertilised egg as the 'mother'. In a nutshell, 'sperms' and 'ova' have started getting generated in the post-adolescence youthful body of the male/female which now has the power to 'procreate'. This is undoubtedly a great power for a common man or a woman.

Thereafter, Lalon says: (In Bengali: "*Choy masher ek kanya chilo, noy mashe tar garbho holo*") (In English: "*There was a daughter of six months age who became pregnant at the end of nine months*"). The meaning would be like this. Although a man and a woman can mate and utilise the power to procreate, the foetus inside the woman's womb carries both good and bad genes—which will lead to virtuous and sinful activities both. A daughter 6 (six)-month old is his way of talking about the 6 (six) vices or bad qualities: lust, anger, greed, infatuation, attachment or obsession, and envy.

Lalon continues: (In Bengali: *"Abar egaro mashe tin ti santan, kon ta korbe fakiri?"*) (In English: "*Again, in eleven months there come three offsprings, which one will become a 'Fakir'?*"

Having 3 (three) kids in 11 (eleven) months is an allegory. We have 9 (nine) outlets in our body: 2 eyes, 2 ears, 2 nostrils, 1 mouth, 1 genital and 1 anus. At the onset of puberty, the mouth and the genitals have twin functions—ready for erotic love. So, 9 + 2, we get 11. Who are Lalon's 3 (three) kids? One is the male semen, another is the female secretion during sexual arousal, and the third is 'honey'. What Lalon means by 'honey' I've no idea, but if I look at it from a neuro-scientific angle, it is 'Dopamine' ('D')—the reward molecule, which provides temporary, transient—in my language, 'SMART Happiness' and 'SHORT-LIVED' or 'SHORT Happiness'.

When the human body is in full bloom, three paths or three directions open up in front of the young person. He (no gender bias) has to choose one amongst these. A typical male who has 'semen' in his possession and a typical female who has the vaginal fluid in her possession would naturally like to go for earning the 'reward molecule' 'D' by having a live-in relationship or by setting up a family and going for 'procreation' which is the goal of majority belonging, moving upward in the five-level 'Pancha Kosha' model to the third from the bottom 'Monomaya Kosha' level. *(Reference 28)* The third path is the path of the mendicant—the life of a 'Fakir' where you have laid before you the path for 'SUSTAINED Happiness' which comes to you as you sing songs—not for 'entertainment' of others, but for 'enlightenment' of yourself.

Lalon's song's next line goes like this: (In Bengali: "*Ghar ache, tar duar nai, lok ache tar bakya nai go, Abar ke ba Tahar ahar jogay, Ke dyay sandhyabati?*") (In English: "*There is a room which has no doors, there is someone there but speechless, who is feeding that person and who is praying for him in the evening by lighting a lamp?*")

Inside the womb, the foetus has a room to stay, but the room has no doors. So, the foetus cannot come out. It gets its nutrition and manages its excretion entirely through the mother via the umbilical cord that has to be severed at the time of taking the baby out of the womb.

'Male' power is in the penis—the 'phallus'. Losing semen too frequently to earn the reward molecule 'D' (leading to 'Smart' or 'Short Happiness' again & again) means losing power leading to powerlessness. When you stop losing your semen by finding your 'True Passion' which allows you to enter the 'FLOW Brain State' ('FBS'), you may get acquainted with 'Anandamide'—the 'Bliss Molecule' and 'DMT: Di-Methyl Tryptamine'—the 'Spirit Molecule'—the first one released from your brain's pituitary glands and the second one from your brain's unpaired pineal gland. These two are earned in addition to the 'reward molecule' 'Dopamine' ('D'). In Lalon's terms, you will experience three flows—red, white and black, if you maintain a celibate life.

Although physical death comes to common man only once in materialistic worldly life, he encounters death every moment due to loss of the seed ('semen') at every ejaculation on being excited at the touch of the opposite sex. In Lalon's metaphorical language: (In Bengali: "*Chele more Ma ke chule go!*") (In English: *"The son dies on touching the mother!"*). Lalon concludes by saying: (In Bengali: *"Ei tin kathar artha noile tar hobe na fakiri!"*) (In English: *"What I want to convey through my this message is that if it happens, then he cannot become a celibate 'Fakir'"*).

The lyric of the song and the deeply insightful philosophy it conveys are unparalleled!!

Discovery 5

Guru-Shishya Relations
(Song in Bengali: *"Bhakta amar prana-sakha"*;
In English: *"My devotee is my life's companion"*)

I just happened to bump into a beautiful Baul verse describing the ideal Guru-shishya (Mentor-mentee) relations. I am tempted to share it with you below: *(Reference 29)*

"My devotee, my disciple, my mentee—is my life's companion
A true devotee is most welcome in the temple of my heart
I've kept a golden seat for him with great care!!

If my mentee offers me food, only then I will eat
otherwise I will remain without any, steadfastly,

My devotee is my life's companion, I'm his guide,
Wherever he takes me I go to bless him,
I become the guard at his doorstep!!

I become a thief along with my disciple.
Together we steal and burgle into the hall of colours,
And we're caught and put into hell
Again, on release, I stay with him without any anger in my heart!!

The feet of the devotee and the head of the Guru are tied in the same string,
Birth is useless if the beginning and the end are not known.
My disciple is my regular companion…we walk on the same path all the time,
where can I go leaving him alone!!

The one who gets into an emotional outburst at my name,
and ties me up in the garland of love,
I get caught in his net like the robin bird gets caught
in the net of the bird-catching fowler.
And, then, whatever he wants me to utter, I utter,
Bhugol says that these are all the things I can do for him –
my devotee, my disciple, my mentee—my life's companion!!

[This song is written by 'Bhugol Baul' and is to be sung in the 'Prabarta Desh' ('Devotion Phase') of Baul Sadhana; the subject is 'Guru-Shishya' Parampara or 'Mentor-Mentee' Relations]

Why it is a special discovery for me because the normal practice in the Guru-Shishya parampara is that the 'Shishya' surrenders to the 'Guru' totally. Here, the lyric shows just the opposite and it smells of a bonding between the 'Guru' and the 'Shishya' full of 'love'.

Helen Fisher, PhD, research professor of anthropology at Rutgers University, USA has conducted extensive pioneering research on the evolution, expression and chemistry of love. *(References 30 & 31)*

According to her, 5 (five) biochemicals are associated with the entire spectrum of 'Love', starting with erotic lustful love ('kam') and ending in well-bonded spiritual love ('prem').

'Dopamine' is the love chemical released in people who are novelty-seeking, risk-taking—they are very curious to know, so they welcome different types of love-related experiences. They are creative; being very open-minded, they love to experiment. The Sadhak Bauls who change their Sadhan Sangini partners quite often have very strongly active dopaminergic 'reward' circuitry in the brain.

'Serotonin' is the love chemical released in people who are conventional and, therefore, neither novelty-seekers nor change-oriented. They generally follow the social norms. They are cautious and harm avoidant. Bauls & Fakirs who are more performers rather than devotee sadhaks, they would come under this category. They go for marriage and procreation. They are not 'la-sarik' (against creating own progeny).

Lovers who are rich in the male sex hormone 'Testosterone' have a very strong sex drive. They practice competitive sex, and play 'who will do physical with whom first' game. They are bold & daring and strategically most intelligent.

The last lover group are strong in 2 (two) bio-chemicals—the female sex hormone 'Estrogen' and the empathy-understanding-trusting-bonded relationship-building neuro-transmitter 'Oxytocin'. Their goal is to cultivate long-term loving relationship not merely to earn a quick 'feel good' feeling. They are very imaginative and mentally flexible. They possess social and communication skills—both non-verbal and verbal.

An ideal 'lover' model would be 'Dopamine' combined with 'Estrogen-Oxytocin' that is what effective Baul Gurus counsel the Baul interns to develop—which they describe as 'Prem Rati'. However, the Baul verse which has been the focal point of discussion here represents the 'Estrogen-Oxytocin' model.

Discovery 6

The Doctrine of Divine Love

(Song in Bengali: *"Premer Mora Jole Dobe Na'*

In English: *"One Who Dies in Love Does Not*

Get Drowned in Water")

I was stunned as I bumped into a totally unusual Baul song written by an unknown songwriter which starts with: *'Premer mora jole dobe na'* (in English: *"Those who die in love never get drowned"*). What the poet had in mind, I cannot say as the poet is unknown. But, from the first line of the poem, my interpretation is: those—the couple who are in deep love, they never get drowned in a river or even in an ocean, their urge 'TO LIVE FOR LOVE' is so strong. This is what I would like to describe as 'Divine Love' (in Bengali: 'Aishik Prem'). Let us continue reading the verse to figure out what really the poet had in mind when he composed it. *(References 32 & 33)*

The song continues as: (I'm translating in English):

> *"And, who neither understands nor has the feeling of love—how love feels,*
>
> *Neither can you love him/her nor can he/she love you either!!!*
>
> *No no no no no, my friend!!*
>
> *Those who die in love, can never get drowned!!"*

Oh, I see! Now, the poet comes to the point in the next line:

> *"The clothes washing of the washerwoman Rami,*
>
> *And the daily fishing habit of Chandidas on the opposite bank of the watershed."*

During the 14th century, Chandidas was the son of a brahmin landlord in a remote village of Bengal, which is now in Bangladesh. He used to worship a very special goddess in a temple located by the side of the pond where every day Rami, an orphan girl from a low caste—who had lost her husband, used to come to wash a pile of clothes to earn her livelihood. Chandidas, the young brahmin priest used to get distracted. He would give up his worship of the goddess in the temple, come out and sit on the opposite bank facing Rami, with a fishing rod posing as if he was serious about his fishing activity. His real intention was to attract the attention of Rami, who was immaculately beautiful. *(References 34 & 35)*

> *"Alas! He kept up his daily habit of acting out the fisherman role for twelve long years—totally in vain!*
>
> *Not even once, he could catch a single fish as his attention was totally on*
>
> *Rami to whom he was too much attracted!!*
>
> *After twelve long years of waiting, suddenly one day he could hear*
>
> *Rami speak: "Have you caught any fish?"*
>
> *Chandidas was thrilled. At last his dream had become reality—Rami had spoken to him very softly & sweetly.*
>
> *This is how the love story of Rami & Chandidas began!*
>
> *The rest is history!!"*

But the society was not in favour of the love between a high caste young man and a low caste orphan widow. The whole village was after them so much that they had to leave their original village and migrate to a village in Bankura, which is in West Bengal, India!!

The Baul poet is full of acclaim for the couple and says:

> *"Chandidas & Rajakini*
>
> *Oh, my mind!*
>
> *Are the symbol of 'Divine Love'*
>
> *They drown together, deeply in love with each other,*
>
> *How many lover couples can do that—remain deeply in love with each other till the end of life!*
>
> *Those who die in love never get drowned,*
>
> *No no no no……*
>
> *Those who die in love never get drowned!!"*

Lesson for us is: Before you fall in love, ensure whether your target partner can provide a lifelong divine love partnership. And, once you have chosen such a partner, try your best to develop 'PURE LOVE' which is free from the 'Six Enemies of the Mind' ('Sadripus'). *(References 36 & 37)*

Discovery 7

The Fun & Mystery of the Human Body

(Song: In Bengali: *"Ki maja ei manab dehete!";*

In English: *"What a fun in this human body!"*)

I've had the opportunity to listen to and study deeply a number of Baul songs on the 'Doctrine of the Body' (in Bengali: 'Deha Tattva') by Fakir Lalon Shah and a few more minstrel songwriters from West Bengal, India and Bangladesh. But one song by deceased (2023) Sadhan Das Bairagya was brought to my notice by a very talented young Baul singer Naru Gopal who is an ardent follower and admirer of mine. Naru Gopal was musically trained by Sadhan's younger brother Baul Bhajan Das Bairagya.

The song goes like this: *(Reference 38)*

"Oh, my dear friend!

Please tell me what is the fun, what is the mystery in this human body.

Oh, Kheypa! One who has got to know about the mystery of the human body…

He has understood its essential features and thus can keep it under control and does not allow the body overpower his mind!!

Oh! Tell me what is the fun, what is the mystery in this human body."

[Very simple, beautiful message! One or more of our 'Six Enemies of the Mind'—the 'Sadripus' are always ready to attack the body with negative vibrations. So, one who is aware of such inner conduct & behaviour of the body, can keep a vigil and try to keep the body unaffected and uninfluenced. *(Reference 39)*]

"(Nitai Gour, say Hari Bol, Hari Bol; chant the name of Lord Hari!)

This body is the all time Vrindaban

In this permanent abode, I keep my most precious 'Krishnadhan' (Lord Krishna),

He has no old age, no disease, no death... he always stays in joy and happiness."

[The poet is possibly talking about the indestructible 'Soul' which is nothing but 'energy' which can never be created nor does it get destroyed.]

"Oh, Kheypa! How mysterious is the human body!

There are five 'arrows' in the human body!"

[The five 'arrows' represents our five senses, *(Reference 40)* but here the songwriter means 'special powers'.]

"These special powers are 'Madan'—the God who represents 'desire'" (Reference 41)

['Madan Mohan'—one who can influence 'Madan' is another name for Lord Krishna.]

'Sanmohan'—the power to hypnotise,

'Unmadon'—the power to get mad and eccentric in love,

'Soshan'—the power to extract the essence and become love-sick; and, 'Sthamvan'—the power to restrain, control and destroy any desire. (Reference 42)

This body is made of earth, water, air, fire, and space; it is being run by 'Triguna'—Satta, Rajas and Tamas! *(Reference 43)*

"Fakir Sadhan, you've not understood, you've not realised how powerful your body is!

Your mental haze has not been removed as it is filled with 'scriptures' which are not real but theoretical!

The real thing is your body!

Again Ma Gosain says this body is being run only by air!!

What fun is there in the human body; how beautiful, how mysterious is this abode of God!!"

Discovery 8

Calculate Profits, Not Losses
(Song in Bengali: *"Manushta More Gele Kannakati"*;
In English: *"Crying on a Dear's Death"*)

Listening to a Baul song by the Bengali mystic saint Bhaba Pagla (on whom the European scholar Carola Erika Lorea has done extensive research). *(References 44-47)* I was reminded of the glorious time I had in the past (1983-2018) conducting workshops in different corners of India and its neighbourhood. The workshops were meant for the corporate crowd including the very top management.

One very unusual item for the participants was a senior executive talking about the 'Achievements' of her/his team members—and not of 'Failures' and 'Shortcomings' as is prevalent in the Indian culture. Only when someone is retiring or leaving the organisation, the big boss talks all good things about her/him, not otherwise in day-to-day co-ordination as well as performance appraisal meetings. One Managing Director of a Tata Group company (who was later picked up by the Mahindra & Mahindra Group to adorn a 'key' chair) another Managing Director of a Birla Group Company (who was later picked up by the Goenkas & Agarwals of Emamis—the consumer conglomerate) were taken by utter surprise at my 'reverse' (in Bengali: 'ulta' like the Bauls & Fakirs practice in their rituals) approach and when they started implementing it in practice, their profits started multiplying and losses, if any, were eradicated.

Even in the day-to-day parenting of our kids, we only criticise them instead of appreciating their achievements. As a consequence, we create in our families, a culture of criticism. On top of this, the kids face criticism from their teachers right from an early age—so we groom youngsters as 'losers' and not as 'winners'. (Please read my two books: *References 48 & 49*)

To quote the first stanza of Bhaba Pagla's song (no gender bias) (slightly modified by me from the original Bengali verse):

"We shed tears—some less some more
when someone leaves this planet,

We talk about our losses—why would we miss that person!

When he was alive & active amongst us,

We failed to realise his value—how were we gaining from him

How he was helping us to gain profits—both tangible and intangible

Instead, we were criticising him for his failures, lapses
and shortcomings making him lose his motivation!"

When you criticise somebody losing sight of his plus points, you are provoking the person to get into the 'freeze/fight/or flight' mode and, if it becomes a regular affair then you are responsible for any disease that he contracts—as your putting the person's 100 trillion body microbes under threat who will be failing in their duty to produce positive digestive enzymes and three neuro-transmitters—'Dopamine', 'Serotonin' and 'GABA' which are produced to a large extent in the 'Enteric Nervous System' ('ENS'). *(Reference 50)*

In another stanza of his song, Bhaba Pagla gets philosophical and expresses his ideas allegorically:

"You and I are nothing more than oven ashes which are easily flown away when the wind blows,

We are here today, and tomorrow we may be gone,

Living inside a rotten cage, by talking so big,

By wishing to reach the moon,

We spread bad odour all around us!"

The mystic poet is now talking about our temporary existence here, in this planet. He is talking about our mortal life. Since we are here only for a few decades, what is the use of out growing a BIG EGO.

In this context, what I feel is this: If you talk about your own 'Achievements', that is the sign that you're blowing your own trumpet, you're inflicting your own 'Big Ego' on others making them feel small and inferior. That is a sign of bad taste, wrong culture. Let others talk about your 'Achievements'—you remain humble and cool. Perhaps, this is the message the mystic Baul madman Bhaba wanted to convey through this beautiful song. *(Reference 51)*

Discovery 9

Desire to be 'Human'

(Song in Bengali: *"Manush hobi bole"*

In English: *"If you want to be 'Human'"*)

I trust you'd recall that I had, from the point of evolution, classified 'Homo Sapiens' into three categories: 'Pre-human', 'Human' and 'Post-human'. 'Pre-humans' are not after social bonding. Their forebrain—cerebral cortex/neo-cortex is not well-developed. Their goal is purely biological: survival and replication. Their hunger is for the neuro-transmitter 'Dopamine' which is fulfilled through 'kam-rati' or 'lustful sex'. 'Humans' go for social bonding and bonded relationships. The temporal lobes of their forebrain are well-developed and their hunger is for 'Oxytocin'—the love-understanding-empathy-bonding molecule. 'Post-humans' have exploratory and investigative nature—they would have spiritual inclinations. Their hunger is for 'Anandamide'—the 'Bliss Molecule' and, at the highest level for 'Di-Methyl Tetramine' ('DMT')—the 'Spirit Molecule'. At the initial stage, 'Post-humans' may be socially attached yet detached.

Amal Gosain's Baul song says:

(In Bengali: *"Manush hobi bole re mon dhoro manushe re"*)

(In English: *"If you want to be 'human', get hold of a 'man'!"*)

[Otherwise, 'pre-humans' and 'post-humans' would not be in a position to satisfy your 'human' needs—that is need for the neuro-chemical 'Oxytocin'—the need for 'love' (in Bengali: 'prem')].

The song continues:

(In Bengali: *"Ei manush i sei manush naro roop dhore,*
Manush hobi bole re mon dhoro manushere!")

(In English: *"It is the 'humans' only who take the 'human' form,*
So, if you want to be 'human' get hold of someone who is also 'human'!!")

(In Bengali: *"Lata jemon brikkha ghire take joriye thake thore thore,*
Temni tor deha ghire sei manush biraj kore!")

(In English: *"Just like a creeper grows around the solid trunk of a tree,*
In a similar fashion, the 'human' exists all around your body—outside & inside!!")

(The songwriter is indirectly hinting at the invisible vibrations coming out of your body—your 'aura'. The 'aura' of a 'pre-human', a 'human', and a 'post-human' are all different from each other.)

Now, the songwriter is talking about the 'soul' or 'atman'.

He says:

(In Bengali: *"Vede ache jar katha, sei ache tor hride gantha,*
Abar janle tare jay re bytha chirokaler tore!")

(In English: *"What is mentioned in the Vedas, the same thing is impregnated in your heart,*
If you come to know him then all your pains will disappear for good!")

According to modern research, the heart has 'neurons' or brain cells and it radiates electro-magnetic waves which provides positive attraction to other humans. However, my perception is that the poet is talking about the love molecule 'Oxytocin' that acts as an emotional balm.

The poet continues:

(In Bengali: *"Amal koy manush jadi hobi re mon,*
tabe Guru pade karo mastak mundon,
Abar Guru I je sei amulya dhon...milay sei manushere!
Manush jadi hobi re mon dhoro manushere!")

(In English: *"Amal says if you want to be 'human', get a Guru and become his disciple*
Guru is the precious resource who can get a proper 'human' for you!
If you want to be 'human', get a 'True Man'")

(A 'True Man' is one who can feed you with 'Oxytocin')

[This piece is based on the song "Manush hobi bolere mon" sung by Baul Naru Gopal, posted on YouTube].

Discovery 10

True Passion

(Song in Bengali: *"Preme te pagol hoyechi";*

In English: *"I've become mad in love"*)

The nature of the human mind is 'restless'. Possessing an unfocused, restless mind was essential for the 'pre-humans' in the pre-historic days to keep track of the emerging 'opportunities' and 'threats'. You can tame your restless 'human' mind today and get rich dividends by getting engaged in tasks related to your 'True Passion'. Such 'Task Engagement Mode' makes your brain totally focused and minimise the expenditure of its costly energy.

'True Passion' is what puts your brain in the 'Flow Brain State' ('FBS') when you lose like a madman ('kheypa' or 'eccentric'), the track of time, place, space, the people around you, and self (your 'Selfish Ego'). *(References 52 & 53)* The Baul song that is the focal point here talks about that kind of a circumstance. 'True Passion' takes place when there is a 3-D convergence: convergence between your 'Dream', 'Drive' and the chosen 'Domain'. *(Reference 54)*

The poet's 'Dream' has been to get drowned in love, the source of 'Drive' is the 'Anandamaya Kosha'—the last sheath enveloping the 'Soul' or the 'Jivatma'—according to the 'Pancha Kosha' model of the Taittiriya Upanishad. *(References 55 & 56)* The 'Domain' that he has chosen is the Baulsphere/Fakirsphere.

The song goes like this:

(In Bengali: *"Ami lajja ghrinar matha kheye ei pathe tei nemechi,*

Premete pagol hoyechi...premete baul hoyechi...premete fakir hoyechi!")

(In English: *"I've forsaken my feeling of embarrassment, shame and disgust to choose this path!*

I've become mad in love...

Love has made me a Baul

Love has made me a Fakir!!!")

'True Passion' means you're in LOVE ('prem' in Bengali) with the subject that you have chosen to delve deep into. The poet says that he has chosen the domain of Bauls & Fakirs out of pure love. He is driven by the 'bliss' that he will earn from such activities. That has attracted him.

The song continues:

(In Bengali: *"Amar nai ko kono jat-kul-man, Ami noy ko Hindu noy Musalman,*
Ami noy ko Jaino, noy ko Christian...Ami nijei jani na to ami ki!")

(In English: *"I've no community, caste or clan,*
I'm not a Hindu nor a Muslim,
I'm neither a Jain nor a Christian,
I myself do not know what I am!!)

(In Bengali: *"Amay nanan loke nanan bole... Ogo jar ja khushi, se tai bole,*
Amar kan thaki teo hoi go kala, mukh thaki teo boba hoyechi...!")

(In English: *"Different people call me by different names,*
Whatever they feel like, they address me that way,
Although I have ears I turn deaf,
Although I've a mouth and voice, I turn dumb.")

The singer is so engrossed in love with it that he is least concerned about his community, caste, clan and religion. Different people call him by different names but he is bothered in the least, he is so focused.

The last stanza of the song says:

(In Bengali:
"Ami premer ghorei basat kori...Ogo, prem sagarei bhasai tori,
Amar Ma Gosain koy binoy kori...Ami ei manusher premei mojechi!")

(In English: *"I live in the apartment of love,*
I sail my boat in the ocean of love,
My lady partner says most humbly,

'I'm deeply in love with this person only......
(who is 'human' and not 'pre-human'!)"

The portion inside brackets is my addition.

My female partner says with a lot of humility that she is deeply in love with me only, because in my company only she can earn the 'love molecule'—'Oxytocin'!

(I've been introduced to this song by my Baul friend & follower—Naru Gopal) *(Reference 57)*

References

[1] Saheb Khandare, "Baul Songs of Bengal", *academia.edu*; https://www.academia.edu

[2] "What is Cosmic Energy?"—*Quora.*

[3] *Pancha Bhoota*—Wikipedia.

[4] 'Lokayata/Carvaka—Indian Materialism'—*Internet Encyclopaedia of Philosophy (IEP).*

[5] Siddhartha Ganguli, *Human Engineering for Better Management.* Kolkata: Kwality Book Co, 1978.

[6] "Performing Arts: Shaktinath Jha on Baul and Fakir traditions of Bengal": Video on YouTube.

[7] Atis Dasgupta, "The Bauls and Their Heretric Tradition", *Social Scientist*, Vol. 22, Nos. 5-6, May-June 1994.

[8] Debaprasad Bandyopadhyay, "Non-Linguistics of Silenceme: Lalon", 2009, Shaktinath Jha ed. *"Ochin Pakhi: Lalon Smarok Grontho"*, Vol. XX, Nadia, West Bengal, Lalon Mela Samiti, pp 16-24.

[9] Paul Zak, "Trust, morality—and oxytocin?" TED Global 2011.

[10] Paul Zak, "How to Bond with Anyone" YouTube.

[11] Paul Zak, "The Connection between Trust, Oxytocin & Group Flow", YouTube.

[12] Paul Zak, "How the Era of Remote Work Impacted Trust & Oxytocin", YouTube.

[13] Zach Bush MD, "A hug is the most powerful way to begin communication with another person", Facebook.

[14] Zach Bush MD, "If you do one thing today, let it be a hug. A big one. Oxytocin levels rise...", Facebook.

[15] "When Does the Soul Enter the Body?" Sadhguru, Video, YouTube, June 10, 2016.

[16] "UNLOCK the Creative LIGHT-FORCE Within"—Dr Zach Bush, Video, YouTube.

[17] "Cosmic Energy and Cosmic Consciousness" *COSMIC ENERGY, Soul Energy, God Is Love.*

[18] "What is the soul made out of? Is it a form of prana energy?" *QUORA.*

[19] Tom Rush and Adrienne Santos-Longhurst, "Everything You Need to Know about the Hallucinogenic Drug, DMT", *healthline*, 24th May 2023.

[20] Rick Strassman, "DMT—The Spirit Molecule: A Doctor's Revolutionary Research Into the Biology of Near-Death and Mystical Experiences", Rochester, Vermont: Park Street Press, 2000.

[21] "Sri Sri Krishna Lila Prasanga" (In Bengali edited by Dulal Acharya), Kolkata: Girija Library, 2021, pp. 11-12.

[22] Tom Rush and Adrienne Santos-Longhurst, "Everything You Need to Know about the Hallucinogenic Drug, DMT", *healthline*, 24th May 2023.

[23] Rick Strassman, "DMT—The Spirit Molecule: A Doctor's Revolutionary Research Into the Biology of Near-Death and Mystical Experiences", Rochester, Vermont: Park Street Press, 2000.

[24] Gerald Edelman & Giulio Tononi, "A Universe of Consciousness: How Matter Becomes Imagination", New York: Basic Books (Hachette Book Group), 2001.

[25] J. Allan Hobson, "REM sleep and dreaming: towards a theory of proto-consciousness", Nature Reviews Neuroscience, 2009, Vol. 10, pp. 803-813.

[26] "Chander gaye chand legeche"—Bengali Lyrics.

[27] "Sringara"—Wikipedia.

[28] "Pancha Kosha"—Vikaspedia.

[29] Shaktinath Jha, *Bastubadi Baul* (in Bengali), Kolkata: Dey's Publishing, Refurbished First Dey's Edition 2010, p. 558.

[30] Helen Fisher, *Why We Love: The Nature and Chemistry of Romantic Love*, New York: Holt Paperbacks, 2005.

[31] *Big think.com*, "The brain has 3 systems for mating…" says Biological Anthropologist Helen Fisher PhD.

[32] "Premer mora jole dobe na!"—Song by Bhajon Das Bairagya—YouTube.

[33] "Premer mora jole dobe na!"—Bengali Non-Film Hitz Vol. 4, Prahlad Brahmachari, You Tube.

[34] "Kothay Chilo Tader Bari—Chandidas o Rajakini r Amar Prem Kahini" (in Bengali), "Khulnar Khabar. YouTube.

[35] Md. Abu Naser Majnu, "Chandidas ar Rajakini r Itihas Janun" (in Bengali), *Eye News BD*, 6th January 2021.

[36] *Arishadbargas*—Wikipedia.

[37] Gaurav, "The Six Enemies of the Mind (Arishadvarga/Shadripu", *Brahma*, 6th July 2020.

[38] "Ki maja ache manab dehete" (in Bengali), Dehatattva Baul Song by Naru Gopal, YouTube.

[39] *Arishadvargas*—Wikipedia.

[40] Sri Sri Ravi Shankar, "Five arrows of Love".

[41] *Madan Kamdev*—Wikipedia.

[42] Deepam Chatterjee, "Vasant Panchami: The Indian Valentine's Day and The Five Arrows of Love", *The Daily Guardian*, January 27, 2023.

[43] "Triguna Theory of Ayurveda", *Planet Ayurveda*.

[44] *Bhaba Pagla*—Wikiwand.

[45] Carola Erika Lorea, "Lyrics of Bhaba Pagla and the Bauls of Bengal".

[46] "Carola Erika Lorea—National University of Singapore"—Academia. edu

[47] Carola Erika Lorea, *Folklore, Religion and the Songs of a Madman: A Journey Between Performance and the Politics of Cultural Representation*, Leiden: Brill, 2016.

[48] Siddhartha Ganguli, *The Making of A Winning Child*, New Delhi: Allied Publishers, 2012.

[49] Siddhartha Ganguli, *Smart Leading & Parenting of Teenage Kids in the Digital Era: A Neuro-managed Way*; New Delhi: Allied Publishers, 2021.

[50] *Enteric Nervous System*—Wikipedia.

[51] "Manush ta more gele kannakati"—Bengali Baul song by Baul Naru Gopal, YouTube.

[52] Zawn Villiness, "What a flow state is and how to achieve it", *Medical News Today*, 19th April 2022.

[53] Mihalyi Csikszentmihalyi, *FLOW: The Psychology of Optimal Experience*, New York: Harper Perennial Modern Classics, 2008.

[54] Siddhartha Ganguli, *SMART Leading and Parenting of Teenage Kids in the Digital Era: A Neuro-managed Way*, New Delhi: Allied Publishers Pvt. Ltd., 2021.

[55] *Pancha Kosha*—Vikaspedia.

[56] *What is Pancha Kosha?—Definition from Yogapedia*—Yogapedia.

Essence of Baulsphere

I have hovered around over the 'Baulsphere' for quite some time now. Having taken an eagle eye view, the first essential observation that I have made is that there is no 'standard' specification for a 'Baul' or a 'Fakir'. I have seen different characters from different backgrounds are putting on the robes of a Baul or a Fakir, carrying an ektara and a khamak wearing anklets with small bells, or playing a dotara—some with and some without accompanying instrumentalists—and posing as Bauls.

Some of them are from the Baul lineage, while a few are first generation Bauls. Some have taken lessons from Gurus to sing, whereas a few others are self-styled and self-trained. The professional light music vocal artists who also include Baul songs in their repertory would certainly not be regarded as Bauls.

In conclusion, I have come to classify Bauls into three main categories. The first category consists of just musicians. I would call them 'Gayak Bauls' or 'Singer Bauls'. They have no idea of the different doctrines of the deep-rooted Baul-Fakir philosophy (Baul Tattva). For many of them, the literacy level and perceptive power are very low, so they don't even understand the inner meanings of the songs they sing. Their performances, therefore, are not effective.

The second category comprises the Sadhak Bauls who again can be sub-divided into two groups: 'Tantric Sadhak Bauls' and 'Vedic Sadhak Bauls'.

Tantric Sadhak Bauls

The nature and characteristic of the 'Tantric Sadhak Bauls' are portrayed well in a song by Late Sadhak Baul Gour Kheypa, which goes like this: (*Reference 1.* Translation is mine. Since absolutely literal translation was not possible, pardon my trivial alterations from the original verse)

"It is not a child's play to become a 'Baul'

To be a 'True' or a 'Real' 'Baul', you have to follow the path of 'True Devotion' whole-heartedly.

Oh! My absent-minded mind! Oh! My madcap mind!

To be a 'Baul' is not a child's play."

"Baul was Nityananda, Srirup Sanatan; Chandidas & Joydeb also had performed devoted worship as a 'Baul'.

They had followed rituals with 'Pancha Rasas'—sweet, sour, salted, bitter and astringent.

The 'Real' Baul spends his every day with the 'Four Moon' ('Char Chandra') ritual by chanting the name of Gour Hari,

It is not a child's play to become a 'Baul'!

Oh! My absent-minded mind! Oh! My madcap mind!

To be a Baul is not a child's play!"

"Gour Kheypa says acquire 'Self-knowledge' ('Atma Tattva')

Find out the nature and character of your five senses—how you respond to sound, sight, smell, taste and touch,

If you continue to meditate without stopping, without moving—sitting on the same seat at the same place for twelve long years,

You can attain 'siddhi'—fulfilment/attainment of your spiritual goal!!

To become a 'Baul' is not a child's play,

If you wish to be a 'Real', a 'True' 'Baul', you have to follow the 'Baul path' with true devotion—whole-heartedly."

The contents of the song are self-explanatory. The lyric wonderfully explains what is the 'Tantric' form of 'Baul Sadhana', consisting mainly of body-based rituals, which many sadhak bauls still follow.

Vedic Baul Sadhana

Vedic Baul sadhaks concentrate only on the philosophical aspects of the Baul Path and not the body-based rituals. This I have already explained in Lalon's Baul philosophy under 'Baul vs Fakir: Role Minimisation' in 'The Appetizer' portion.

The Western Baul Movement

Lee Kheypa Baul (Real Name: Lee Lozowick) (1943-2010) was an American spiritual teacher, author, poet, lyricist and singer from Prescott, Arizona, USA. He became a student of 'Silva Mind Control' in 1970 and got interested in the human potential movement. He came to believe that the human mind has tremendous unexplored potential which has got to be tapped. But since he did not know how, he started searching for ways and means for 'Super Mind Development'.

With several of his students, he made a pilgrimage to India in 1977, where he met Yogi Ramsuratkumar. By 1980s, he felt very close connection with the Yogi and became known to many people the world over as the "Heart-Son" of the great Yogi. He formed a spiritual community called 'Hohm' and set up ashrams in Arizona, USA, Ferme de Jutreau in France and Tiruvannamalai in India. According to scholar Helen Crovetto, who has studied the Hohm community, "Lee said the word 'Hohm' has no translation and chose not to elaborate on its significance". (*References 2 & 3*) I have a 'gut feeling' that perhaps Lee was moved by the divine sound 'AUM' ('OM') which rhymes with 'Hohm'.

Lozowick came to identify with the Baul tradition of Bengal, speculating that his Guru Yogi Ramsuratkumar may have had some connection to that community as well during years of his early life that he no longer remembered or refused to disclose, although Ramsuratkumar was not a Baul by lineage. Subsequently, however, the Hohm community did establish relationships with a number of Bengali Bauls, such as Sanatan Das Baul and Purna Das Baul.

The focus of spiritual practice in Lozowick's teachings is 'Guru Yoga' just as the Bauls claim that you cannot be a 'Real' or 'True' 'Baul' unless you are under the tutelage of a Guru. Lozowick was known to discourage his potential students with the 'sexual content' of much of his talk or by 'loud obnoxiousness' that underlie the Tantric Baul practices. His 'Western Baul' movement recommends lacto-vegetarianism and lays importance on the 'chakras' (energy system) of Subtle Body. His followers incorporate music in their spiritual practice.

One main theme in the Western Baul path is that you have a separate existence other than what you are in your worldly life. That realisation is the first step in your journey towards spirituality. There has to be a 'Dream' in you to reach and taste that existence. There has to be a 'Drive' in you to embark on the journey towards fulfilment of that 'Dream'. And, the 'Domain' is that separate existence. Not everyone is fortunate enough to achieve the 3D (Dream-Drive-Domain) convergence state. The separate existence is the 'Godly' existence. We are not separate from God. God exists very much within us—not in temples, mosques or churches, as the Bauls & Fakirs of Bengal believe. So, one has to go for self-observation, self-realisation and self-purification as is also recommended in the Baul path.

Energy is all around us in different forms—heat, sound, magnetism, wind, light, chemical energy, biological energy. God is also energy—cosmic energy. Since we are a bundle of energy, we are not separate from or different from God. It is only a matter of self-purification to be united with God.

The goal thus is: inner transformation. *(Reference 4)*

The Eastern Baul tradition, which arose in and around the 14th century, is known to adapt and utilize principles of other spiritual traditions, as I have already discussed elsewhere.

The Western Baul movement is very organised and information on them are readily available. *(References 5-7)*

References

[1] "Baul hoa mukher katha noy" (Song in Bengali by Gour Kheypa; shared by Sourav Sarkar (aka 'Rob Kheypa', disciple of Late Gour Kheypa).

[2] *Lee Lozowick*—Wikipedia.

[3] Helen Crovetto, "Embodied Knowledge and Divinity: The Hohm Community as Western-style Bauls", *Nova Religio: The Journal of Alternative and Emergent Religions*, Vol. 10, Issue 1, p. 72.

[4] Mary Angelon Young, "Speech/Yogi Ramsuratkumar Ashram Centenary Celebrations", Vela Videos, video presentation posted in YouTube.

[5] *Lineage*—Western Baul.

[6] *Basics*—Western Baul.

[7] *Activities*—Western Baul.